Th ... ...

Far away, visible over the rooftops and church spires of the city, a puff of black smoke curled toward the sky. Three more booms came in quick succession.

Mrs. Morley peered fearfully out. "What is it, Jane?"

"I'm not sure," Jane replied quickly. "It must be cannon fire."

"Oh, Lord, have mercy! Come back inside, quickly!"

But Jane had caught sight of the schoolmaster rushing toward the front gate. "Mr. Cordwyn!" she called down to him. "What's happening?"

He glanced up at her without slowing down. "No school today, Jane."

"But where are you going?"

"To tell my friends on Queen Street to get out while they still can!" He was out the front gate and down the street in an instant.

With the booms rumbling and rolling across the sky, Jane was suddenly seized with a wild impulse. She ran for the stairs, calling over her shoulder. "I'll be back later, Mrs. Morley. I'm going to Cousin Hugh's!"

"No, dear, you mustn't!" Mrs. Morley cried.

But Jane was already gone.

Just Jane

*A Daughter of England Caught
in the Struggle of the American Revolution*

WILLIAM LAVENDER

SCHOLASTIC INC.

New York Toronto London Auckland Sydney
Mexico City New Delhi Hong Kong Buenos Aires

ISBN 0-439-81070-1

Copyright © 2002 by William Lavender. All rights reserved.
Published by Scholastic Inc., 557 Broadway, New York, NY
10012, by arrangement with Harcourt, Inc.
SCHOLASTIC and associated logos are trademarks
and/or registered trademarks of Scholastic Inc.

12 11 10 9 8 7 6 5 4 3 2   5 6 7 8 9 10/0

Printed in the U.S.A.   01

First Scholastic printing, September 2005

Text set in Bembo

Display set in Caslon Antique

Designed by Cathy Riggs

*To Mary and Debbie—two strong
right arms of support*

The Prentice Family
of England and South Carolina

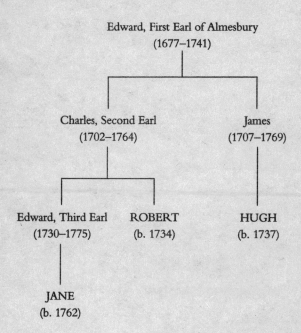

Edward, First Earl of Almesbury
(1677–1741)

Charles, Second Earl
(1702–1764)

James
(1707–1769)

Edward, Third Earl
(1730–1775)

ROBERT
(b. 1734)

HUGH
(b. 1737)

JANE
(b. 1762)

Capitalized names designate characters in this story.

PART I

Point of No Return—1776

Chapter 1

Jane Prentice awoke with a start in the cramped, air-less cabin that had been her world for forty-six days and nights. Always there was the endless motion, the creaking and rocking of the sailing ship surrounded only by ocean and horizon. A lantern, now dark, swung gently on a beam overhead, as Jane's elderly companion snored softly in the opposite bunk.

Suddenly from the crowded deck above, shouts rang out in the gray, cheerless dawn. Sailors starting their morning chores called to one another across the decks. According to the ship's rules, that meant Jane could go up, too. Shivering with a mixture of cold and excitement, she quickly dressed and ran up on deck to greet the new day. *Maybe,* Jane thought—as she had every morning for the last week—*just maybe,* this *will be the day.*

Her stout, gray-haired companion found Jane leaning over the railing on the bow, looking straight into the spray-filled wind. She was straining to see a sliver of land through the mist.

"Jane! Gracious, child, you'll catch your death—"

"Mrs. Morley, look!" Jane was too excited for a scolding. "Do you see? It's the Sea Islands, the lookout told me. Charlestown's* only three more hours' sail. That's South Carolina you're seeing—we're finally here!"

Squinting into the distance, Mrs. Morley could barely see a dark line low on the horizon. "Lord above! Can it be?"

"I wonder what it'll be like," Jane murmured.

"A backwoods outpost, I dare say." Her companion sniffed. "Like all the American colonies."

"That can't be. Uncle Robert and Cousin Hugh have lived here for years. And Uncle Robert wrote to us that Charlestown's quite as civilized as London, only smaller."

"Civilized, indeed! We'll be spending half of every year at Mr. Robert's farm, miles from town and surrounded by wild beasts and savages!"

"It's not a farm, it's a big plantation," Jane corrected her.

"Besides, there's all this talk of quarreling between the Americans and King George, our lawful ruler. It worries me."

But Jane's mind was on her uncle's plantation. "Rosewall!" She breathed the name as if enchanted.

_____

*In colonial times, the name of Charleston, South Carolina, was usually spelled Charlestown, often Charles Town.

"Uncle Robert says it's a beautiful patch of England, transplanted to America. I'm sure it's lovely now, in June."

"A tangled wilderness, I'll warrant." Mrs. Morley was not to be influenced. She pulled her long overcoat tight against the chill, looking quite miserable.

Jane scowled. "If you already hate it, why did you come?"

"You know very well why," Mrs. Morley replied indignantly. "Because I've been your companion since your dear mother died so long ago, and because I promised your poor father. What a wasted life he led! Earl of Almesbury at thirty-three, and his fortune and estate lost to drink before he was forty! It was his dying wish that I remain with you."

"Well, I could have come alone," Jane replied, absentmindedly pulling at the small gold locket she always wore—and always tugged at when she felt nervous.

"A girl of fourteen sailing off alone to a strange land to live with an uncle she's never met? I think not!"

Jane gave her faithful companion a hug. "I'm glad you came, Mrs. Morley, but I want you to be glad, too. From his letters, Uncle Robert sounds wonderful, and I'm dying to meet Aunt Clarissa. He says she's very beautiful, and from a good Charlestown family. Her brother's a rich merchant and belongs to the South Carolina Assembly, or whatever it's called. And Cousin Hugh is—"

"A cabinetmaker!" Mrs. Morley scoffed at the mention of Robert's cousin Hugh Prentice. "Imagine! No more than a lowly woodworker, and him with all that schooling. All the Prentice boys had a fine education, you know. Their grandfather, Edward, the first Earl, saw to that. He'd turn over in his grave if he knew that after Hugh came to America, he tossed aside his books for a hammer and chisel!"

"I don't see why. Surely, woodworking's an honest occupation."

But Mrs. Morley had already turned to go back belowdecks. "I tell you this, my girl," she called over her shoulder, "we may be a long way from home, but I intend to remain English through and through till the day I die. These colonies can't change that. And stop pulling on that chain, dear. You'll break it for certain. You know I wasn't even supposed to let you have that locket until you turned eighteen."

"I know, and I keep telling you, I won't break it." Engraved with her parents' initials—*EP to RP*—Jane's beloved gold locket contained her only memento of her mother, the Countess Rachel, who had died when Jane was just three years old. Curled inside the heart-shaped locket was a wisp of chestnut brown hair. The locket, and a slim volume of poems that had belonged to her father, were the two treasures she had brought with her to America.

"And I know how you feel about England, Mrs. Morley. I feel the same way. I'm sure all our friends and kinsmen in America do, too. But you'll see— we'll have an exciting new life here, and I'm . . ."

Jane turned her gaze again to the mysterious horizon shrouded in morning mist.

I'm afraid, she thought.

Chapter 2

While Harriet Ainsley was often considered pretty, she looked plain in comparison to her husband's beautiful sister, Clarissa Prentice. But Harriet possessed an inner beauty that would last, everyone said, far longer than Clarissa's glamour. While the elegant Clarissa was widely admired, it was the warmhearted Harriet, with her sunny disposition, who was genuinely loved by all who knew her. Harriet was blessed in other ways as well. Her husband, Arthur, was a prosperous merchant, respected public figure, and devoted family man. Their handsome eighteen-year-old son, Brandon, was famous around Charlestown for his superb horsemanship. All in all, the Ainsley family was the picture of life at its very best.

Harriet's second-floor sitting room in the Ainsley house, on Church Street, opened onto a narrow covered veranda running the length of the house. Late on this warm June afternoon, her husband found her there enjoying the view of Charlestown Harbor from the floor-to-ceiling windows.

"Well, Arthur," Harriet asked, "has Miss Prentice arrived at last?"

"She has, but she's completely exhausted. Nellie is showing her directly to her room."

"Good. I thank heaven she's safe, what with all these rumors of British ships approaching."

"Being a loyal British subject, she'd likely see no danger in that. She doesn't seem to know much about the quarrel between England and the colonies. And it's probably just as well."

"Well, ignorance is bliss, the poet says. I hope she'll remain blissful as long as possible. What's she like, Arthur? Is she pretty?"

"I daresay she will be, once she's spruced up with some decent clothes. Slender, graceful, lovely complexion. Long brown hair. Huge dark eyes, like a frightened doe. But frightened or not, she's remarkably poised for one so young. I could tell she was disappointed that Robert wasn't at the dock to meet her. But I explained how busy he is at Rosewall in June, and that we'll do everything we can to make her comfortable until he arrives."

"Of course." Harriet became thoughtful. "I wonder if she'll expect to be called Lady Jane. After all, she *is* the daughter of an English earl."

"I suppose we should, until she becomes accustomed to American ways. Soon enough she'll realize we don't much use titles of nobility."

Just then Jane appeared in the doorway. "Come in, my dear," said Arthur, with a kind smile. He introduced her formally: "Harriet, may I present Lady Jane Prentice."

"Lady Jane! We're delighted you're here!" Beaming, Harriet embraced the girl. The warm hug and the sweet scent of the rose water Harriet wore took Jane's breath away for an instant. It was the same rose water her mother had worn, she was certain of it. Jane had only a few memories of her mother, and it was comforting to feel that Harriet was in some way like her.

"Thank you, Mrs. Ainsley." It was nice to be so warmly received.

Harriet bubbled cheerily. "Now, dear, until Robert and Clarissa return to their house in Charlestown, please consider our home and our family as your own. Our son, Brandon, is also at Rosewall just now, but he returns soon. And we'd be so pleased if you'd call us Uncle Arthur and Aunt Harriet. Wouldn't we, Arthur?"

"Indeed we would," Arthur agreed amiably.

Jane, with her English reserve, was taken aback by this display of friendliness. "I don't know how to thank you. You're both so kind. And..." She hesitated. "It's true that I'm called Lady Jane at home. But I'm told that things are different in America. So, now that I'm here, I'd like everyone to call me just Jane."

Arthur and Harriet exchanged pleased smiles. "As you wish, Jane," he said with a nod. "And don't worry, despite the disagreements we've been having with the king's government, no one will forget that you're English, or try to influence you in political

9

matters. Your uncle Robert would never permit you to set foot in this house if he thought there was any danger of that."

"Thank you, sir," Jane responded, waiting expectantly for further explanation of the "disagreements" Arthur had mentioned. But none came.

Quickly, Harriet said, "Such talk will make Jane's poor head spin, Arthur." She gave Jane's arm a little squeeze. "My dear, why don't we let you rest a bit. I'm going to send notes around to some of our close friends, inviting them to stop in this evening to meet you. Nothing formal, just a light supper and a little conversation. I think you'll enjoy it."

"I'm sure I shall." Jane smiled politely, but her insides felt like a thousand butterflies had just taken flight. She would be the center of a great many strangers' curious attention on her very first day in Charlestown.

That evening Jane was pleasantly surprised by the friendliness directed toward her, but mortified by the dowdiness of her only halfway decent dress. Somehow she had expected to be able to get at least one new dress in America before being introduced to her relatives' respected friends. She only picked at the "light supper," which turned out to be a feast of roast game, succulent hams, and all manner of breads, cakes, and pies. There was more food than Jane had ever seen in one place, certainly not aboard ship, where even bread had become scarce toward the end. Glad when the evening finally ended, she peeked into Mrs. Morley's room to say good night.

"How was it, dear?" Mrs. Morley inquired. "Did they treat you properly?"

"Everyone was very nice. I've never seen so many fancy-looking ladies and gentlemen, all dressed in such beautiful silks. I felt like a milkmaid among them in this old thing—it's so babyish!"

"Nonsense!" Mrs. Morley sputtered. "Don't forget, you were the only highborn English lady there, even if your dress isn't new. And you're growing into quite a shapely young lady, at that. You'll be lacing up a fine set of stays before long, and the young men will be buzzing around you."

"Well, I didn't feel highborn or grown-up when I met the president of the Republic, Mr. Rutledge. He is a most impressive gentleman."

"President? Of what Republic?"

"They're calling this place the Republic of South Carolina."

"Are they, now! That sounds ridiculous, indeed."

"I also heard Uncle Arthur's neighbor Mr. Heyward talking about arguments with the king over things like commerce and taxation," Jane went on. "That's why you'll find no English tea in the shops."

"I can't understand why your uncle Robert would bring us into this nest of rebels, fine people or no!" Mrs. Morley exclaimed.

"Oh, they're not *rebels*, Mrs. Morley," Jane explained. "I'm sure they're all as loyal as we are—it's just that this colony has a few complaints. Don't worry, everything will be fine. Good night now. Sleep well."

———

Back in her own room, Jane lay awake a long time. Her mind whirled with visions of beautiful new dresses, sumptuous food—and echoes of the shocking word Mrs. Morley had used. *Rebels? The Ainsleys? Surely they are loyal British subjects. And yet . . .*

It seems I have much to learn about these Americans, she thought. *How will I ever find my right place here?*

She drifted off, at last, to a fitful sleep.

Chapter 3

The next day, Brandon Ainsley returned from Rosewall.

Arthur had sent a rider with word of Jane's safe arrival, and Brandon immediately set out for Charlestown. As his horse's hooves clattered through the gate, black servants ran out, shouting, to greet him.

The commotion brought Harriet outside as well, laughingly scolding her son. "Brandon, dear, don't bring that dirty old horse into the courtyard!"

Dismounting with a flourish, he turned his dappled gray mare over to a groom. "Why, Mother dear! Dare you call Princess a dirty old horse?"

Jane already knew he was eighteen, and now she saw that, with clear blue eyes and straw-colored hair falling in disarray over his forehead, he was handsome like his father, his face full of the joy of life.

Harriet enveloped him in a warm embrace, chiding him, "Do behave, or Jane will get a bad first impression of you."

Just then he caught sight of the girl standing in the doorway, gazing at him in wonder. "Oh, my . . . ," he breathed, and with wide-eyed wonder of his own, stepped toward her. "Lady Jane!" Bowing low, he kissed her hand, then held on to it, beaming. "Enchanted, I'm sure!"

She quietly withdrew her hand. "It's just Jane, please, Master Brandon. Or Cousin Jane, if you like."

"You are lovely, whatever you're called," he said casually, studying her all over. "Lady Jane, Cousin Jane, or simply Jane—I expect I'll marry you someday."

Too taken aback to respond, Jane was grateful that Harriet quickly came to her rescue. "Brandon, stop that. You're embarrassing our guest. Now, what news of Robert and Clarissa? Will they be coming soon?"

"As soon as possible," he replied. "They're delighted that you're here, Jane, and send you their warmest welcome. But you see, Uncle Robert's just bringing in his rice crop and needs Aunt Clarissa's help. You can't imagine what it's like running a large plantation. Well, I must see to Princess. But then I'll come looking for you, Cousin Jane. I never want you out of my sight again!" Taking long, confident strides, he hurried away.

Harriet smiled apologetically as he strode off. "He's a dreadful show-off, dear, but quite harmless. Shall we go in?"

Jane was slow to answer. Again she felt the sting of disappointment that the two people she most wanted to meet would remain names without faces for yet a while. Meanwhile, two others had just left her in a daze of astonishment. She had never met a young man quite so brash, so cockily sure of himself, as Brandon Ainsley—or a mother so openly adoring.

"I'd like to walk in the garden a bit, if you don't mind, Aunt Harriet." Graciously excused by Harriet, Jane set off for the cool shade.

Like many fine Charlestown houses, the Ainsleys' was long and narrow, with a short side facing the street and one long side looking out over a secluded garden. The house had covered verandas on three levels, overlooking flagstone paths winding through a miniature forest of fragrant orange and gardenia, jasmine and honeysuckle. Beyond that were the huge stone-floored kitchen, servants' quarters, storehouse, carriage house, and stables.

Off to one side sat another small building, with a hand-lettered sign above the door:

SCHOOLROOM
S. CORDWYN, SCHOOLMASTER

Impelled by curiosity, Jane approached the glass-paned door and tried to peer inside. Suddenly the door swung open, and she stepped back with a gasp. A tall, dark-haired young man with piercing gray eyes stood there frowning at her, as if annoyed by this intrusion. Jane hastily offered apology.

"I'm sorry. I was being nosy. I hope I didn't disturb you."

A sudden smile transformed his piercing gaze into a

15

gentle one. "You must be Miss Prentice, lately arrived from England." His resonant voice had an accent quite different from the Ainsleys'. "I'm Simon Cordwyn, schoolmaster, at your service." He opened the door wide in welcome. "Would you like to come inside? There are no classes on Saturday afternoon."

Jane hesitated for only a moment. "Thank you, sir." She stepped into a room full of long tables and rows of straight-backed chairs. In front was a desk covered with books and papers.

"It's an old storehouse," Simon explained, "converted to a higher purpose, thanks to Mr. Ainsley's enlightened generosity."

Jane smiled. "It reminds me of my village school back home. Of course, I had to stop going when my father died. There was no money to pay for it."

"Well, I'd be pleased to have you attend this school, if you like," he said. "You could come with the older boys in the afternoons. It would certainly overturn tradition, since the gentlemen here see little value in education for girls. But I do. That's one of the ways we differ."

How wonderful it would be to study with books again, Jane thought wistfully, but brightened when she spoke. "I must say, it's nice to meet a schoolmaster who believes in education for girls. I should imagine that's quite as unusual here as it is in England."

Simon pulled up two chairs. "Well, I'm convinced they'll see the light eventually. Now, please, sit down. Tell me how you like it here so far." His tone was so kind and gentle that Jane somehow found herself telling this stranger just how she felt about her new home.

"The Ainsleys have been wonderful to me, and I'm sure my uncle and aunt will be, too," Jane said. "But everything is so different here. I guess I'm a little homesick."

"I know what you mean. After almost five years, I still don't feel truly at home here."

This was the opening for the question Jane longed to ask. "Where are you from, Mr. Cordwyn?"

"Pennsylvania, in the North. And it's very unlike South Carolina."

"It is? How so?"

"Society is so much more class-conscious here in the South. There's a more gracious style of living here, too—for those with money. And in the North, thank God, we don't have slavery."

"Slavery." Jane's face darkened at the word. "That's not an easy idea to get used to. But the Ainsleys' Negroes seem to be treated kindly."

"Yes," Simon conceded. "And they're lucky to have such decent folks as owners. Actually, many Southerners treat their slaves kindly. But it's still an evil system, and someday it will have to be abolished."

This grim topic had only increased Jane's curiosity. "Feeling as you do, Mr. Cordwyn, how did you happen to come here?"

"By accident, really. Mr. Ainsley advertised in Philadelphia for a tutor for Brandon, and I applied. I was only twenty at the time, but I'd had two years at Philadelphia College, and Mr. Ainsley thought I'd do." Simon shook his head. "I regret to say, I failed miserably with Brandon. He cares only for horses and racing. He soon deserted my classes altogether."

"He'll regret that someday, I don't doubt," Jane said.

"I don't think so," Simon replied. "When he inherits his father's business and the Ainsley estates, he'll devote his life to his thoroughbred horses and fine racecourses, and have no regrets at all."

Jane was puzzled. "Yet even after he left, you go on teaching here?"

"Oh yes. This school was well established when Brandon quit, and the Ainsleys urged me to continue—even though their own son wouldn't benefit. So, here I am. But enough of all that. Tell me about yourself, Lady Jane."

"Please, I'm just Jane here. I'm in America now."

"Indeed you are—and a very long way from home. Why is that?"

"It's not much of a story. My mother died when I was very young, so I barely remember her. My father, the Earl of Almesbury, died just last year, but I never really knew him. He was—well, not exactly a devoted father. I was brought up by my companion, Mrs. Morley. She's been almost like a member of the family since long before I was born, and I'm glad to say she's with me still. At one time the earldom included a large estate, but my father squandered it all away, leaving me an orphan without means. Fortunately for me, Uncle Robert, his younger brother, has agreed to take me in. So—as you said about yourself—here I am."

Simon nodded thoughtfully. "Seems to me you've been mostly on your own in life so far, Jane. That's regrettable, but in a way also beneficial. No doubt it has taught you a degree of self-reliance, which will serve you well from now on. And you know—this may sound foolish, but it strikes me that we have something important in common, you and I."

"Really? What's that?"

"It could be said that we're both, in a sense, aliens in a foreign land, trying to find our way."

Jane stared at him. "What a fascinating thought, Mr. Cordwyn. Yes, I do believe you're—"

At that point a knock sounded at the open door. "Ah, there you are, Jane." It was Brandon, looking in.

Simon greeted him with a smile. "Master Brandon! Come, join us."

"Thank you, sir, I can't stay. I just came looking for my cousin. I was worried about you, Jane. I thought perhaps you'd gotten lost."

"Lost? Hardly—I'm not a helpless child!" Rising, she turned to the schoolmaster. "But I'm afraid I've taken up too much of your time, Mr. Cordwyn. Forgive me. I'm very glad to have made your acquaintance."

"Not at all, Jane. My pleasure." He was up, extending his hand to her. "And don't forget—Monday, one o'clock. I'd be honored if you'd join us."

"Thank you. Perhaps I will. Good-bye." Going to the door, she took the arm Brandon offered, and they started back to the main house.

After they had gone a short way, Brandon fixed a disapproving frown on his companion. "Jane, what can you be thinking of? An English lady such as yourself doesn't strike up casual acquaintances with strangers. And as for attending his school—good Lord, you couldn't possibly do such a thing!"

"Why ever not? I've attended school before, and I love it."

"He's not one of us, that's why. He's a Northerner and common folk, and suspect in both his politics and his morals."

"What can you mean by that?"

"No, I'll say no more. But make no mistake, associating with the likes of him won't help you take your proper place among us. You've got a lot to learn about American ways, I can see that. But never fear. I'll see to your instruction in these matters."

Jane suppressed her urge to smile, but her answering tone was gently mocking. "How very nice of you, Brandon! Yes, I'm sure I have a lot to learn." Her next thought she left unspoken:

But I rather think, sir, it will not be you who teaches me.

Chapter 4

The idea of attending Mr. Cordwyn's school appealed to Jane, but she was not sure about being the only girl in a schoolroom full of rowdy boys. Mrs. Morley agreed with Brandon on the matter, that it was simply not a proper thing to do. In the end, Jane decided to seek Arthur's opinion.

"I see no harm in it, Jane," he said. "Cordwyn's a fine fellow, and an excellent teacher, I believe. And if you find it to your liking, you'll be welcome to use my modest library to help you in your studies."

Jane thanked him. And so it was settled—she would go to school again.

The next morning, Brandon saddled up Princess and rode off with friends for a tour of far-flung racecourses that would keep him away for a week or more. And that afternoon, Arthur and Harriet took Jane for a carriage drive to see the city. Arthur explained that Charlestown stood on a peninsula between the mouths of two rivers. And he amused Jane by adding, "The natives are a proud people. They like to say that Charlestown is where the Ashley and Cooper Rivers come together to form the Atlantic Ocean."

Up and down the cobbled streets they drove, Jane admiring the curbside shops, the stately houses, and the many churches with their tall steeples. That morning, she had gazed up into the lofty interior of Saint Michael's Church, where the Ainsley family regularly attended services.

"Unfortunately, we are temporarily without our church bells," Arthur told her. "The royal governor had them removed several years ago, in a dispute with our citizens."

"How sad," Jane said. "Even sadder that all this quarreling is going on between England and the American colonies."

"It's just petty politics, Jane," Arthur told her. "Believe me, it'll all blow over in time."

Next he showed her the Dock Street Theater, where she might enjoy seeing a play performed. And as they drove along East Battery Street near the docks, he pointed out his own Ainsley Emporium.

"I hope to be able to invite you very soon to come in and choose some new dresses," he said.

Thrilled at that prospect, Jane eagerly studied the Emporium building. But there was no activity around it, and, as she had noticed on her arrival a few days before, there were almost no ships in the nearby harbor. She asked Arthur why, but all he would say was,

22

"Overseas trade is very spotty these days. Unfortunately, stock is rather low just now." He hurriedly drove on.

On Legare Street stood Robert and Clarissa's imposing two-story house, regal in tree-shaded seclusion behind a beautiful wrought-iron gate.

Seeing it reminded Jane of her other relatives. "I understand that my father's cousin Hugh Prentice also lives in Charlestown. Could we—"

"Visit him?" Arthur shot a glance at Harriet, shaking his head. "No, Jane, I'm afraid not."

"May I ask why? Is something wrong?"

"Nothing that I could easily explain. It's just that your uncle Robert considers it unsuitable for you to meet him. He forbids it, in fact."

"But why? Does it have something to do with the quarrel between—"

"Oh, you know how men are, Jane dear," Harriet said. "Endlessly quarreling! And Robert and Hugh disagree on things so violently, that—well, it's just too tiresome to worry your pretty head about."

Jane found the Ainsleys' reluctance to answer her questions most unsatisfactory. But the carriage was moving on, and because they were plainly determined to say no more, she had to let the matter drop—for now.

Free from Brandon's disapproving frown, Jane looked into Simon Cordwyn's schoolroom at one o'clock the next afternoon. While the schoolmaster sat intently reading some papers at his desk, a dozen boys, aged ten to fourteen, chattered in their seats. Jane slipped into a seat at the rear and cringed as the boys turned to stare at her, whispering and snickering.

Simon looked up, then rose, scanning his male charges with narrowed eyes. "Gentlemen," he began. "Today we welcome a new student, Miss Jane Prentice, from England. You will regard her as your equal and treat her with the utmost respect, or you will incur my extreme disfavor. I expect not to have to say this again." His voice was quiet, but its hard edge made clear his absolute authority. The unwelcome attention directed at Jane evaporated.

The day's lesson began, and soon Jane discovered that Mr. Cordwyn encouraged his students to participate in classroom discussion. She herself listened eagerly to everything but remained silent. Toward the end of the session, the schoolmaster turned to her favorite subject—history.

"It was in 1663," he said to open the discussion, "that King Charles the Second bestowed upon his favorites a tract of land in North America to be known as the Colony of Carolina. The charter described this territory as lying between the thirty-first and thirty-sixth degrees north latitude, and extending westward to the South Seas. Who can tell us what the king might have meant by the South Seas?" He waited. "Anyone?"

After a long silence, no hand being raised, Jane finally lifted hers.

The schoolmaster responded instantly. "Yes, Miss Prentice?"

"I believe he meant the Pacific Ocean, sir."

"Exactly correct. And how far away is that, would you say?"

"I don't know, sir. And neither did King Charles, most likely. He might have been astonished to learn that he had made one of the largest land grants in all history."

Simon threw back his head and laughed heartily. "Very good, Miss Prentice! By heaven, that's what we've been missing in this classroom, gentlemen. An occasional display of intelligent wit!"

Jane blushed in pleasure and embarrassment.

Soon class was over. "Tomorrow," the schoolmaster said, "we shall turn to our geometry. And I shall be immensely pleased if a few of you can exhibit slight familiarity with the properties of a triangle. Good afternoon."

In a burst of foot-shuffling disorder, the boys bolted for the outdoors. Jane rose slowly, wondering if she might engage Mr. Cordwyn in further conversation. Perhaps he would be willing to answer some of the unanswered questions in her mind. Had he not taken a sincere interest in her—even discovering something they had in common? Already she was beginning to develop a warm feeling for the gentle schoolmaster.

To her pleasant surprise, as the other students dashed out he headed straight toward her. "I'm glad you spoke up, Jane," he said with a smile. "Glad you decided to join our school, too. You'll be an asset to the class."

"Well, I know *I'll* greatly benefit, sir. Thank you for inviting me."

"Now, would you walk outside with me? I have something to tell you."

"Certainly." Jane tingled with curiosity and anticipation.

As they strolled through the garden, Mr. Cordwyn said in a low tone, "I've been asked to bring you warm greetings from Mr. Hugh Prentice."

"*You* know my cousin Hugh?"

"Yes, he and his wife are good friends of mine. I dined with them just last evening near here in Queen Street. Although Hugh's never seen you, he holds you in great affection and hopes someday you two might meet."

"*Might* meet!" Jane stopped short. "Mr. Cordwyn, I just don't understand. I'm told my uncle Robert forbids me to meet Cousin Hugh. But why? Because they disagree violently! About what? They came to America together years ago. Now they don't speak? It doesn't make sense!"

"Maybe I can help." Simon beckoned toward a shaded bench, and the two sat down. "Simply put, the quarrel between the Prentice cousins is the quarrel between England and the American colonies. Hugh is a former Englishman who has become an American. Robert, though he lives in America, will be an Englishman forever. Then there's Arthur Ainsley, who

26

tries very hard to occupy a middle ground. He agrees with many of his friends that the British have treated us unfairly, but he believes we should resolve our differences by peaceable negotiations."

"And what, pray tell, *are* these differences that are causing so much bad blood between friends and kinsmen?"

"You must understand, Jane, this quarrel didn't start just yesterday. It's been simmering for years. England maintains that by defeating France in the Seven Years' War, it saved the American colonies from those 'awful French.' So, out of gratitude, the colonies ought to pay their share of the costs of that war. This has led to severe restrictions on our overseas trade, unreasonably high tariffs, and, worst of all, punishing taxation. Of course, paying taxes has always been a part of life. But what infuriates many Americans is what they call 'taxation without representation.' That is, without representation in Parliament, where they have no voice at all."

"That does sound unfair," Jane said. "Especially for a merchant like Uncle Arthur, whose business is suffering directly. But where do *you* stand, Mr. Cordwyn? If I may be so bold as to ask."

"I'm with moderates like Mr. Ainsley. They're reasonable men who might save us from disaster—if only their voices could be more clearly heard."

"Why can't they be?"

"Because the firebrands have taken over, and their voices are much louder and more dramatic." A dark foreboding came into Simon's tone as he went on. "You see, there's something besides reason at work here. Passion. A passionate certainty on each side of the rightness of its position, and an equally passionate determination to prevail at all costs. Look at the Prentice cousins. Robert's a staunch Loyalist, willing to die for the king and British rule if he has to. Hugh, quite the opposite—a more mild-mannered man than Robert, but a member of the rebel faction, and just as fixed in his views as Robert is in his. Patriots, as people on that side call themselves, are convinced the colonies must declare independence from England altogether."

"Independence!" Jane recoiled in horror. "Wouldn't that be treason?"

"Of course, and the Patriots know it. But it does not deter those madmen one whit. 'Give me liberty, or give me death!' says Patrick Henry of Virginia, and he's speaking for the lot of them. You can easily imagine how such fiery speech stirs up all the hotheads in the land. They're itching to take up arms and rush off to do glorious battle."

"Surely you don't think there might be an all-out war!"

"I hate to say so, but I fear it's already begun. Shots were fired in Lexington, Massachusetts, more than a year ago. Down here in the South, the so-called Carolina Sons of Liberty drove the royal governor away, and the British burned Norfolk, Virginia. Meanwhile, the British fleet stops merchant ships from bringing us goods—"

"A blockade!" Jane's eyes flashed in sudden comprehension. "So *that's* why there are no goods in Uncle Arthur's store!"

"Not only that, now we hear that British warships are headed this way. If they try to take Charlestown, and Hugh's fire-breathing Patriot friends put up armed resistance—well, all I can say is, God help us all."

Jane stared off across the garden. It seemed so strange that sitting there among the flowers on a warm summer afternoon, she could feel a chill creeping up her spine.

Suddenly Simon was apologetic. "Forgive me, Jane. I shouldn't be talking like this, it's—"

"But I need to know these things," she interrupted. "They concern my family. And you're the only one who's willing to talk to me about it. I can't tell you how grateful I am."

"Nevertheless, I've said too much. Anyway, perhaps I'm being too gloomy. There's still time for tempers to cool. Put all this out of your mind now, and I'll see you tomorrow. And I hope you'll speak out in class more tomorrow than you did today." Giving her hand a gentle pat, he rose and hurried away.

Watching him until he disappeared from sight, Jane could still feel his brief touch on her hand. How kind and patient he was in explaining things to her. But for all that, the chill on her spine remained. All this awful talk of war and rebellion—and on top of it all, to be told that Cousin Hugh was a rebel! She sagged in dismay. *What in the world is going on here?*

Chapter 5

Weeks passed, and still Uncle Robert and Aunt Clarissa did not come. Jane understood that the work at Rosewall was demanding, and that it was a good thirty miles from Charlestown—a day's journey over a rough, muddy road. Still, she couldn't help feeling a little hurt by their prolonged absence.

Meanwhile, life at the Ainsley house was pleasant. Arthur was genial, and Harriet as kind and loving as any mother. They took tea together every afternoon, cheerfully pretending that the brew, made from garden herbs, was real English tea. Mrs. Morley also seemed content. Thanks to the tactful Ainsleys, her status—above that of the black servants but not exactly the same as a member of the family—was smoothly established.

Brandon, when he was at home, grumbled about Jane's attending school, but he was usually off somewhere, either riding his beloved Princess in a race or training her for the next one. Sometimes Jane yielded to his entreaties that she attend a race, but she hated the noisy crowds and the clouds of dust raised by the galloping horses. She was relieved when a big race in some distant county took Brandon away for days at a time.

Most of all, Jane enjoyed Mr. Cordwyn's school—where she was soon speaking up as often as the boys. And she enjoyed spending long hours in Arthur's library, working on reading and writing assignments. For her first essay, she chose a topic from one of Shakespeare's history plays. It dealt with the Wars of the Roses, terrible civil wars that had torn England apart three hundred years before. She was deeply moved by a scene in *King Henry VI,* in which a boy is killed in battle by his own father as they fight on opposite sides. The father cries out in anguish, "What showers arise, blown with the windy tempest of my heart, upon thy wounds..."

Jane worried constantly that the colonies' quarrel with England might result in such a war in America. In her essay, she wrote with deep feeling about this fear, expressing the hope that both sides would calm their anger and work together to preserve peace. Her work earned the notation *Excellent* from the schoolmaster, setting her aglow with pleasure and pride.

But she soon noticed that despite Mr. Cordwyn's policy of encouraging classroom discussion, "the troubles," as they often were called, were a strictly forbidden topic. One day she lingered after class had been dismissed and inquired as to the reason for this.

"Some of these boys come from Loyalist families, some from families with rebel sentiments," the schoolmaster explained. "The minute the subject is touched upon, heated argument ensues. The next thing I know I've got a brawl on my hands, and the classroom is in chaos for the rest of the day. The only thing to do is to ban the topic altogether."

"I see. Well, I was just curious, so—"

"That's fine, I'm glad you are. You're curious, you're observant, and you think about things. As a schoolmaster, I take great delight in that."

Encouraged by his friendly attitude, Jane fell into the habit of lingering after class for further discussion. At first their talks centered on "the troubles." But gradually—almost without Jane's realizing it—they drifted over into personal subjects. Curiosity, an element he admired in her, was something he demonstrated as well, asking Jane detailed questions about her life in England and listening intently to her answers. Thus he learned that although she possessed all the poise, dignity, and elegant manners expected from the daughter of an English earl, she had come from shabby surroundings. Her mother long dead, her dissolute father usually absent, she had survived a lonely childhood in diminished circumstances, cared for by her nanny, the widow Mrs. Morley, who was her only constant companion.

"But I'm embarrassed to be telling you all this, Mr. Cordwyn," she said in the end. "It sounds as if I'm complaining, and I don't mean to. I really feel that, considering everything, I've been lucky."

Simon nodded in sympathetic understanding. "And considering everything, Jane, I'd have to say you are a most remarkable young lady."

Coaxed by Jane, he, in turn, talked about his own background. Born to hardworking Pennsylvania farm folk, he and his older sister, Rebecca, had been orphaned before they were fully grown. Rebecca, called Becky, had looked after her brother until they parted company a few years later, when Becky got married and Simon went to Philadelphia in pursuit of education. Becky had married a man named Jack Herndon, a prosperous owner of a mercantile store in the town of Lancaster, Pennsylvania.

"I owe everything to Jack and Becky," Simon told Jane. "They sent me to college. I would have settled in Lancaster and opened a school there, except that it was already overcrowded with schools and schoolmasters. I do miss them. And especially do I miss my niece and nephew. Jack Junior was just three when I left, and the little girl, Frances, was a baby. They're eight and six now. I love those children as if they were my own, and I hate not being there to see them grow up."

"I understand how you feel," Jane said sympathetically. "But we need you here. I need you here, to stuff some education into my head."

This made him chuckle. "Jane, my dear, stuffing education into your pretty head is a pleasure I hope to enjoy for a long time to come."

"Good." She said it with a smile, wondering what it was that had made her tingle—his calling her pretty, or his calling her *my dear*? Either or both, it didn't

33

matter—the tingle was lovely and strange, something she had never felt before.

Each time Brandon came home from one of his racing excursions, he complained anew to Jane about her going to Simon's school. "Why must you do that?" he demanded one day. "Didn't you get enough education in England?"

She looked up from the book she had been reading. "No, Brandon, I didn't. I attended a village school run by a doddering old gentleman who couldn't remember my name, let alone anything else. Mr. Cordwyn is the only competent schoolmaster I've ever had, and an excellent one he is."

"He's also suspected of being tainted with rebel sympathies."

"Suspected? By whom?"

"By me, for one. And Uncle Robert, for another. I warn you, Jane. When Uncle Robert hears about this, he'll be very upset."

"Oh, I hope not, Brandon. Because I'm not doing anything wrong. But I thank you for your concern. Now if you'll excuse me, I have a reading assignment for tomorrow." She gave him a smile and returned to her book.

Often when alone, Jane found herself thinking of the gentle schoolmaster—and realizing that it was not solely for education that she valued their time together so highly. *What else, then?* she wondered. In pondering this mystery, she remembered something he had said to her the day they met.

We have something important in common, you and I. We're both aliens in a foreign land, trying to find our way.

Never mind being called pretty, or addressed as *my dear*. It was in *that* statement, coming back to her again and again, that Jane found real meaning. In a few words it seemed to identify the two of them as kindred spirits.

There was no doubt in her mind: A strong bond was growing between them.

Chapter 6

So the summer days passed tranquilly. Then one sultry morning in late June, the tranquillity was shattered. Jane sensed an undercurrent of anxiety flowing through the house. Arthur and Harriet spoke in low, worried tones. The servants whispered to each other. Grim-faced men came to see Arthur, and Jane, hovering near his closed study door, caught fragments of their ominous conversation.

". . . an enormous fleet . . . hundred guns . . . gallant fools on the island . . . people evacuating the city . . . a tragic sight . . ."

Looking down from an upper-floor veranda later, Jane saw the "tragic sight"—families, their possessions piled high on carts, hurrying up the street, as if fleeing an unseen menace.

Suddenly Brandon was standing beside her. "Don't waste your sympathy on them, Jane. Last year they forced our English governor to run for his life. Now he's coming back, and they'll pay for their insolence."

"And you take pleasure in their wretchedness?" Jane asked coldly.

"Not pleasure, of course not. But neither do I sympathize with them, as I fear my foolish father does. And I should think that as a loyal British subject, Jane, you certainly should not."

"Nevertheless, I do." Tugging at the locket around her neck—a sure sign she was upset—she turned away and went to her room.

A while later, Mrs. Morley joined her there, her face clouded with worry. "Something's wrong, Jane. I can feel it in the air."

Jane was just about to reassure her when a deep boom in the distance shook the room. Hurrying out onto the third-floor veranda, she looked toward the harbor. Far away, visible over the rooftops and church spires of the city, a puff of black smoke curled toward the sky. Three more booms came in quick succession.

Mrs. Morley peered fearfully out. "What is it, Jane?"

"I'm not sure," Jane replied quietly. "It must be cannon fire."

"Oh, Lord, have mercy! Come back inside, quickly!"

But Jane had caught sight of the schoolmaster rushing toward the front gate. "Mr. Cordwyn!" she called down to him. "What's happening?"

He glanced up at her without slowing down. "No school today, Jane."

"But where are you going?"

"To tell my friends on Queen Street to get out

37

while they still can!" He was out the front gate and down the street in an instant.

With the booms rumbling and rolling across the sky, Jane was suddenly seized with a wild impulse. Queen Street! Cousin Hugh!

She ran for the stairs, calling over her shoulder, "I'll be back later, Mrs. Morley. I'm going with Mr. Cordwyn to Cousin Hugh's!"

"No, dear, you mustn't!" Mrs. Morley cried. "You know your uncle—"

But Jane was already gone.

"Mr. Cordwyn, wait!" Breathless, she caught up with him a block away. "I'm coming with you!"

Scowling at her, he swept an arm toward the invisible rumblings. "You hear that, Jane? British warships are attacking Charlestown Harbor. You shouldn't be out on the streets. It's not safe. Go home and stay there."

"Mr. Cordwyn!" Jane stood her ground, eyes ablaze. "For all their kindness, the Ainsleys treat me like a child. You're the only one who has been honest about what's going on. Please, don't let me down. I need to go with you."

Simon hesitated, struggling with indecision, then finally sighed in resignation. "I'll regret this. But all right, come along."

"Oh, thank you, Mr. Cordwyn!"

Over the rumbling cannon fire, Simon explained more as they walked on, threading their way through a mass of fleeing refugees.

"The Patriots are holed up on Sullivan's Island, outside the harbor. All they've got is a couple of guns and a little powder, behind a few palmetto logs they call a fort. With that they plan to turn back a huge British fleet! It's positively pathetic."

Soon after turning onto Queen Street, he knocked on a door beneath a swinging sign reading, HUGH PRENTICE, CABINETMAKER. Tacked on the door was a handwritten note reading, CLOSED UNTIL FURTHER NOTICE.

"Perhaps they've come to their senses and left," Simon remarked.

Then a bright-eyed woman with abundant red hair stuck her head out of an upstairs window. "Simon—what a nice surprise! I'll be right down."

"That was Lydia, Hugh's wife," Simon told Jane while they waited. "Prepare yourself, Jane, you're about to enter a nest of rebels. But you're also going to learn that rebels can be very nice people."

It was, Jane would decide later, a remarkable learning experience. First there was Lydia, who ushered the visitors into a large, stone-floored room littered with wood shavings, pieces of decorative woodwork on several tables, and a clutter of carving tools. The cabinetmaker's workshop.

Lydia's lively personality seemed to match her flame-colored hair, and she enveloped Jane in a great hug upon being introduced. "You'll call me Lydia. We're all family here," she said. "Now come on upstairs. Hugh and my son, Peter, are up on the third floor watching the battle through a spyglass. And oh my, Hugh's going to be delighted you're here!"

She led them upstairs and through a second-floor kitchen and eating area. At one end, cooking utensils hung on the wall next to a huge stone fireplace. At the other sat a large oak table and chairs. Hugh's work, Jane assumed, admiringly. At the top of another flight of stairs, they entered what appeared to be a large storage room. Before high windows stood two men, the younger one peering through a telescope. Both turned at the sound of footsteps. When the older man's eyes fell on Jane he stared in disbelief.

"Can this be . . . Jane?" he breathed.

She smiled. "Yes, it's Jane. And you must be Cousin Hugh." In a few seconds, she found herself wrapped in another enormous hug.

"Jane, my dearest girl! I never thought it would be here in my humble American home that I'd finally meet Lady Jane of Almesbury. But fate has so decreed it, so welcome, Cousin, welcome!" Beaming, he kissed her cheek.

She already knew he was thirty-nine. And now she saw that he was a large, broad-shouldered man with thick dark hair and a roundish face. And when he held her at arm's length for a better look, she realized that in spite of his size, there was a gentleness in his eyes and in his touch.

"Thank you, Cousin Hugh," she said, and thought: *I like him.*

Then as Hugh turned to shake hands with Simon,

the younger man stepped forward to greet Jane. He was nineteen or twenty, she guessed, with his mother's vivid red hair and twinkling eyes.

"I'm Peter Quincy," he announced with a grin. "Hugh's stepson and apprentice, and the despair of Mr. Cordwyn, who thinks I'm much too belligerent in my devotion to the Patriot cause. He, of course, pretends to be neutral, but—"

"I *am* neutral," Simon put in sharply. "Seeing nothing but foolish belligerence on both sides, I find it the only sensible course."

Peter's grin disappeared. "There can be no neutrals in this fight, schoolmaster! Sooner or later you'll have to decide which side you're on. The side of tyranny, or the side of freedom!"

"Hush, Peter!" Lydia scolded. "Remember, Jane's an English lady."

His amiable grin returned as quickly as it had vanished. "Don't mean to offend you, Lady Jane. You're among friends here."

"Oh, please, don't mind me," Jane said. "I want to listen and learn all I can." And once more, she patiently asked to be called simply Jane.

"Come over here. Let me show you something." Peter led her to a high window where a panoramic view of Charlestown Harbor lay before them. Drifting black smoke hung low, darkening the water. The booming guns were unseen, but were still booming, and their sound seemed alarmingly closer.

"Have a look." He picked up his telescope and

offered it to Jane. "That big building down by the docks is the Exchange, which used to be a busy place before they cut off our shipping. Nothing in there now but tons of rotting English tea. Over on the other side of the harbor is Sullivan's Island, where our men are returning the enemy fire, shot for shot. And standing way over yonder offshore is the British flagship *Experiment*. A nice target, eh?"

"So is that ridiculous pile of palmetto logs they call a fort, on Sullivan's Island," Simon remarked, joining them. "It won't last long."

"You forget, schoolmaster, palmetto logs are spongy," Peter countered. "They bend, but they don't break. Meanwhile, the British ships sit out there like ducks on a pond. They're the ones that won't last long."

"And if they're driven off, you think they won't return?" Simon asked.

"If they do, we'll drive 'em off again!" Peter replied hotly.

"You're an idle dreamer, Peter. You dream of American independence, but unfortunately, your ragtag rebels have no way to achieve it."

"I think we do, Simon." This was Hugh, his mild manner a soothing contrast to Peter's fiery style. "We Americans can't go on living under a distant king forever. A king who bleeds us for taxes but cares nothing for our welfare. No, we must become independent. It may not happen soon, but it will happen. It's in our destiny. I can see it very clearly."

Simon scowled. "Look here, Hugh. What you need to see—and what I came to tell you—is that when the British make it to shore, they'll be coming after people like you. You've got to get out while you still can!"

"We appreciate your concern, my friend. But running is not our way."

Lydia drew Jane aside. "Sorry about all this rebel talk, love. But don't take it personally. Remember what Peter said: You're among friends—"

Just then, Peter, squinting through his telescope, shouted, "Look at that—the *Experiment*'s taken a direct hit! And she's listing badly, turning about!"

Hugh took the glass and confirmed the news. Then he and Peter swapped backslapping congratulations that even Lydia couldn't resist joining. Simon looked on stone-faced, Jane in wide-eyed wonder.

"Come on, Cordwyn!" Peter cried. "Give a cheer for the valiant defenders of Sullivan's Island!"

Simon snorted. "You want me to cheer for suicidal recklessness?"

Peter turned to Jane. "How about you, Miss Jane? I realize you can't give your countrymen's enemies a big cheer. Maybe just a little one?"

Jane hesitated, searching for words. "What can I say? I'm a loyal subject of King George. Yet, here in a house that stands against his rule, I'm told I'm among friends—and I truly believe that is so. I have no idea where right lies in all this. So I'll just say three cheers for the valiant men, and may God protect them all, Englishmen and Americans alike!"

"Hear, hear!" exclaimed Hugh, delighted with Jane's diplomatic reply.

Soon then, while the men stayed upstairs, Lydia invited Jane to come down to the kitchen with her while she prepared a bite to eat. There she busied herself while refusing Jane's help.

"You sit, love. Just talk to me. Tell me about yourself."

Jane sat at the table and, in reply to Lydia's questions, spoke of her life in England—this time trying to make it sound pleasant—and her voyage across the sea, which she admitted was a grueling ordeal. In her turn, Lydia told of how her first husband, Peter's father, had started a tavern in Charlestown years ago. When her husband died, soon after Peter's birth, she couldn't keep the business going. Then she met Hugh, a lonely bachelor, and—

"Well, you can see my story has a happy ending," she said with a smile.

Jane smiled back. "Just the kind I like."

Soon the men came downstairs to take seats at the table.

Simon was ready to admit he'd been mistaken. "The British fleet does seem to be withdrawing. But I still say celebrating is not in order. Even if they're driven away today, they'll surely be back before—"

He was interrupted by an urgent knocking at the door downstairs.

Lydia went tense. "Who could that be?" she wondered.

44

"I'll go," Peter said, and headed down to the ground floor.

The others waited, listening. They heard the creaking of the heavy front door as Peter opened it, followed by the sound of mumbled voices. Then with explosive suddenness, the mumbled voices became angry shouts. One of the angry voices was Peter's. The other, immediately recognized by Jane, brought her to her feet in wide-eyed amazement.

"It's Brandon Ainsley!" she cried, and flew downstairs.

Chapter 7

By the time Jane reached the ground floor, Peter and Brandon were eye to eye, snarling insults at each other.

Brandon, shaking himself loose from Peter's grasp, said, "Get your filthy hands off me, you—"

Peter responded, "Watch your manners, you prissified dandy!"

"I'll teach *you* some manners, villain!"

"Try it, Sir Dandy! Just you try it!"

They were coming at each other for physical combat when Jane stepped between them. "Stop it at once, both of you!" Her sharp tone startled them both into sullen obedience. Turning to Brandon then, she spoke in her usual calm manner. "Brandon, why are you here?"

He was still glowering from his tiff with Peter. "I am here because I was sent to fetch you. Uncle Robert and Aunt Clarissa have arrived in the city. And you, dear girl, are in trouble."

Her calm destroyed, Jane paled and clutched her throat.

Then Simon was standing beside her. "Don't worry, Jane. I'll explain to your uncle that it's all my fault. I shouldn't have brought you here."

"No, thanks all the same, Mr. Cordwyn. But I chose to come, and I'll accept responsibility for my own actions." She turned back to Brandon, and noticing that he and Peter were still glaring at each other, said, "Perhaps you could wait outside, Brandon. I'll be only a minute."

"Gladly!" he snapped, and went out.

Peter began to look sheepish. "Sorry, Jane. But he barged in here like he owned the place. Rubbed me the wrong way, that's all."

Jane gave him a sad smile. "It's plain to see, Peter, that you and Brandon are two people who should never, ever be in the same room together."

Brandon waited outside beside his carriage while Jane said her hasty good-byes, but on their ride home he was still in an ill temper. "Who *was* that ruffian who treated me so rudely?" he demanded.

"Cousin Hugh's stepson, Peter Quincy," Jane told him.

"Hmph! Next time I see him I'll give him a good thrashing."

More likely the other way around, Jane thought. "Of course you will, Brandon. Now tell me about Uncle Robert and Aunt Clarissa."

He explained that rebel raids at Rosewall had delayed their return to the city. "Backwoods thieves thinking they're Patriot heroes, raiding the slave quarters," he muttered. "Scum of the earth!"

Finally able to get away, Robert had arrived with high hopes. "He wanted to be here to welcome back our royal governor the minute he stepped ashore when the British fleet docked. And, of course, he was also eager to meet *you*."

But Robert had found his house on Legare Street so badly vandalized as to be uninhabitable. Meanwhile, the fleet was encountering stiff resistance, making the governor's return impossible for the time being.

"And on top of all that, he learns that you've disobeyed his express orders and gone off with Cordwyn to visit that disreputable Hugh Prentice! I warned you about Cordwyn, Jane. But you wouldn't listen."

Jane gazed glumly out of the carriage window as she pondered her bad luck. How eagerly she had waited to meet her uncle! At last, it was to happen— but a meeting that should be joyous was now spoiled.

As Jane stepped out of the carriage at the Ainsleys' house, she caught her breath at the sight of an elegantly gowned woman coming out onto the veranda. Her lustrous blond hair framed a perfect face, and she moved with exquisite grace. Jane knew instantly who she was, and came forward with hand extended.

"Aunt Clarissa? I'm Jane Prentice."

"So I assumed." Clarissa coolly looked her up and

down. Then she touched the worn fabric of Jane's dress, and a pained expression distorted her beautiful face. "Oh, dear! You actually go out in this?"

Jane felt like a peasant under royal scrutiny. "It's the best I have."

"And you, the daughter of an earl!"

"A penniless earl, I'm afraid."

"Evidently. Well, if we ever get free of this infernal blockade and Arthur gets some decent merchandise again, we'll fix that. Meanwhile, Robert's waiting for you in Arthur's study. And he's quite angry. Of course, I understand how easily a young girl can fall under the spell of a devilishly attractive man like Simon Cordwyn, but—"

Jane recoiled in shock. "Oh, no, it's not like that at all, I just—"

"Explain yourself to Robert, dear. He's waiting."

So was Mrs. Morley, at the top of the stairs on the second floor. "I'm sorry, Jane—I hope you're not angry with me. I had to tell them where you were."

"Of course, Mrs. Morley. I understand."

Moving on down the hall, Jane paused in front of the closed door of Arthur's study. Inside, a furious argument was going on.

First Arthur: "That's unfair, Robert. I've looked after her very well."

Then Robert: "By allowing her to consort with a scoundrel like Cordwyn?"

"She does not *consort* with him. She attends his school."

"And permitting her to be exposed to low-life rebels like Hugh!"

"Good Lord, Robert, I don't know what you're so agitated about. Both Simon and Hugh are perfectly decent, honorable men!"

Taking a deep breath, Jane knocked at the door.

Arthur opened it. "Come in, Jane. Your uncle wishes a word with you."

She would have recognized Robert easily from the family resemblance. His dark hair, finely chiseled face, and piercing eyes were remindful of his late older brother—Jane's father. His kinship with Hugh was not so readily seen. A few years older than Hugh, he was shorter, more compact and muscular—a tougher man, Jane surmised, than his easygoing cousin.

She stepped toward him. "Hello, Uncle Robert."

He spent a moment examining her features, then, to her pleasant surprise, spoke gently. "Ah, yes. I see my dear brother, Edward, in your face." But then he became stern. "I had hoped, Jane, to embrace you when we met and welcome you into my family. Regrettably, however, I am plagued by one misfortune after another. And now the unkindest cut of all—your willfully disobeying my orders by going with an unsuitable companion to a place specifically forbidden to you. Is it any wonder I'm ill-tempered?"

"No, Uncle," Jane replied. "I'm truly sorry about your misfortunes, and I greatly regret that I've spoiled our meeting. It's just that I wanted so badly to meet Cousin Hugh, I—"

"And since no one bothered to stop you, you just did as you pleased! I should have known better than to let you be brought to this house."

"What the devil do you mean by that?" Arthur demanded hotly.

"I mean that I've always suspected this place of rebel sentiment!" Robert shot back. "We all know one of your friends is that notorious John Rutledge, who dares call himself president of the *Republic* of South Carolina!"

"Rutledge is an old friend of many years' standing. Should I renounce him because we differ in our political views?"

"If he favors treason, yes, just as I have renounced Hugh! A man is known by the company he keeps, Arthur."

"He is better known by his words and actions, Robert. I have never favored treason, and you know it. I refused to attend the Continental Congress in Philadelphia precisely because I feared some foolhardy action by that assembly."

"Does that prove you're loyal, or simply that you're a coward?"

In the heat of argument, they seemed to have forgotten Jane's presence, but now they were interrupted by Simon appearing in the doorway.

"Cordwyn!" Robert thundered. "How dare you take my niece to mix with street rabble, and expose her to all manner of traitorous talk!"

Simon came forward, ready with a calm reply. "I

beg your pardon, sir, but Mr. Hugh Prentice is not street rabble. He's an honest, hardworking citizen and a good friend. As for Miss Jane, you need have no fear of her being affected by rebel talk. She's an exceedingly intelligent young lady with a mind of her own."

But this only made Robert angrier. "Well, *you* have no right to take her anywhere. You owe me an immediate apology for your actions!"

Simon's voice was now tinged with anger as well. "If I have caused Miss Jane to incur your disfavor, sir, I am very sorry, for she is innocent of so much as any thought of wrongdoing. If an apology is due, it is to her, and I offer it now." He bowed slightly to Jane, who stared back in astonishment. "But I fail to see how my escorting Miss Jane to her cousin's home requires an apology to you, and I must decline to give it."

Robert was outraged. "The devil you say!" Arthur again became the object of his anger. "Arthur, I told you years ago that bringing this man here was a grievous mistake. He's an insolent scoundrel! He's got to go!"

"That'll be all, Simon," Arthur said quietly. "Thank you for coming."

Simon nodded, and after a long look at Jane, went out.

Arthur then turned to Robert. "I find this discussion very tiresome, so I'll excuse myself as well." Starting for the door, he paused in passing Jane to speak softly to her. "Don't let him frighten you, my dear. He's not as ferocious as he pretends to be."

He seems quite ferocious enough, thought Jane. "I'm truly sorry for any distress I've caused you, Uncle Robert. But Mr. Cordwyn is not at fault. I persuaded him to take me to Cousin Hugh's. Blame me, please, not him."

"I *do* blame him, for his insolence," Robert snapped. "And Arthur, for leaving you unsupervised. And *you*, for being disobedient. That I cannot tolerate. Only the fact that you're a highborn English lady prevents me from sending you to your room without supper, as a badly behaved child should be!"

Now a glint of defiance came into Jane's eyes. "In that case, sir, I suggest you disregard my highborn status. If it would please you to punish me, then do so."

Robert blinked, taken aback by her sudden show of spirit. When he spoke again it was in a calmer tone. "I must go now. Thanks to rebel thugs, I need to see about repairs on my house. Please pack your things tonight, because we leave for Rosewall first thing in the morning. This is no fit place for you, Jane. Perhaps out in the country, away from the undesirable influences here, you may learn to behave like the proper lady you were born to be."

"I shall do my best, sir. And now, if I may be excused?"

Head high, with serene dignity, she turned and went out, heading upstairs to her room. Her thoughts were in turmoil. *Learn to be a lady, must I? But how am I ever going to learn to get along with that tyrant?*

Fretfully she felt for her locket. Only this time, it wasn't there.

Chapter 8

Mrs. Morley looked in on Jane later, to find her slumped in her bedroom chair. "What happened, dear? Was Mr. Robert terribly angry with you?"

"I fear so, yes. He told me I must learn to behave like a lady."

"Hmph! You're already the finest lady he's ever likely to meet."

"He was also furious with Mr. Cordwyn, which was extremely unfair. But we have to remember, it hasn't been a good day for Uncle Robert. His house has been vandalized, and the royal governor's return was postponed."

"And some even worse news just arrived," Mrs. Morley said. "The British ships suffered so much damage in the bombardment, they've given up and sailed away."

"Really!" Jane had noticed that the distant cannon fire had long since stopped, a fact accounted for by this latest news. So Peter Quincy had been right—and to Jane's surprise, she couldn't decide whether to be sad or glad.

"I have some bad news of my own, Mrs. Morley," she said then, rising from her chair. "I hate to tell you this, but you'd notice eventually, anyway. My locket came off somewhere, and now it's missing."

"Oh, merciful heavens!" Mrs. Morley cried. "What's to be done?"

"I have to find it, that's what's to be done. I'm going to start immediately after supper, if Uncle Robert will allow it."

But Robert was not at the supper table—only Harriet, Clarissa, Jane, and Mrs. Morley gathered there. Arthur had gone off on some unspecified "business," and Robert, accompanied by Brandon, had gone to see about his damaged house. Conversation between Harriet and Clarissa was mostly limited to domestic matters, as if both were determined to steer clear of the day's important events.

Jane waited, and when the opportunity arose, she brought up the subject of her missing locket. "Not that it's especially valuable," she explained. "Except to me. It's the only thing I have that belonged to my mother."

"After supper we'll launch a thorough search," Harriet promised.

"What worries me is that I might have lost it at Cousin Hugh's," Jane went on. "So I was wondering,

Aunt Clarissa—if we don't find it, do you suppose Uncle Robert would mind awfully if I ran back to Hugh's, and—"

"Good gracious, Jane!" Clarissa exclaimed. "I wouldn't dare suggest such a thing to him! He's so hostile toward Hugh, the mere mention of the name sends him into an apoplectic fit."

Harriet offered a solution. "I'll send a servant to inquire."

It was done. In the meantime, the women spent an hour after supper scouring the house in search of the locket. It was nowhere to be found. The servants were questioned, but none could recall seeing it. The one who had been sent to inquire at Hugh's returned, saying that the people there had found no locket.

Clarissa tried in vain to console the inconsolable Jane. "Now don't fret, dear. Losing a locket is not the end of the world. I'm sure we can find you another pretty necklace to wear."

Jane forced a smile. *Another pretty necklace—to replace my mother's!* How little understanding the beautiful Clarissa possessed. With a sigh of resignation, she began to pack for the trip to Rosewall the next morning.

Rosewall. Suddenly she had the feeling that going to the backcountry plantation, a day's journey away, would be like going to another foreign land.

It was stiflingly hot that night. Jane was a long time getting to sleep, slept fitfully, and awoke after an hour feeling limp and exhausted. The French windows leading to the third-floor veranda were open, but no breath of air stirred. Jane rose and went out onto the veranda, hoping to find a cool breeze. There was none, but the garden below was enchanting under soft moonlight. All was quiet. All the world was asleep.

But not quite. Gradually, Jane became aware of low voices drifting up on the still air. She tiptoed down the veranda toward the rear corner of the house. Two people sat on a garden bench below, half hidden in the shadows. The blond hair of Clarissa Prentice shone like spun gold in the moonlight, and Jane could make out the broad shoulders of Simon Cordwyn beside her.

"I had intended to apologize," Simon was saying. "But the way he went after me set me off. Now he's demanding that Mr. Ainsley send me packing."

"Don't give it a thought," Clarissa said soothingly. "Do you think for one moment I'd let that happen? Never, my darling, I couldn't bear it!"

My darling? Jane stifled a gasp.

Clarissa's fingers played in Simon's hair. "Now, go back to your room. If I can get away later, I'll come to you, I promise." She slipped her arms around his neck and pulled his lips to hers.

Turning away, Jane crept back to her room and crawled into bed, to lie staring at the ceiling in wide-eyed shock. Which was worse? Her sharp disappointment at the kind and gentle schoolmaster, whom she had come to respect and admire so much? Or the disgust she felt for the lovely Clarissa, the shameless, deceiving wife? She knew only that there would be very little sleep for herself that night.

Two carriages were drawn up in front of the house the next morning. It was all arranged: Robert and Clarissa would travel in the first, Jane and Mrs. Morley in the second. While the drivers loaded the baggage, the Ainsleys and their guests said hasty good-byes in the courtyard. Brandon fervently clasped Jane's hands and promised to visit her soon and often, since her sweet company was essential to his existence. She gave him a distracted smile, and after embracing Arthur and Harriet with warm thanks for all their kindness, climbed into her carriage beside Mrs. Morley. Watching them, she noticed that although Arthur embraced and kissed his sister, he barely mumbled a word to Robert. How sad it was to see the brothers-in-law harboring resentment against each other. Harriet gave Robert and Clarissa expansive hugs and waved cheerily to her departing guests.

Jane settled back, eager to be gone. But as the first carriage pulled out, Simon suddenly appeared beside the second, delaying its departure.

"I know your uncle wouldn't approve of my speaking to you, Jane. But I couldn't let you go without saying good-bye. I'll miss you."

Her eyes fixed on the carriage driver's back, Jane replied with cold formality. "Really? How nice. I'm sorry I can't say the same."

He regarded her with a puzzled frown. "What's the matter? Are you angry with me about something?"

Still she refused to look at him. "No, not angry, Mr. Cordwyn. Just disappointed." Leaning forward, she spoke to the driver, "Move out, please."

As the carriage clattered away, Mrs. Morley looked back to see Simon staring after them with a look of slack-jawed astonishment. Her own face wore a look of shocked disapproval as she turned to the girl beside her.

"I must say, Jane! That was really quite rude of you!"

Jane tossed her head crossly. "I don't care! I hate him, and I hate his boring school, and I can't *wait* to get to Rosewall!"

And if that's true, she thought, tears stinging her eyes, *why do I feel so miserable?*

Chapter 9

As a young bride arriving in the South Carolina backcountry, Clarissa Prentice had taken one look at the fourteen-foot-high stone wall encircling her husband Robert's plantation house and its gardens, and called the place a fortress. To soften its appearance, she had ordered hundreds of climbing English roses brought in, which she had planted along the base of the wall. Soon the great expanses of stern, forbidding stone disappeared beneath fragrant blood-red blossoms and thorny growth, and the name Rosewall was born.

A great iron gate guarded the only entrance to the grounds. Shimmering in the distance, a quarter mile beyond, the winding Edisto River lay, like a twisted thread on a deep green carpet. The three-story brick-and-timber mansion sat a hundred yards back from the gate. Surrounding the house was a garden paradise, complete with grape-laden arbors, masses of flowers, giant moss-hung oaks, lush green lawns, and meandering gravel footpaths. Gazing about, Jane felt that she had entered a world of almost unearthly peace and serenity. As she stepped into the house a few minutes later, the magnificent interior of high ceilings, richly paneled walls, and fine furnishings took her breath away. The Ainsley house in Charlestown was grand, but even in England Jane had never seen such splendor as this.

A muscular giant of a man appeared, ebony black, completely bald, and barefoot. He was Omar, the butler, and he moved with uncommon grace and dignity. Omar bowed to each person in turn, with an especially low bow for Jane.

"Omar here to serve you, miss," he said in a resonant voice. "What you ask be Omar's command."

Thanking him, Jane turned to meet the lighter black woman who now stood at his side. Cuba, the cook and housekeeper, was Omar's wife. Her broad face crinkled with a warm smile. "Praise God, you be sent from heaven, child!" she exclaimed. "You'll liven up this big ol' house right quick, I'd say." Jane returned her smile and, just this once, didn't mind being called a child.

Clarissa showed Jane up to a sunny, pale pink room on the second floor.

"This is your room, dear. We hope you'll like it. We truly enjoyed getting it ready for you."

"It's beautiful," Jane exclaimed, gazing around her at tall windows with lacy white curtains, a tall four-poster bed, and soft, fluffy pillows. "Thank you for everything you did to make it so."

"Oh, it was mostly Cuba, really. Robert may be the owner here, but it's really Cuba and Omar who run the place. Cuba works miracles managing the house, keeping us all fed and everything in perfect order. And Omar—there's a man of many talents. In another life, he could have been a great leader."

Jane thought of the Ainsleys' servants. Though kindly treated, they had seemed more like phantoms than people, gliding silently in and out, eyes downcast, speaking only when spoken to. Omar and Cuba, though, seemed to see themselves as valued persons in their own right, perhaps because their owners—or at least their mistress—openly acknowledged their importance.

Jane felt tempted to soften her attitude toward her beautiful aunt. But when she recalled the whispered conversation in a moonlit garden—and the promise of a tryst to follow—the temptation vanished. In time, she hoped to overcome Robert's anger toward her. But how could she ever get over her disgust at seeing his wife betray him? *And why,* she wondered, *do I, too, feel somehow betrayed?*

The summer daylight was beginning to fade when they gathered in the dining room an hour later. To Jane's relief, her uncle seemed in an amiable mood as he inquired if her room was satisfactory. She assured him that it was more than satisfactory, it was beautiful.

"Indeed," she added, "Rosewall is quite beautiful altogether."

Robert gave a pleased smile. "Actually, you've seen very little of it so far. Later I'll take you upstairs, where you can see its full extent."

"Feel honored, Jane," Clarissa said dryly. "You'll get to see Robert's favorite place, his observatory. He reads his precious poetry up there and stares off for miles in all directions. Everything you can see from up there is Rosewall land. The kingdom of His Majesty, King Robert the First!"

Shocked by Clarissa's sarcasm, Jane shot a curious look at her. But Robert only chuckled indulgently. He didn't seem to mind her words a bit.

The observatory, it turned out, was the entire third floor of the house. Reached by a steep, narrow staircase at the end of a long hallway, the chamber was almost bare, except for a table and chair in one corner and a desk stacked with old books in another. A portrait of King George, complete with crown and long jeweled robe, hung above the desk. Robert stood watching Jane while she gazed around her. The golden light of the setting sun shone through high, open windows on all four sides of the room, and the rich fragrance of the thousands of roses far below seemed to fill the air they breathed.

Jane looked out beyond the massive rose wall at a panorama stretching to the distant horizon. Robert pointed out the intricate system of ditches bringing the flooded rice fields their life-giving water. There were barns, vegetable gardens, and fruit orchards, and two long rows of small brick houses for the slaves working the crops. Beyond the rice fields lay endless wilderness, with the river winding through a brooding swamp. Barely visible in the twilight, plumes of smoke rose from the chimneys at the plantation of Robert's friend Louis Lambert and his family, several miles to the north.

Robert pointed to a pair of large birds soaring in the luminous sky. "Eagles. The swamp is their home, and the alligators' as well. This land belonged to the wild creatures long before it was ours, Jane. We are the interlopers here." He drew a long sigh. "Clarissa mocks me, calling this my kingdom and all that. She doesn't love it the way I do. That's because it reminds her of the one great sadness that has darkened our lives. Our little daughter was taken by the fever in her infancy, years ago."

"Yes, Aunt Harriet told me about that. I'm so sorry, Uncle Robert."

"But now that you're here, Jane—" His wistful smile touched her heart. "Perhaps you'll be the daughter we always dreamed of having." Now, at last, he embraced her tenderly. "Welcome, my dear. Welcome home."

As the long midsummer days passed, Jane settled comfortably into her new life at Rosewall. The only difficulty was that she missed the lively city of Charlestown, missed the Ainsleys and their charming home—and, most of all, missed Mr. Cordwyn. But she could not forget what she had learned about him and Clarissa, and she made a solemn vow never to speak to or even think of him again. Meanwhile, Brandon visited occasionally, providing a welcome diversion, even though he spent most of his time talking to Robert—partly about "the troubles," and partly about his favorite topic, horses and racing. Playing the beautiful German harpsichord in the parlor was another pleasant diversion, as was strolling in the garden among the many-scented flowers.

Mrs. Morley kept insisting to Jane that she disliked living "out in the wilderness," as she called it. But she got along well with both master and mistress, and though finding Omar a little frightening, she formed an easy relationship with the cheerful Cuba. Soon Mrs. Morley found ways to keep busy: mending clothes, darning socks, and doing other useful chores.

Despite Clarissa's observation that Omar and Cuba ran the place, the true ruler was clearly Clarissa herself. She fulfilled her many duties with confident efficiency. Jane was glad for the chance to learn from her, and Clarissa instructed her patiently. But their long hours together produced no real bond between them. And, sadly, it seemed to Jane that her aunt took no pleasure in the privileged life she led—with one exception: She genuinely loved the garden. The cool early mornings nearly always found her out surveying the flower beds, directing her several gardeners to clip a wayward camellia branch here, or pluck away faded azalea blossoms there. A large corner of the garden Clarissa reserved for her dozens of imported rosebushes, and these she tended herself. She allowed Jane to help her, dressed in an old frock and a too-big sun hat that Clarissa no longer used.

One morning, gazing up at the wall looming above them as they worked, Clarissa fell into a somber mood. "When all is said and done, it really is rather like a prison here, don't you think?" She smiled at Jane's shocked look. "Don't worry. In a few years you'll marry and leave here, while I . . ." She shrugged and went on working.

Jane stepped closer. "Rosewall is your home, Aunt Clarissa, not a prison. Your husband seems a fine man, and I'm sure he loves you dearly."

"It's true, I am one of two things Robert loves best in the world. The first is Rosewall, and I'm definitely second. Notice I said *thing*—a lovely ornament at Rosewall. And now you are one, too."

"It seems to me that you're much more than an ornament here," Jane said as they worked. "I've watched you. You're busy all day long, attending to a thousand details. I only hope I can be of some help to you."

"Of course you will," Clarissa said. "And in a few years, there'll be a fine wedding here. You'll become the wife of some carefully selected son of a good Carolina family and go live in a big house of your own."

"Carefully selected?" Jane echoed. "You mean by Uncle Robert?"

"Well, not literally, I suppose. But he'll expect you to be guided by his judgment. You *are* his ward, after all."

"Only until I'm twenty-one."

"But surely you'll be married by then."

"Perhaps not. Perhaps I won't make any important choices in life until after I'm twenty-one. Then I can make my own, using my own judgment."

Clarissa paused in her work to stare at her young assistant. "I must say, Jane, that refined English-lady manner of yours is quite deceiving. You've got a lot more grit in you than I thought."

Not sure whether she had just received a compliment or a scolding, Jane let this pass without comment.

The next morning, Clarissa unexpectedly announced that she was going into Charlestown. "Someone must see to our house repairs," she told Robert, "and you're needed here more than I am."

Jane asked if she could come along. "I'd so like to see Aunt Harriet and Uncle Arthur again."

But Clarissa shook her head. "I'm sorry, dear, not this time. For a few days, *you* must be mistress of Rosewall."

Omar swung open the iron gate for her carriage, and Clarissa, in her best finery, was on her way. Jane watched glumly, afraid the trip had less to do with house repairs than with a lonely woman flying to her lover's arms. *Is she unfaithful to Uncle Robert because she feels no love in their marriage?*

Robert, standing beside her on the veranda, looked fondly and longingly after the departing carriage. "She's my treasure, Jane. I'd be lost without her. I'm a lucky man."

Jane nodded. So much for the theory that Clarissa was unloved by her husband. "Yes, Uncle Robert. And she's a lucky lady."

If only she had the good sense to realize it.

Chapter 10

Gloom descended over Robert in Clarissa's absence. His duties took him away from the house for hours each day, but when he was at home, he roamed the house restlessly. *He really is lost without her,* Jane thought.

But at the same time, she was pleased to notice a real friendship developing between Robert and Mrs. Morley. More precisely, the warm relationship that had existed between them when Robert was a boy began to grow again. In the evenings while Clarissa was away, Robert, Mrs. Morley, and Jane sat together in the parlor, sipping sassafras tea and talking. Robert asked if Mrs. Morley was comfortable at Rosewall. Was her room satisfactory? She replied that her airy, second-floor room right next to Jane's, with its nice view of the garden, was perfect, thank you, sir. Tactfully, she refrained from mentioning the complaint she often voiced to Jane, about living "out here in the wilderness." Mostly Jane listened as the other two reminisced about old times in England, long before she was born, occasionally chuckling at stories of Robert's boyhood pranks with his brother, Jane's father.

"You know, Mr. Robert's really a kind soul," Mrs. Morley told the girl later. "You were very lucky when he consented to become your guardian."

"Indeed I was, Mrs. Morley." Jane readily agreed, happy that her old companion was starting to settle in. But Robert's own discontent was past helping until Clarissa's return. Fortunately, in a few days she was back—and his gloom lifted.

"I bring news," she began. They were seating themselves in the parlor while Cuba brought refreshments. "First, the house will be ready very soon."

Robert nodded, pleased. "That's excellent."

"Second—and you won't like this, Robert—the whole city's talking about the Continental Congress in Philadelphia. It's rumored they're about to adopt a resolution by Mr. Thomas Jefferson of Virginia—"

"Stop right there," Robert growled. "I know about Jefferson. He's a dangerous lunatic. I'll hear no more of him. What else?"

"Well, I'm sure there's nothing to that, anyway. Third, I've invited a few people for the weekend. It's so dull here. I thought, at least for Jane's sake, we should have some friends in."

"You might've asked me first," Robert grumbled.

"And you'd have raised all sorts of objections, as usual. It's just the Dunnings, the Lamberts, and Arthur and family. They'll come on Saturday, and we'll have a grand feast." Clarissa glanced apologetically at Cuba. "Sorry to announce this so suddenly, Cuba."

"Oh, no trouble, missus!" Cuba flashed her ever-ready smile. "Saturday two days away. Plenty time."

"You invited Arthur here?" Robert asked, glowering at Clarissa.

"He *is* my brother, Robert! Can't you try to get along just for a day or two? Arthur's willing. Is it too much to ask?"

"I hope Brandon's coming, too?"

"Indeed, he's longing to see Jane again. He's quite taken with you, dear. Fancies himself becoming your husband one day."

"And you could hardly do better, Jane," Robert put in. "He's a young man of fine character, and his loyalty to the Crown is beyond question. Which, unfortunately, is more than can be said of his father."

Clarissa gave him a sharp look. "That was uncalled for, Robert."

The conversation had taken a turn that made Jane uncomfortable, and she was glad when Robert excused himself and went out a moment later.

"Now tell me, dear," Clarissa asked her, "what have you been doing?"

"I finished trimming the roses in the east bed, and started on the south side," Jane replied. "I hope you'll be pleased."

"I'm sure I will."

"About Saturday, Aunt Clarissa—who are the guests you've invited?"

Clarissa explained that Morton and Penelope Dunning were old friends with a fifteen-year-old daughter, Lucinda. Morton had been a merchant in Charlestown whose business, like Arthur's, had suffered severely from the British blockade. Unlike Arthur, he had given up his store in the city and removed to a smaller town only a few hours' ride from Rosewall. Brothers Louis and Jacques Lambert were co-owners of a nearby plantation. The younger brother, Jacques, she described as an outrageous flirt, in contrast to the dignified, sober Louis.

"They're of French descent," Clarissa said. "And Jacques thinks he must flirt with every woman he meets. No doubt you'll get your share of his attentions. But he's really quite harmless."

"I'm sure it won't be a problem," Jane remarked. "But I wonder—would it have been out of the question to invite Cousin Hugh and his wife?"

"Good heavens, yes! Robert will have a hard enough time being civil to Arthur, but Hugh—don't even think of it!"

"And I don't suppose..." Jane hesitated, a mischievous thought forming in her mind. "Could one have invited Mr. Cordwyn?"

This time Clarissa's response was even more emphatic. "I should say not! What could you be thinking—he's not our sort at all!"

"Isn't he?"

Clarissa slapped the arm of her chair angrily. "Look here, I disagree with Robert on many things, but he was absolutely right about your spending time with that low-class adventurer! Believe me, Simon Cordwyn's not worth five minutes of your time—or anyone else's!"

Before the surprised Jane could say a word, Clarissa was heading for the door. "Excuse me, I really must rest now. It was beastly hot on the road."

She doesn't want to see him? How interesting, Jane thought, mentally kicking herself for mentioning the very person she had vowed to forget.

Friday was spent in bustling preparations. It was now early August, and Robert complained that the terrible heat made this the worst possible time for entertaining. Busy planning the menu with Cuba one minute and arranging flowers with Jane the next, Clarissa paid no attention to his grumblings.

Luckily, Saturday turned out to be unseasonably cool. With that good omen, it remained only to set the huge dining room table with glittering crystal and fine china. Watching Clarissa direct this operation, Jane ran her fingers across the gleaming mahogany tabletop as it disappeared beneath an elegant damask tablecloth.

"What a beautiful table, Aunt Clarissa. Is it Cousin Hugh's work?"

"*Shhh,*" Clarissa whispered. "Don't let Robert hear you. Yes, it was a wedding present from Hugh, years ago. When those two fell out it was all I could do to keep Robert from chopping this table up for firewood."

Jane gave silent thanks that Clarissa's cool, sensible views sometimes prevailed over Robert's temper.

Finally, all was ready. The Lamberts were first to arrive. Louis was a heavyset man of courtly manners and few words. His wife, Alice, was a buxom, pink-cheeked, chatty woman. Louis's bachelor brother, Jacques, was lean and handsome, his dark eyes glinting in constant amusement. When introduced to Jane, he promptly lived up to his reputation as an outrageous flirt.

"Ah, mademoiselle!" He clasped her hands as if entranced. "What a ravishing beauty you'll be! I always thought one day I'd entice your enchanting aunt Clarissa to run away with me. But perhaps I shall wait a few years and entice you, instead."

Jane smiled at how quickly he proved the emptiness of his words by turning his flirtations on Clarissa, despite disapproving frowns from Robert.

When the Dunnings arrived, the smiling Morton, fully as handsome as Jacques Lambert, soon became his rival for Clarissa's attentions, while pale, sickly looking Penelope Dunning tried not to notice. Their daughter, Lucinda, tall and reddish blond, with her father's good looks, was introduced to Jane with Clarissa's prediction that they would become fast friends. Jane saw immediately that this would not happen, as Lucinda's only interest was what time Brandon Ainsley would arrive. *Ah,* Jane smiled to herself. *It seems that I, too, have a rival.*

The Ainsleys, who had stayed overnight in a small country inn midway between Charlestown and Rosewall, arrived around noon, accompanied by Brandon, who cut a dashing figure alongside their carriage on his prancing Princess. Lucinda rushed to greet him, while Jane and Clarissa welcomed Arthur and Harriet as they emerged from the carriage. Robert waited on the veranda, and Jane watched anxiously as Arthur walked up the steps. Clarissa was watching, too, and Jane saw her fleeting smile of relief as the two men shook hands, exchanging pleasant words of greeting. All would be well.

Soon, to Lucinda's annoyance, Brandon had Jane in his ardent clutches, declaring his undying devotion and assuring her that every day he spent without her was utter misery.

"It's good to see you, Brandon," she said with a fond smile. It occurred to her that unlike Jacques, who didn't pretend that he meant what he said, Brandon honestly believed his own romantic declarations. She did not, but she had to admit to herself, she found them charming.

Soon enough, Brandon deserted both young ladies, displeasing Lucinda still further by attaching himself to Robert. He wanted to talk to his uncle about building a racetrack on a section of unused Rosewall land. Jane noticed that Robert listened carefully. It seemed to her that he was the only member of the family who took Brandon's enthusiasm for horses and racing seriously.

For two hours, the house and grounds rang with social chatter as guests lounged in the parlor or strolled with their host and hostess along the garden paths.

Then in midafternoon, Omar appeared, announcing in his deep voice, "Dinner be served!" The guests filed into the dining room, scanned the place cards, and seated themselves at the huge table—Robert at the head, Clarissa at the other end.

While Cuba served the first course, Omar worked his way around the table pouring wine. Then Robert tapped his glass for quiet.

"Ladies and gentlemen, I would like to propose a toast." When all glasses were raised, he continued. "I should like to honor a new family member. Like a beautiful English rose, she has brightened all our lives immeasurably since she has been with us. Indeed, as the great Shakespeare wrote, 'She doth teach the torches to burn bright.' Would you all please join me in honoring the daughter of my late brother, Edward, Third Earl of Almesbury—my beloved niece, Lady Jane Prentice."

"To Lady Jane," chorused the guests, drinking the toast.

Jane glowed with pleasure as the friendly faces beamed at her. She knew she couldn't decline being called Lady Jane this time. *How sweet of Uncle Robert,* she thought. *And how clever of Aunt Clarissa, to enliven these drowsy summer days with a lovely party.*

Chapter 11

After dinner, the women moved into the parlor while the menfolk remained in the dining room sipping brandy and indulging in what Clarissa called "man-talk." The "woman-talk" in the parlor failing to hold Jane's interest, she wandered over to a window and stood admiring the soft golden slant of afternoon sunlight on the grounds outside. Thus, she was the only one who saw the horseman arrive at the front gate; saw Omar open the gate to admit him; saw the visitor dismount, hand the horse's reins to Omar, and walk hurriedly toward the house. Feeling the color of excitement rising in her cheeks, Jane turned to see that Clarissa was watching her.

"What is it, Jane? Something going on out there?"

Jane tried to make her reply sound casual. "Mr. Cordwyn just arrived."

Clarissa stiffened slightly, stared rigidly at Jane for a moment, then turned back to her guests.

Robert was discussing the prospects for next year's rice crop with his friend Louis Lambert when Omar came into the dining room and leaned over him.

"'Scuse, sar. Mr. Cordwyn from Charlestown desires admittance."

"Cordwyn!" Robert scowled. "What the devil is he doing here?"

"It must be urgent for him to have ridden all this way," Arthur Ainsley said. "We'd best find out."

"Very well, show him in," Robert said gruffly.

Simon appeared before them, his face grimy, his shirt damp. "My apologies for this intrusion, Mr. Prentice," he began. "I was sent with a message for Mr. Ainsley. But in truth, it's important to everyone here."

"All right, Simon," Arthur said. "Let's have it."

"It's from Mr. Rutledge with the Continental Congress in Philadelphia, sir." Simon's tone was solemn. "The Virginia Resolution is adopted. The American colonies are declared free and independent from England."

Frozen as if in disbelief, the men at the table stared at the messenger, then at one another. Red in the face, Robert came to his feet.

"This party," he growled between clenched teeth, "is at an end."

Suddenly everyone was up and shouting at once. Sweeping into the room, Clarissa brushed past Simon without a glance and approached her husband.

"Don't let this upset you, Robert," she said in a

soothing tone. "Those wild men in Philadelphia are surely bluffing."

Simon was quick to dispute this. "I'm afraid not, Mrs. Prentice. I've seen Mr. Jefferson's resolution. It's called the Declaration of Independence now, and it ends with the words, 'We pledge our lives, our fortunes, and our sacred honor.' It's no bluff." Turning from Clarissa's cold gaze, he addressed Arthur again. "Sir, Mr. Rutledge wishes the Declaration to be read from the steps of the Exchange Building on Monday. And he hopes that you, as well as all the other respected and influential men of the city, will be present, to stand in a show of solidarity and support."

"No, Arthur!" Clarissa pleaded. "You wouldn't!"

"Not unless he's a complete fool!" Robert snapped. "Joining a mob for a public declaration of treason? Unthinkable!"

Again Simon disagreed. "Three-quarters of Charlestown's population is no mere mob, ma'am. People are dancing in the streets at the news. This will not soon pass."

Robert lashed out at him. "Damn you, Cordwyn! I've always suspected your loyalty. Now I see I was right!"

"You're mistaken, sir. I deplore the rebel movement as both ill-advised and doomed to failure. I report to you only what I've seen with my own eyes."

Dismissing Simon with a snort of disgust, Robert turned back to his brother-in-law. "Well, Arthur. The time has come when you must state once and for all where you stand. With King, Crown, and orderly rule? Or with the rebel mob? Which is it?"

The ladies had silently filed in to stand with their husbands, who were on their feet, watching and waiting. All eyes were on Arthur—some suspicious, some openly hostile. But beside him stood a faithful ally.

"I'm with you, Arthur," Harriet said softly, "whatever you must do."

"Thank you, my dear." Drawing strength from her, he spoke. "Friends, not long ago I met with Mr. Rutledge, Mr. Heyward, and the others who were going up to Philadelphia to the Continental Congress. It was decided that they would speak moderately and explore all avenues for reconciliation with England. But if a strong course of action was determined upon, we would stand steadfastly together. I pledged myself to that. Now that such decisive action has been taken, I will keep my word. I will be there on Monday. And heaven help our cause, which is just and right."

Brandon slammed his fist down on the table in rage. "For God's sake, Father, come to your senses! Even the learned schoolmaster says this rebellion is doomed. You could lose everything—maybe even your life!"

Arthur smiled sadly. "We're a strange pair, Brandon. A father moving into the future, a son clinging to the past. Seems as if it should be the other way around. I wish you'd join me on Monday. After all, it's your generation that will have to carry on the work of mine. But if it's not to be—"

"I cannot speak for my generation, Father," Brandon declared hotly, "but for myself, it's certainly not to be. I am a King's man, and you speak treason. Henceforth, sir, we are enemies!"

Harriet and Clarissa gasped in horror, but Robert beamed approval. "Well said, my boy!"

Arthur turned on Robert, seething with bitterness. "It seems he *is* your boy, and none of mine."

Robert, too, was seething. "I can only tell you that if you do this, Arthur, you'll never set foot in my house again. Nor I in yours."

Clarissa appealed to both of them. "Now, Robert, there's no need for such talk. Please, Arthur—don't do this to us!"

Their guests stood spellbound by the sight of a family disintegrating. In all the turmoil, no one noticed that Simon had quietly slipped away. Or that the guest of honor was nowhere to be seen.

Simon found her sitting on a garden bench under a grape arbor. "Hello, Jane. May I join you?"

She gave a disinterested shrug. "If you like."

"Thank you." He drew a heavy sigh as he slumped down beside her. "I believe I've made myself very unpopular here today."

"I know. I was listening from the hallway. Well, they say it's human nature to blame the messenger for bad news."

"And it's bad news, indeed. This so-called Declaration of Independence will be taken by the British as a declaration of war, nothing less. Until now there was still some faint hope for a peaceable settlement. But now I'm very much afraid we've passed the point of no return."

"The point of no return," Jane repeated dully. "So now we must watch helplessly while friends go to war against friends. Kinsmen against kinsmen. Fathers and sons become sworn enemies! My heart bleeds, Mr. Cordwyn."

He nodded somber agreement. "As does mine. As any thoughtful person's must. But I've learned that yours is a particularly sensitive heart. It's one of the many charming things about you that never ceases to—"

Jane rose abruptly and moved off a few steps. "It's getting late," she said, her tone now cool and distant. "Shouldn't you be going?"

"Indeed, I should. Even at full gallop, I'll be long after dark getting back to town. But we're not quite done here yet." He got up and came to where Jane was standing. "When I volunteered to bring the news out here today, I knew I wouldn't be welcomed. But I gladly took on the duty, because I wanted to see *you* again. There's something we need to talk about."

"Really?" Jane looked off into the distance. "I can't imagine what."

"I think you can. The morning you left Charlestown, you were very cold to me. And unless I'm imagining things, you still are. I've racked my brain ever since, wondering what on earth I did or said to displease you. But it's quite beyond me. So, won't you tell me now?"

This was something Jane had intended never to discuss with anyone, least of all Mr. Cordwyn. But now that he had confronted her with the question, she forced herself to answer. "The night before we left Charlestown, I saw you and Aunt Clarissa together in the garden. Heard you, too."

"Oh, dear Lord!" Simon held his head, groaning. "So *that's* it! I am so sorry, Jane. If you'd been there to overhear us again the other day, you'd know that's all over now. I was a lonely bachelor, she was a discontented wife—but that's no excuse. It was a shameful thing that never should have happened, and when she visited last week, I put an end to it."

"And that's why she's angry with you now?"

"Exactly. We had a bit of a row. She became furious, accused me of deceiving her, which I certainly never meant to do. In any event, it's finished. And I'm terribly sorry you heard about it. I expect you'll think ill of me forever now, won't you?"

"Well . . ." Jane's hostility was slipping away. "Since you've put an end to it, I suppose I can feel more kindly toward you."

"I'm very relieved to hear that. Because, you see, this will be our last meeting, and I'd deeply regret it if we couldn't part friends."

Her mouth dropped open as she stared at him. "Whatever can you mean?"

"I'm leaving now. Going back to Pennsylvania,

where I came from. I've always intended to go back one day. I couldn't live my whole life in a society that depends on human slavery. Besides, I'm worried about my sister and her family. They have those two young children to look after, and now I've heard my brother-in-law's in poor health. When war explodes all around them, which it's bound to soon, they'll need me."

"Of course they will. I understand," Jane said. "But before you go, will you be my schoolmaster one last time? I need your guidance. I'm still so...so *uneducated*, I scarcely know who or what I am. I'm English, but I live in America now. And all around me there are people I care about on both sides of this terrible conflict. What shall I do? Where should my allegiance lie?"

Simon smiled as he shook his head. "You don't need guidance from me, Jane. Nor from anyone. Knowing you, I'm quite confident that you'll do what you always do. You'll listen, you'll observe, you'll think things through for yourself, then make your own decision. And whatever it is, it will be a wise one. Because you *are* wise. And that's even better than being educated. So there you are. And now I really do have to be on my way."

Her grave eyes held him. "You'll be greatly missed, Mr. Cordwyn."

"I'll miss a few people myself. The Ainsleys. They've been good to me. Hugh and Lydia—dear friends. Even hotheaded Peter. And, of course, you, Jane. You're the best, the brightest student I ever had.

Let's not say good-bye, all right? Let's just tell each other"—he took her hand and held it—"'may God keep you safe till we meet again.' Will you share that parting thought with me?"

She nodded, no longer trusting herself to speak.

"Don't forget me. I won't forget you." He kissed her hand lightly, then let it go and strode rapidly toward the gate.

Jane watched until Omar had closed the gate behind him and the sound of his galloping horse's hooves had died away in the distance. Then, feeling numb, she started slowly back to the house. Others would be leaving soon, of course. As Robert had so rightly said, the party was over. Jane wanted desperately to be alone, but her good manners would not permit that. Putting on her most gracious demeanor, she went back inside to attend to her social duties.

After all, she was supposed to be the guest of honor today.

Light was failing in the west when at last she escaped to her room and found merciful solitude. As seen from her window, the deserted garden, its flowery abundance softened by lengthening shadows, was especially beautiful—but she was in no mood to appreciate beauty. She was thinking of the gentle schoolmaster, and things he had said that she knew would haunt her forever.

"May God keep you safe till we meet again," he said. *"Till we meet again"*—his very words. *"Don't forget me. I*

won't forget you," he said. *Lovely words, words full of promise. But promises given in haste, and on the brink of chaos and upheaval that may last for years, can have no real meaning. "We are aliens in a foreign land, trying to find our way," he had once said. That had meaning. That was true. Now one of the aliens had found his way back to the land of his birth, where he belongs. While the other—*

Made dizzy by a sudden wave of despair, Jane sank down on her bed. *The other wishes she had never left England . . .*

PART II

Interlude
1776–1778

Chapter 12

Even the most stouthearted Patriots knew that declaring independence for the American colonies did not make it so. Rather than an accomplished fact, independence was a thing to be worked for, fought for, died for, if need be. In South Carolina, the thunderclap of news from Philadelphia produced no immediate change in people's lives. Jane, resigned to the prospect of living most of the time at Rosewall, patiently settled in and worked hard at learning all she could about this tumultuous place called America. Unfortunately, the plantation's remote location made it difficult to hear of events beyond its borders. Information from the North took months to wind along the rutted roads into the South Carolina backcountry. Oddly enough, it was mostly through Brandon that occasional bits of secondhand news arrived.

Brandon so passionately disapproved of his father's decision to align himself with the Patriots that he had left home and moved in with friends in Charlestown. After that, he came often to Rosewall, never failing within minutes of arriving to renew his pledge of undying love to Jane. Gradually, she grew fonder of Brandon. Not for one moment did she believe his ardent declarations of love. But she could easily see that he himself believed them, and she found his sincerity, coupled with his boyish, impetuous manner, quite charming. So did the other women in the household—not only Clarissa, but Mrs. Morley and Cuba as well. Only the solemn Omar was immune to Brandon's charm—but then Omar was not one to be readily charmed by anyone.

During his visits to Rosewall, Brandon always spent hours talking war with Robert. After the unsuccessful attack on Charlestown in June 1776, the British had not returned, which disappointed them both. For his part, Brandon burned with military zeal, craving a spot in the British cavalry. Robert advised him to be patient, certain that each of them would get his chance to serve their king. Clarissa seldom joined these discussions, and Jane was expected to stay out of them. But at the risk of incurring Robert's disfavor, Jane always managed to hover nearby, her sharp ears picking words out of the air. In this way, she kept herself reasonably well informed.

She learned that the Continental Congress had named the new nation the United States of America. Robert and Brandon scorned this outrageous rebel insolence and laughed over the British Redcoats' easy occupation of the important port of New York. But the rebels continued to nip at the British soldiers' heels. It seemed that the Americans' Continental Army Commander, a Virginia planter named George Washington, was somehow able to keep his inexperienced troops just out of reach of the vastly stronger British. "They say he's a stodgy old farmer pretending to be a military leader," Brandon reported, failing to notice that it was mainly the astonishing leadership qualities of that "stodgy old farmer" that were keeping the rebellion alive.

In the fall of that year—1776—Robert moved the family back to the city and the newly refurbished Legare Street house, saying they would now resume their former custom of dividing their time between Rosewall and Charlestown. But despite Clarissa's entreaties that he soften his attitude, he still refused to have any further contact with the Ainsleys.

By December, Clarissa's patience was exhausted. "You may stick to your stubborn principles all you like, Robert. But it's Christmas, and Jane and I wish to visit Arthur and Harriet. You needn't join us."

They found Arthur genial as usual, but distracted by worry, and Harriet grieving about her absent son. "He comes to see his mother now and then," Arthur told the visitors. "But only when he's sure I'm not at home."

Feeling the sadness that now filled this once-cheery house, Jane and Clarissa visited the Ainsleys often after that. Jane hoped that Robert might eventually allow her to visit Hugh again, as well. But any mention of his name brought her a stinging rebuke. Hugh and Lydia were not fit company for a loyal British subject, she was told. The cabinetmaker's shop was off-limits.

A favorite diversion of Jane's when in Charlestown was to go with Harriet and Clarissa to visit Harriet's elderly mother at Goose Creek, a small community about twenty miles from Charlestown on the main route to the north. And because it was a relatively short and easy journey by carriage, Jane often took Mrs. Morley along on these excursions.

One of the finer houses at Goose Creek was a stately Georgian mansion set among ancient oaks. Known locally as the Dudley house, it was the family home of Harriet Ainsley, born Harriet Dudley. Once it had been the seat of a prosperous plantation, but now only Harriet's widowed mother, frail of body and growing dim in her mind, still lived there. Attended only by her personal maid and by her physician, Dr. Jeffers, a neighbor and longtime family friend, Grandmother Dudley seldom left her small upstairs apartment.

Ordinarily, old Mrs. Dudley cared nothing for company, so it was a surprise to everyone that from their very first meeting, she and Mrs. Morley responded warmly to each other. Jane was especially delighted to see the two elderly women sitting together, chatting contentedly as if they had known each other all their lives. It seemed to her that Mrs. Morley felt more at home in the Dudley house than she had anywhere else since crossing the ocean.

It was on one of these visits the following summer that Mrs. Dudley proposed that her new friend come to live with her. Mrs. Morley hesitated only briefly. On one hand, the thought of parting with Jane distressed her. On the other, she had never felt quite comfortable at the Legare Street house, and she hated the isolation of life at Rosewall. Besides, as she said to Jane, poor Mrs. Dudley was plainly in great need of a companion her own age.

And so, Jane thought with a smile, *are you, my beloved old friend.*

So it was done. Mrs. Morley's few possessions were brought to Goose Creek, and one day she and Jane hugged each other good-bye in the front garden of the Dudley house. Jane nodded patiently while being reminded of everything she should and should not do. As her carriage pulled away, she felt a little sad but oddly excited as well. She would still see Mrs. Morley on visits to Goose Creek. But for the first time in her life, Jane felt that—in a way, at least—she was finally on her own.

Months went by with maddeningly little news from the North. At last, in the fall, word came that Philadelphia had become the second large American city to fall to the British. The rebel leaders who had their headquarters there fled to nearby York, Pennsylvania. But just as Robert and Brandon were slapping each other on the back over this, they heard the Americans had captured five thousand British troops at Saratoga, New York. In early 1778, the Americans achieved another crucial success: England's age-old enemy, France, joined the American side. Fearing a blockade of Philadelphia by the French navy, the Redcoats fled, and the American government returned to its capital city amid wild celebration.

Thus the war dragged on, surging back and forth across the northern colonies until subsiding at last into a stalemate. And all the while, people in the South watched and waited, wondering when the clouds of war would move down to darken their Southern skies.

During this period, Jane had the feeling that she was living through a kind of stalemate herself—an interlude in which the most notable developments were within herself. In the summer of 1778, two years after arriving in America, she was sixteen, her slight girl's body now fully transformed with the contours of a young woman. Her creamy skin, shining dark hair, and lustrous gray eyes, all enhanced by her kind and gracious nature, earned her a reputation as something of a beauty. But for all her blessings, she found that life as the ward of Robert Prentice was far from ideal.

He was concerned for her safety—that she understood, and appreciated—but his tight rein on her

movements had grown wearisome. When at Rosewall, she was never allowed to venture outside the
plantation walls unescorted. In Charlestown, she could
take walks alone, and this gave her a pleasant sense of
freedom, however brief. But she could see the Ainsleys only if accompanied by Clarissa. She was still
strictly forbidden to go near Hugh's. In her mind, a
personal rebellion was quietly growing—and as it
grew, so did the prospect of an eventual clash with her
domineering uncle.

Friction between them developed on another point
as well. Jane had made friends with Omar and Cuba, a
fact that greatly displeased Robert. "Familiarity between ourselves and the servants is bad for discipline,"
he told Jane. She could not understand this. She liked
Omar and Cuba, was intensely curious about them,
and could not see any "discipline" problem. She
obeyed Robert's rules when he was at home, confin-
ing her conversations with the servants to times when
he was not.

Bothered by the idea that with enough money one
could actually buy and sell other people, Jane badly
wanted to know how Omar and Cuba came to their
present life. They gradually began to trust her, and
spoke freely.

Omar had been brought on a slave ship from West
Africa, where he had attended an Arab-run school before being sold to slave traders. Cuba came from the
Caribbean island for which she was named, where she
was born the property of a Spanish slave trader. She

dimly remembered her mother, who had died young. Omar recalled no parents. After several previous owners and hardships they would not discuss, both had been purchased by Robert Prentice in the Charlestown slave market. Jane often had seen shackled men, women, and children there being traded like cattle, an image that horrified her. Omar had been sullen and unruly when first brought to Rosewall, but he changed dramatically when Cuba arrived a year later. Marriage between slaves was not recognized by law, but they lived together as man and wife.

"I settle him down good," Cuba said with a smile. And Jane noticed that Omar obeyed his wife more readily than he did his white master.

Jane's future marriage was another sensitive topic at Rosewall. Although other eligible young men competed for her attention, Robert soon decided that the only suitor worthy of Jane's hand would be Brandon. He and Clarissa spoke fondly of a lovely wedding at Rosewall, between the two handsomest young people in all of South Carolina. And the more they dreamed of this wedding, the more certain Jane became that it would never happen.

By now Brandon himself was rarely seen. Itching to help suppress the rebellion, he had volunteered to serve in an American cavalry company loyal to the British. Robert constantly praised his heroism. Once Jane ventured to wonder aloud if Brandon was really acting on well-thought-out principles, or merely out of boyish enthusiasm for military adventure. But this so angered Robert that she was careful never to mention the subject again.

All the while, Jane tried hard to banish all memories of a gentle schoolmaster from her mind, but they would not leave her. Sometimes when her uncle was away and the great house at Rosewall was quiet, she climbed the narrow stairs to the third-floor observatory. There, removed from the world, she would read awhile from Robert's books of poetry, then stand at a window and look north toward the hazy blue-green horizon. Somewhere out there lay Pennsylvania. What was it like? Was he surviving in these dangerous times? Though far away now, his face remained clear in her mind. And a few of his parting words lingered still in her ears: "I won't forget you."

Pretty words, she thought. *Pretty words, like a line from a sad song. But best not taken too seriously.*

One stormy afternoon, Jane sat at a small desk in her room, gazing pensively into the flickering flames in her fireplace. Finally, she took up her pen to write.

Rosewall
24 November 1778

Dear Mr. Cordwyn,
   I remember you told your students to read and to write constantly, saying these not only develop our minds but also help us sort out thoughts and feelings. Recalling that good advice, I now pursue both goals,

reading as much as I can and writing to you this modest communication, hoping it finds you well. News reaches us here haphazardly, but it's clear that for those in the North, war has been very much present for some time. How much longer can we escape its ravages? Meanwhile, I wonder if you are safe.

I am about three inches taller now, but you would have no trouble recognizing your most eager student. I think often of our last meeting, here at Rosewall, when you said you were leaving. You spoke some pleasant words, and there were things I wanted to tell you, too. How much I missed your school. How important it was to me to have known you. That it was the happiest time of my life, and how sorry I was that it had ended so soon. Instead, I stood there dumb as an ox. What must you have thought of me?

How I wish that it could be as you said, that we might meet again someday. I would speak to you boldly, and tell you many things that are buried deep in my heart. Perhaps then you would see me not as a child, not as a former student, but as a woman. But forgive me, I do not mean to go on about what cannot be.

I remain always your devoted friend,

Jane Prentice

Like a teacher judging a student's work, she read over the letter with a critical eye. *Almost no information here*, she thought. *And that wish near the end sounds like the aimless prattle of a daydreamer. Besides, you shouldn't tell wishes, or they won't come true. But that's all right—no one will ever see this, anyway.*

She crossed the room and dropped the letter, and her daydream, into the fire.

PART III

War Clouds Move South
1778–1780

Chapter 13

If Jane could have seen all the way to Pennsylvania that November night, her gaze might have fallen on Simon Cordwyn, making his way past mud puddles along a crowded Philadelphia street. She might have seen him stop beneath a hanging sign reading GRIMSBY'S TAVERN and push open the heavy oak door. He threaded his way through a smoky room full of boisterous drinkers and bustling serving girls to a rear corner, where a bearded, rough-looking man sat nursing a glass of rum.

"Mr. Murphy?" Simon inquired. The man at the table nodded. "I'm Simon Cordwyn, Jack Herndon's brother-in-law."

Murphy gestured toward the chair opposite him, and Simon sat down. A serving girl approached, but Simon waved her away. He was not there for drinking but for business. And the conversation that followed would have sent Jane reeling in disbelief.

———

After looking around to make sure he was not being observed, Simon slid a scrap of paper across the table. The man called Murphy scanned it, mumbling to himself as he read.

"Two hundred yards Irish woolen. Three hundred and fifty pair heavy cotton stockings. Good. A hundred pounds coffee. Thirty barrels potatoes. Excellent." He glanced up at Simon. "In fairly good condition?"

"I couldn't say. Jack collected these goods and left them at his store, meaning to deliver them when he returned from his current expedition. Since he hasn't returned, my sister asked me to deliver them in his stead. Which I am doing strictly as a favor to her."

"A fine woman, Mrs. Herndon."

Simon ignored the attempt at flattery. "Just how picky are General Washington and his starving men, anyway? Another winter like Valley Forge, and he'll have no army left."

Murphy smiled as he folded the slip of paper and put it in his pocket. "Surely, Mr. Cordwyn, you aren't only doing your sister a favor. Surely, you are acting out of firm belief in the cause of American independence."

"I believe in the rightness of it. But I also believe we should be working for it peaceably, not through war."

"You're an idealist, sir. Unhappily, we must live in the real world."

Simon grew annoyed. "And what in this real world has happened to Jack?"

"We have no news of him yet, unfortunately."

"He's been gone too long. My sister's very worried."

"In our trade, a man doesn't have a fixed schedule," Murphy said coolly. "Delays are bound to occur. But he'll be along soon, I'm sure. In the meantime, I trust you'll continue to act as his capable replacement?"

Simon's head shake was scornful. "You trust incorrectly, my friend. My sister was anxious that you get these supplies as soon as possible. And I agreed to deliver them because they are meant to sustain life, not destroy it. If they were weapons of war and destruction, I'd never have touched them. In any case, I'll not do this again. I'm a schoolmaster, not a smuggler."

"And I'm a farmer," Murphy countered. "Ordinarily. But in these desperate times, we're all soldiers, whether we choose to be or not."

"Speak for yourself, sir. Do not attempt to speak for me."

"Well, at least allow me to thank you for your help on this occasion. General Washington will be pleased, I'll warrant."

"Well, you may take him some advice from me, along with the supplies. Tell him he ought to distribute what's left of his rations and send his men home, while there's still a spark of life left in them."

"I very much doubt he'll take that advice," Murphy said with a smile.

"In that case, I have nothing further to offer." Simon got to his feet. "I trust you'll inform my sister the minute you have any news of Jack?"

"Tell Mrs. Herndon she may depend upon it."

"Thank you, sir. Good night, and good luck to you." Turning away, Simon strode out of the tavern in the same purposeful way he had come in.

It was two weeks later, in his hometown of Lancaster, Pennsylvania, that Simon again encountered the man named Murphy. Prominent on the dirt road that served as the main street of the frontier village was a barnlike building called Herndon's General Store. A short distance up the road stood a small house with a swinging shingle outside that read, SIMON CORDWYN, SCHOOLMASTER. Just as he had done on the Ainsley estate in Charlestown some years before, the schoolmaster occupied private living quarters in the rear.

He was reading students' essays there late one pale winter afternoon when there came a knock at his door. Opening it, he was surprised to find his sister standing there. Rebecca Herndon was two years older than Simon, a sturdy woman of plain looks but fine, intelligent eyes. Today those eyes were clouded. Behind her stood Mr. Murphy from Philadelphia.

"What is it, Becky? What's wrong?" Simon asked. But he was grimly certain of the answer.

"It's happened, Simon. Jack's been taken. Either taken, or killed." Her low voice was strangely calm, as if she was trying hard to resist the shock that had so suddenly struck.

Murphy stepped forward. "All we know," he said, "is that Jack was bringing a barge up Delaware Bay when he was intercepted by a British patrol vessel just off the mouth of the river. The man with him managed to slip overboard and swim ashore, and he brought me the news. There were shots exchanged, and the last our man saw, the British were boarding the barge, so we have to assume Jack was taken, at best. What his fate will be—who knows? The Redcoats are an unpredictable lot. Sometimes harsh, sometimes lenient. We can only hope."

Simon glanced at his silently grieving sister, then fixed a scowl on the visitor. "We thank you for this pleasant news, Mr. Murphy. We also thank you for enticing a gentle, home-loving man away from his family and, quite possibly, to his death."

Murphy responded with quiet patience. "Jack Herndon never needed enticing. He was eager to do the work. Unfortunately, he always had a reckless disrespect for the enemy. Bringing a barge up Delaware Bay in broad daylight! Many a time I warned him about thumbing his nose at the British like that. He wouldn't listen."

"You warned him, did you?" Simon snapped. "How very decent of you."

Becky gently intervened. "Stop it, Simon. Mr. Murphy's not to blame. Jack was doing what he felt he had to do, the best way he could."

Simon turned a scowl on her. "Did *you* ever warn him, or try to talk him out of it? You knew he wasn't suited to that kind of work, with his poor health. If the British hadn't gotten him, sickness eventually would have."

Becky turned sharply away as Murphy spoke up again. "We are desperate, Mr. Cordwyn. Another winter like Valley Forge and Washington will have no army left—you said so yourself. When a man offers us his services, we don't turn him away, no matter what his weaknesses. Why, if an educated, well-informed, and responsible man like yourself offered to work with us, we'd get down on our knees and thank God."

"Flattery!" Simon almost spat. "The same kind you fed Jack, no doubt."

"He spoke about you often, you know," Murphy went on, ignoring Simon's hostility. "'How I wish we could get Simon in with us,' he'd say. 'He's far more clever than I, and what's more, he knows the South.'"

"What's *that* got to do with anything?" Simon demanded impatiently.

"It's clear we're going to have to shift our operations to the South. With the British watching all our usual landing sites, the only good ones left are the wooded inlets and river mouths along the Carolina coast. The Great Wagon Road, between there and Pennsylvania, has got to become our main supply line. Trouble is, we don't have anyone to oversee operations down there. Southerners are insanely proud men, impossible to deal with. But you lived in the South for several years. You must still have valuable contacts down there. Am I right?"

Murphy paused to wait for a reply, but getting nothing but a stony glare from Simon, he went on. "Surely, Mr. Cordwyn, you can see where your duty lies. Out there, giving your countrymen the benefit of your abilities. Not here, hiding in a schoolroom while men fighting for our liberty are dying for want of supplies. Think it over. You know where to reach me. And now I must be off, so I'll bid you both good day."

Becky put a hand on the visitor's arm. "I thank you for bringing us the news of my husband, Mr. Murphy."

"Madam, believe me, I regret the necessity for it. But we may yet hold good hopes that he survives. Meanwhile, my admiration for you knows no bounds. God keep you, dear lady. You are a true Patriot." And with a curt nod to Simon: "Remember, sir. Grimsby's Tavern, Philadelphia. Anytime." Then, jamming a grimy cap on his head, he turned abruptly and walked away.

In the silence that followed, Simon studied his sister's face. It was blank, the eyes vacant. "I'll stay with you and the children tonight," he said gently.

She shook her head. "No. No, thank you, Simon. I'm all right."

"Well, at least I'll walk you home, then."

It was a quarter of a mile to the Herndon house, and they walked halfway there in silence, immersed in their own dark thoughts. At last Simon spoke.

"Tell me something, Becky. And be honest. Would you really want me to leave you on your own here and rush off to replace Jack?"

Becky drew a heavy sigh. "I'm sure you're doing what you think is right, just as Jack did. But you can't blame Mr. Murphy for trying to recruit you. You'd do a far better job than my poor Jack ever did. Dear God!" Seized by some wrenching emotion, Becky stopped in her tracks. "If only I could wave a magic wand and combine my husband and my brother— what a man that would be!"

She walked on, and Simon followed, saying no more.

The next day the children in Simon's classroom found their normally attentive tutor surprisingly inattentive. He spent much time gazing broodingly out the window at low hills in the distance, leaving the students to do as they liked. That afternoon, he dismissed them early and went for a long walk over those hills, still brooding. And that night, after pacing for a long time in his silent rooms, he sat down at his writing desk, dipped pen in ink, and began a letter.

Mr. John Murphy
c/o Grimsby's Tavern
Walnut Street, Philadelphia

Sir,
This is to advise you that I expect to be in Philadelphia on Saturday next, at which time I would be pleased to confer with you further concerning a matter we recently discussed . . .

Chapter 14

Rumors were flying in Charlestown that the British, stymied in the North, were turning their eyes toward the Southern colonies. Just before New Year's Day, 1779, those rumors suddenly became reality. In striking contrast to their failed assault on Charlestown almost three years before, British forces attacked and quickly occupied Savannah, Georgia, a hundred miles to the south. No Loyalist or Patriot in South Carolina doubted there would soon be another British assault on Charlestown.

Thrilled the city would soon be back under British rule, Robert Prentice moved his family to their Legare Street home. He wanted to be among the first to welcome the Redcoats. And certain that those sympathetic to the rebellion would soon need places to hide, he suddenly felt a burst of compassion for his brother-in-law, Arthur Ainsley, and his cousin Hugh Prentice—both, in his view, sadly deluded. He wrote to them, urging that they renounce the insane notion of American independence before it was too late. Naturally, they would have to explain themselves when the British occupied the city. But Robert, whose loyalty was well known, would gladly offer them shelter and help them reestablish themselves as loyal English subjects.

The note to Arthur went with Clarissa and Jane to the Ainsleys' house. Arthur's simple reply declined the generous offer with sincere thanks. "He's determined to sink or swim with this rebellion tide," Clarissa reported.

"And I must say," Jane dared to add, "I believe he'll prove a very strong swimmer." This only brought an angry glare from Robert.

The note to Hugh was delivered by Clarissa's maid, Nellie, who always came over from the Ainsleys' to Legare Street when the Prentices were in town. In short order, she returned with a brief note from Hugh.

Thank you, Cousin, for your kind offer of protection. But I hardly think the British, if they come, would concern themselves with an obscure cabinetmaker like me. I will take my chances. However, I am glad to hear from you. Lydia and I send greetings to you and Clarissa, and to our dear cousin Jane, whom we once had the pleasure of meeting.

Robert threw up his hands in exasperation. "I don't know which is the bigger fool, Hugh or Arthur. The devil take them both, I say!"

112

He also did not know that Nellie brought a second note—for Jane. "A mutual friend, who has left here, wrote to me recently," Hugh wrote. "He asked to be remembered to you, and he looks forward to seeing us all again soon." It wasn't much, but it lifted Jane's heart with joy. Perhaps there was hope, after all, that one day she might see Mr. Cordwyn again.

After capturing Savannah with ease, the advancing British met months of fierce Patriot resistance. But by May of 1779, they were poised at the outskirts of Charlestown. While their friends in the city eagerly awaited their arrival, the Patriot-minded prayed for another escape from disaster.

One hot night in late May, Robert Prentice paced the floor, unable to rest. The hour was late, the night air heavy with a drizzling rain. But all was peaceful, and peace was not what Robert wanted this night.

Jane appeared in her nightgown at the top of the stairs. "We'll know if they come, and meanwhile, you need some sleep," she said in the uneasy calm.

"In God's name, where are they?" he growled. "The rebel defenses are ridiculously weak. The Redcoats could storm in any time—what are they waiting for?" He continued to pace, muttering to himself.

Her advice ignored, Jane went back to her room. But unable to sleep, she sat absently brushing her long dark hair and worrying. *What will happen to Arthur if the British take the city? To Cousin Hugh and his cocky stepson, Peter Quincy? Aren't they worried?* At last she heard Robert coming upstairs, giving up his vigil for the night. Then she, too, finally went to bed.

In the cold light of dawn, she awoke with a start. Raising herself on one elbow, she froze, listening. Riotous shouting reverberated in the distance. She knew instantly that it was not the Redcoats. Throwing on a dressing gown, she hurried into the hallway. Robert, fully dressed, and Clarissa, in her nightgown, were just leaving their bedroom as well. Nellie stood trembling at the bottom of the stairs, wide-eyed in fright.

"I'm going to investigate," Robert announced, starting down the stairs. "Stay upstairs, and don't open the door to anyone."

The women dressed quickly, then huddled on the stairs. Now they could hear a raucous celebration outside, full of exultant but menacing laughter.

A few minutes later, Robert was back, scarlet with fury. He slammed the door and bolted it behind him. "It's beyond belief!" he shouted. "The Redcoats have vanished like thieves in the night!"

Clarissa gasped. "But why, Robert?"

"The sentry at the powder magazine says Continental troops were coming up fast on their rear. So now we're left surrounded by rebel scum roaming the streets, attacking Loyalists. And they're coming this way!"

Indeed, they had already arrived. The house was assaulted by a mob shouting taunts at the known Loyalist inside. "Open up, Tory Prentice! Tell us what became of your yellow-bellied Redcoats! Are they too spineless to fight?" The words were hurled in contempt, along with sticks, stones, rotting vegetables—anything handy for bombarding the house.

Robert peered out the window at the attackers, then barked at the women. "Back in your rooms, all of you, till I say it's safe. Quickly now!"

Clarissa and Nellie obeyed, but Jane lingered on the landing. Again muttering to himself, Robert dug in his pocket for keys, then hurriedly fumbled with the lock on a heavy cabinet in the parlor. Pulling the door open, he reached in and took out a pistol.

Jane, watching, recoiled in alarm. "What are you doing, Uncle Robert?"

He scowled up at her. "I told you to get back to your room!"

"What are you doing?" she repeated, starting down the stairs.

"I'm defending my property!" he bellowed, heading for the front door.

But Jane got there first, blocking his path. "Are you mad?" she cried.

"What's the matter? Afraid I'll shoot one of our own traitorous kin?"

"You know very well Uncle Arthur's not out there, and neither is Hugh!"

"They're rebels, aren't they? All rebels are alike. Stand aside!"

"Uncle Robert, get hold of yourself!" Jane held on to his arm. "Those are crude, ignorant people. There

115

are plenty of them in England, too. I've seen them. But it's not their fault. They just need education."

"Fine!" Robert waved his pistol. "I'll educate them!"

"Not like that! They don't deserve to be shot!"

"Don't lecture me, you impudent girl! Get out of my way!"

"No!" Eyes blazing, Jane threw herself across the door. "You must not go out there!"

Robert was so astonished by this unexpected show of defiance that he could only stand and stare. Jane stared back, equally astonished, but she did not retreat. Then to her vast relief, Clarissa intervened. "I must say I agree with Jane," she said coolly from the top of the stairs. "If nothing else, Robert, think of your own safety. You would do battle single-handedly with an angry mob? You could get yourself killed."

Even as she spoke, the noise outside began to subside. Tiring of the sport, the boisterous crowd was moving on. Robert went back to the cabinet and put his pistol away. Then he turned to Jane, his anger still hot.

"It is not your place to instruct me," he said with simmering rage. "How dare you defend a gang of thugs who want to run me out of the city. I won't abide such insolence, from you or anyone else!"

Jane tried to respond calmly. "I wasn't excusing them, Uncle Robert. But look at their situation. For years they've been subjects of a distant king they think doesn't care about their welfare. With no voice in their own government, they resort to—"

"Good God, what am I hearing!" Robert's rage flared anew. "Has rebel fever infected you, too? I should never have let you traipse around unsupervised. Obviously, you still can't be trusted!"

Clarissa hurried downstairs, again trying to intervene. "Now, Robert—"

"No, you both listen to me! We have survived an ugly incident this morning without serious harm. But apparently neither of you has the sense to realize the danger we're in here. Well, no more! We're going back to Rosewall, and we're going to stay there until this city is safely back under British rule, once and for all!" With that Robert stormed out through the back of the house, doors slamming behind him.

Next Clarissa turned accusingly on Jane. "Now see what you've done!" she snapped. "Your divided loyalties just got us sent back to prison, thank you very much! In future, kindly remember that handling Robert is *my* job, not yours." She wheeled about and rushed upstairs.

Left alone, Jane stood for a long time gazing out the window. Something Clarissa had said had stuck in her mind. *Divided loyalties—is that what ails me?* she wondered. *If so, things may get a lot worse before they get better.*

Chapter 15

Despite its grand name, the Great Philadelphia Wagon Road was little more than a rutted old Indian trail, winding south from Pennsylvania through Appalachian foothill valleys into western Virginia and the Carolinas. Years before, the king's mapmakers had surveyed the road as far as Salisbury, North Carolina, pronouncing it 453 miles from Philadelphia.

Some distance below Salisbury, at a shallow crossing on the Pee Dee River not far from the village of Badin, there was a run-down inn operated by a rough-hewn frontiersman named Josiah Hobson. Traders' wagons, farmers' carts, and packhorses with their sweating drivers often turned the Hobson Inn's bare courtyard into a tangle of dust and confusion.

Here, in June of 1779, the Continental Army's top supply agent in the Southern colonies set up headquarters. No one knew his name. He was called only The Schoolmaster.

Into the inn's courtyard one afternoon rode an olive-skinned man with thick black hair, a broad mustache, and an aristocratic manner. He regarded the grimy rustics around him with unconcealed distaste as he found the proprietor and, in Spanish-accented English, stated his business. A minute later he found himself in a small building across the courtyard from the inn. Simon Cordwyn sat working over a ledger book. Deeply tanned and wearing homespun, he looked as much the frontiersman as any native mountain man.

"Mr. Roca?" Simon stood and greeted the Spanish gentleman.

"Fernando Roca, at your service, señor." He presented some papers for Simon's inspection. "Have I the honor to address The Schoolmaster?"

Simon glanced over the papers, then replied, "The same, sir. I'm glad to meet you at last. Please, be seated."

"It was difficult to find you here," Roca remarked, taking a chair.

"I apologize for the inconvenience. But for an operation such as ours, a remote location is essential. So, shall we get down to business?"

"First, I bring you greetings from Charlestown, from our friend the merchant and his charming wife. They are well, and much relieved that the British attack on their city last month failed."

"Or was abandoned, some say. I'm glad to hear they are well."

"Indeed so. Now, to business. I can inform you,

señor, that my country will soon join France in its war against Britain. This does not mean that King Charles of Spain wishes to be seen as aiding revolutionary forces in America. However, it cannot be denied that Britain is our common enemy. In sum, certain interests in Spain are now ready to supply your valiant fighters. And as their agent, I am here to arrange this matter with you."

Simon smiled. "This is welcome news, sir."

"The first supply ship should arrive off North Carolina around July first. Another comes in the fall." Roca brought forth a map. "Our landing site is a heavily wooded cove near Cape Fear, far from normal shipping lanes." He pointed to the spot. "You may keep this, but guard it carefully."

"You may be sure of that." Simon carefully folded the map and put it into his pocket. "I can't tell you how desperately General Washington needs supplies. Food, clothing of all kinds, medicine, blankets, boots—"

"And weapons, of course."

"I don't handle weapons, if I can avoid it."

Roca's eyes went wide. "*¡Dios mio!* Are you Americans not at war?"

"Sir, General Washington loses more men to disease, hunger, and cold than to enemy fire. My chief aim is to keep those poor wretches alive. Hasn't Mr. Murphy, our contact in Philadelphia, made that clear to you?"

"His communications with us never mentioned any such thing."

"*Hmmm,* an unfortunate oversight. Well, Mr. Roca, when I undertook this job I said I'd handle life-sustaining supplies only, not deadly weapons."

"And Murphy agreed to this?"

"Not exactly, but he was forced to agree that we would leave the matter open for the time being. He desperately needed a supply agent, you see."

"No, no, no, señor, this will not do!" Roca's agitation brought him to the edge of his chair. "Our ships carry all sorts of supplies—guns and ammunition, and all the rest. The matter cannot be left open. You will accept all of our cargo, or none of it."

Simon heaved a discouraged sigh. "Murphy said I'd run into this situation sooner or later. I was a fool to pretend otherwise."

Roca waited. "Well, señor? Are we doing business, or are we not?"

A knock at the door spared Simon the necessity of answering. "Yes?" A fresh-faced, sandy-haired young man stuck his head in. "What is it, Billy?"

"'Scuse me, sir. Gillis is here with a load o' goods. And he's got a couple o' prisoners with him."

"Prisoners?" Simon frowned. "What sort of prisoners?"

"British soldiers, seems like. Gillis says they're spies, and he means to stand 'em up in front of a firing squad."

Grim-faced, Simon got to his feet. "I'm sorry, Mr. Roca, I must deal with this. Mr. Gillis is a mountain man with a very short temper."

"Take care, señor," Roca warned. "I hear such people can be dangerous."

"They are dangerous, tough, and fearless. That's exactly why this rebellion didn't collapse long ago."

A tall, weather-toughened man with shaggy blond hair stood with several others in the courtyard. "How do, Mr. Schoolmaster!" he called with a grin as Simon approached. "Brought you a fine load of corn, leather, molasses, and—"

"And two prisoners, I hear. Who are they, Gillis?"

Gillis's grin vanished. "Them ain't for you. They're mine."

"I said, who are they?"

"British deserters, they say. I found 'em down near Cheraw, on the river. They're spies, plain to see, and I'll give 'em what spies deserve!"

Against the other man's bluster, Simon spoke quietly. "Sorry, Gillis, but prisoners aren't your personal property. Bring them here at once."

Gillis glowered. "Don't you be orderin' me around, Schoolmaster."

"Bring them here now, or you no longer work for the Continentals."

Their brief stare down ended when Gillis sputtered, "All right, dang it! But remember"—he shook an angry fist at Simon—"they're none o' yours!"

The two strode off in opposite directions. Word spread quickly, and when Simon returned a crowd had gathered around Gillis and his two captives. One was only a boy, the other a bit older. Their soiled and tattered shirts once had been white, and their mud-spattered pants were remnants of British army uniforms. Hands tied behind their backs, they stood glassy-eyed with fear.

While Gillis scowled disapproval, Simon inspected the prisoners. "Identify yourselves, please."

The older of the two spoke first. "Andrew Jennings, formerly Sergeant, His Majesty's Sixtieth Regiment of Foot."

Then the other: "Edward Bailey, sir. Private, Sixtieth Regiment of Foot. Formerly, that is."

Simon's gaze lingered on the boy. "How old are you, Bailey?"

"Seventeen, sir."

"Seventeen!" Simon shook his head. "Did you both leave your regiment voluntarily?"

Jennings gave the reply. "Yes sir, we did. We were moving north from Savannah, you see, and—"

"And you deserted. Why?"

"Well, sir, we both have kin in the colonies. My brother's in New Jersey, Bailey's uncle and cousins are in Virginia. We know they're fighting on the American side, and—how can you take aim at a rebel knowing he might be your own flesh and blood? It's no good, sir. We just wanted out of it."

"You're out of it, all right!" Gillis barked. "Out of luck, too!"

"Not necessarily," Simon told them. "Going back to your regiment is out of the question, of course. You could, however, join the Americans."

"The devil you say!" Gillis bellowed in outrage.

123

The captives stared at Simon, hope flickering in their eyes for the first time. "Is that so, sir?" asked Jennings.

"Assuredly. There are two or three thousand former British soldiers serving in the Continental Army. Many have been commissioned for their excellent service. When the Americans win this war, everyone who served honorably will receive grants of land. Congress has pledged itself to that."

The two Englishmen exchanged amazed looks.

"Of course, should we lose," Simon went on, "I'd suggest you resort to your disappearing act again. And next time, keep clear of people like Jim Gillis here."

Laughter rippled through the circle of onlookers, most of whom—except Gillis—were enjoying the entertainment. The prisoners whispered to each other, then Jennings announced their decision.

"Thank you kindly, sir. You're a gentleman. We'd be proud to join the Americans."

As the spectators cheered, Gillis snorted in disgust.

Simon turned to him with a curt order. "Untie these men."

"Damned if I will," Gillis growled. "They're my prisoners, and if you try to take 'em, I'll..." His right hand rested on a pistol in his belt.

The crowd fell silent.

Undaunted, Simon studied Gillis's angry face. "You're one of our best suppliers, Gillis. How much does the army owe you for your services so far?"

Gillis blinked at the unexpected question. "My bills

of credit are up to four hundred dollars. And that re-minds me—when do I get paid?"

"These things take time. But how much do you think you'd ever collect if you shot the army's chief supply agent in these parts?"

Gillis scratched his stubbly beard, opened his mouth to speak, then closed it again. He had met defeat.

Simon turned to his young assistant. "Billy, untie these men and get them food and drink. I'll give them further instructions later."

Billy went to work and the spectators dispersed, many looking disappointed that there was no fight. Gillis edged up to Simon with a sheepish look on his face.

"Lookee here, Mr. Schoolmaster, you didn't think I meant to harm them fellows, did you? I was only fooling."

"Of course you were, Jim." Simon clapped Gillis on the shoulder. "I never doubted it for a minute."

Returning to his meeting with Roca, he found the Spaniard standing in the doorway.

"Tell me, señor," Roca said with a skeptical look on his face, "was it really worth risking your life for two deserters?"

"It's a matter of necessity, Mr. Roca. If I let a man like Gillis get away with something like that just once, I might as well go home. Besides, even if I have to handle weapons, I like to save a life whenever I can."

Roca smiled. "You are a man of quality, Señor

Schoolmaster. May I look forward to seeing you at Cape Fear on July first?"

"We'll be there, sir, to take delivery on all cargo."

"Till July, then." Roca bowed stiffly, shook Simon's hand, and strode off, glad to leave that strange place behind.

Simon was again working on his ledgers when Billy returned. "They're resting, sir. And dying to tell you what a fine, upstanding chap you are."

"I'll see them in a few minutes."

Billy sat down. "Sir, if you don't mind my askin'— who was the foreign gentleman?"

"A Mr. Roca. He brings us greetings from friends of ours in Spain."

"I'll be jiggered!"

Simon pushed his book aside. "There's a busy summer ahead, Billy. We'll pull up stakes here soon and go down to the coast to meet a Spanish ship—and pick up more supplies than you ever dreamed of."

"Bully, sir!"

"It'll be some job, hauling it all up the Wagon Road. In the fall there'll be another ship, and we'll do it again. But in between we can grab some time off. I want to get down to Charlestown to see some friends."

Billy frowned at this. "Beggin' your pardon, sir, but that don't seem too healthy these days. Not with the Redcoats so close by. You want to see those friends that bad?"

"As a matter of fact, I do. One, in particular. Although it's been so long, I'm not sure she'll remember me." Simon was suddenly gazing out the window, as the face of a dark-haired girl floated before his eyes. Her beauty seemed close enough to touch. His next words were spoken in a distant voice, as if to himself.

"I said I wouldn't forget her. And I never have."

Chapter 16

After Charlestown survived the second invasion threat, the number of Patriot-minded citizens swelled. Robert Prentice was not the only Loyalist who removed his family from the city for safety. But Patriot celebrations at the British retreat soon dissolved into dread. The enemy ruthlessly destroyed rebel strongholds north of Savannah. Fear was in everyone's mind: They'll be back. Meanwhile, spring faded into a surprisingly tranquil summer.

But for Jane, with visits to Charlestown forbidden, life at Rosewall had become so oppressive that she almost agreed with Clarissa's view of the plantation as a prison, even if a beautiful one. She spent as much time as she could with Omar, whose lordly manner was somehow comforting, and with Cuba, whose cheery personality brightened the shadowy house. Sometimes she accompanied her aunt and uncle to the Lambert plantation, a few miles away. But Jacques no longer lived there, having quarreled with his brother, Louis; and without his lively presence, Jane found these visits rather dull.

One day toward the end of summer, Brandon appeared, on short leave from his cavalry unit. In high spirits, he swung down from his horse, beaming at Jane, who had come out to meet him. She was so starved for company that she gave in to an impulse to hug him—then promptly regretted it, fearing he might interpret it as a sign of budding love.

But this time he was preoccupied with an eagerness to be admired. "How do you like my new uniform, Jane? Don't I look fine?" He flourished his tricornered black hat with a gold insignia, then twirled to display his tan coat with red collar and cuffs, white ruffled shirt, and leather breeches. He did indeed look fine, and Jane told him so.

He was also eager to show off his new horse, a huge chestnut stallion named Warrior, his beloved Princess having been "retired from active duty."

"Warrior's better suited for the man's work of war," he explained. "Although, the damned rebels are too cowardly to stand and fight, so we haven't actually seen any action yet. We mostly just chase them around."

Jane hoped that "chasing them around" was the worst her action-hungry young friend would ever have to do. But there was something else that concerned her, and as they strolled in the garden later, she brought it up.

"Brandon, when did you last see your parents?"

"Oh, I know what you're going to say, Jane. They're sad because I left home. But when Father rejected everything that loyal, law-abiding Englishmen in America stand for, he rejected me, too."

"That's not true. He never did. Anyway, what about your mother? Isn't she a kind of innocent victim in all this?"

"Look here, I feel terrible about Mother. She's such a kind, generous, warmhearted person. And Father, having taken leave of his senses, is leading her straight down the path to ruin. I worry about her, I miss her dreadfully, and I go to see her as often as I can. Truly, I do."

"I hope so," Jane said with a sigh. "And I daresay that's all we can expect of you, isn't it?"

Brandon had come saying he could stay only one night, because he had to get back to his regiment the next day. All afternoon, he chatted pleasantly with Clarissa about her gardening, and that night he held a long war council with Robert. Brandon had brought exciting news. The British were massing a huge force in Savannah, one far stronger than needed to hold that small city.

"Obviously they're planning a major offensive toward Charlestown, Uncle. Probably not until spring, they say. But the third time's the charm, you know. This time it cannot fail."

Robert clenched his fists. "Gad, how time will drag till then!"

The next morning, Jane accompanied Brandon to the gate, where Omar waited holding Warrior's reins. There, clasping Jane's hands, Brandon recited his habitual declarations of devotion. "Be patient, dearest girl. Though we're far apart, you're in my heart every moment. And when the world is finally put right again, we'll have a happy future together."

She accepted a kiss on the cheek, wished him well, and waved good-bye as he swung expertly into the saddle and went galloping away. *Dear, foolish Brandon,* she thought. *He's been talking like that since the day we met, and it never occurs to him to wonder how I might feel about our "happy future." Why don't I set him straight? Is it because he hasn't thought to ask? Or because I dread hurting him?*

Suddenly Omar, standing beside her, spoke, his deep voice and solemn manner imparting immense weight to his words. "Young master want you for wife, miss. But you not want him."

"Oh, I didn't know it showed," she said with a light laugh.

Omar's solemn face betrayed no hint of amusement. "You wise, miss. Young master talk fancy, but he just a boy that never grow up. You wait for real man. One day he come."

"How kind you are, Omar. But I really don't think that's going to happen." She smiled up at the big man towering over her, then turned back toward the house.

As summer heat gave way to the coolness of fall, Clarissa and Jane finally told Robert: Either we spend some time in town, or we lose our minds. Which shall it be? But after so many weeks in isolation, even Robert was ready to give in. Not for the social diversions Clarissa craved, but to get the war news, which was almost impossible to do holed up at Rosewall. Trips to the Charlestown house once again became part of the family routine.

In town, Robert attended long sessions with Loyalist friends, while Clarissa made daily rounds of visits with Loyalist wives and daughters. Jane sometimes accompanied her but found the gentle ladies' conversation drearily familiar—all about the scarcity of goods in the shops, or the high prices of goods that were there, or the folly of breaking with the king, which, of course, would soon be stamped out. She was often invited to parties, but the young men she met seemed to be only pale copies of Brandon, forever boasting of their horses and their horsemanship as they eagerly awaited the arrival of the Redcoats. It was all too tedious.

One afternoon, Robert returned elated from a Loyalist meeting. "Great news from Savannah!" he fairly shouted. "French and American forces dared challenge the British there—and were utterly destroyed! Now those scurvy rebels see what their French alliance did for them—nothing! The Redcoats are again moving north from the Savannah River, this time in overwhelming force. Of course, we know what that means. They'll soon be here!"

Where was Brandon? Jane wondered uneasily. And that question led to another: Where was that fire-breathing young Patriot Peter Quincy? Could it be that they were both at Savannah? Even if not, it was surely possible that one day the two might try to kill each other on a field of battle.

Jane cringed at the thought. *What an awful insanity this war is!*

During these tense days, Jane often took long walks along the Battery—the broad, curving boulevard bordering the harbor. A few rusting ships dozed at the docks. Clearly, the British blockade had taken its toll. Shortages of every kind had reduced life in the city to the minimum essentials of survival. Yet the streets teemed with vitality—tradesmen, street vendors, idlers, women, and children—ordinary folk going about their business as if not even the approach of an invading army could dampen their spirits. Even the nearby Ainsley Emporium, though almost empty and far from the commercial beehive it had once been, was still open. Contemplating all this, Jane suddenly knew something not yet discovered by Loyalists like Robert and Brandon: These people would not be easily conquered.

And often, on the way home from her walks, she gazed up Queen Street, at the swinging sign of HUGH PRENTICE, CABINETMAKER, and was struck by a thought that vexed her constantly: *How ridiculous that I'm forbidden to see him.*

One crisp October afternoon, Arthur Ainsley, of all people, presented the opportunity. Drawing her aside at the end of a visit, he asked in a low voice, "Jane, could you come again tomorrow at three o'clock? Alone?"

"I suppose so," she replied, instantly curious. "What's the occasion?"

"Your cousin Hugh Prentice will be here," was his surprising response. "And your presence is urgently desired. Make whatever excuse you need to, but come! And say nothing of this to anyone."

Despite her pleadings, Arthur would say no more, leaving her to spend the next twenty-four hours wondering what on earth was afoot.

Chapter 17

L uckily, both Robert and Clarissa had engagements the next afternoon. Robert's Loyalist group was holding a special meeting with refugees just arriving from Savannah. Clarissa had been invited to a formal luncheon, where one of her friends had promised there would even be real English tea. Pleading a headache, Jane declined, and retired to her room.

At precisely three o'clock, she was knocking at the Ainsleys' front door. Harriet opened it and quickly drew her inside.

"Hurry upstairs, dear. They're waiting for you."

Seated at his study desk, facing the door, Arthur called out, "So glad you could come, Jane!"

Two other men were seated with their backs to the door. One of them—Hugh—rose and came smiling to greet her. "Jane, what a delight!"

"Cousin Hugh! It's so good to see you again, I—" She stopped short as the third man rose and turned toward her. "Mr. Cordwyn!"

"Jane," he murmured, coming closer. His smile seemed a bit shy. "Is it really you?"

Thoroughly flustered, she struggled to regain her composure. "Yes, Mr. Cordwyn. Jane Prentice, your former student." He looked a bit older and—oddly, for a schoolteacher—as tanned and fit as a woodsman. The same piercing gray eyes that had stared down at her from the schoolroom door so long ago now gazed intently into hers. For a moment, she didn't know what to say. Then she shot a playful look at the chuckling Arthur.

"You, sir, have tricked me." This brought forth a round of laughter, in which Jane and Simon fully shared, smiling at each other with her hand still clasped in his.

At first everyone seemed to talk at once. Jane told Hugh how Robert was convinced she'd be infected with rebel fever if she visited Queen Street, and how much she had missed seeing him and Lydia. Hugh told her about Peter's marrying a sweet girl named Marianne Ellis.

"He's in the militia, the Sons of Liberty. We pray for his safety."

"And so shall I," Jane declared. She longed to know why Mr. Cordwyn was there—and she felt his gaze upon her.

Meeting his eyes at last, she said half teasingly, "Mr. Cordwyn, I do believe you're staring at me."

"I beg your pardon," Simon apologized. "But it's so hard to believe the lovely young woman sitting here is the schoolgirl I once knew."

Glowing with pleasure and embarrassment, Jane hastened to change the subject. "What brings you back to Charlestown?"

Simon told her about the small school he'd started in Lancaster. But, he said, his brother-in-law, Jack Herndon, had fallen ill, so he had closed his school to help his sister run the family store. "It's a tough job, so I came to seek advice from Mr. Ainsley. He's been able to keep his Emporium open for years in spite of the blockade, so obviously he's an expert."

"I see," said Jane, but secretly she was puzzled. It was hard to picture the schoolmaster running a store—even temporarily.

Simon continued. "I'm also still trying to persuade my rebel friends here to leave before it's too late. General Henry Clinton's in command of the British now. The next attack will not fail. But everyone's as stubborn as ever. Surely you agree this is good advice, don't you?"

Flattered to be asked, Jane considered the question carefully. "Yes, I think it probably is, Mr. Cordwyn. Uncle Robert also offered to help everyone. But people are who they are, and I doubt anyone can change that."

"The voice of wisdom!" cried Hugh.

Simon gave up. "All right, it appears that I'm hopelessly outnumbered. I'll wish them luck, and say no more."

All too soon, Jane noticed the lateness of the hour. "I must go," she said, rising. "Uncle Robert gets so agitated if I stay out long." She looked at Simon.

Would these few minutes be all they would see of each other?

It was as if he could read her mind. "I have a hired carriage," he said. "May I drive you?"

"That would be lovely," she replied, trying not to sound too eager.

Good-byes were said, and in a few minutes Simon and Jane drove away in the carriage. Simon chatted pleasantly as he drove, inquiring after Robert and Clarissa and saying how nice it was to be back in Charlestown for a short visit. Jane was pleased that he even remembered her old companion Mrs. Morley, whom he also inquired after. All the while he drove in a direction that showed he had no intention of taking her straight home. It almost seemed as if there were something important he wanted to say, but he couldn't quite bring himself to say it.

Finally she ventured, "It's delightful to see you again, Mr. Cordwyn, but you've told me very little about your present life. How are things for you in Pennsylvania?"

"There's not much to tell, really, except what I've already said."

"Well, have you . . ." She hardly dared ask. "Have you married?"

"Oh, no, that would be quite out of the question. I have as much responsibility as I can handle these days, with my sister's family all depending on me. There was one young lady who might have been interested, but she grew tired of my maddening indecisiveness and married someone else."

"Oh, that's too bad," she said, hoping her sudden happiness at this news was not betrayed in her voice.

They were riding along the bay shore now, where Simon stopped the carriage at a quiet spot and turned to Jane with a long, pensive look. "I can't get over how you've blossomed, Jane. When I saw you last you were just a slip of a girl. Now I find you're . . ."

"A woman?" Jane suggested slyly.

"Exactly—a woman! And, I hope, one who doesn't mind the way she was tricked. But I wanted to see you again, and it seemed the only way. I'm sure your aunt and uncle wouldn't be pleased if I came knocking at their door."

"No, I dare say they wouldn't," Jane agreed.

"And I must say, I'm greatly relieved to find that you, uh . . . well, the truth is, I was afraid you might be Mrs. Brandon Ainsley by now."

She gave a light laugh. "*Afraid,* Mr. Cordwyn?"

"I just never felt Brandon was right for you. No doubt he's convinced he is, and I'm told your uncle thinks so, too. But it seems to me a young woman should have the right to make her own decisions in such matters."

"Yes, and I intend to," she replied firmly. "Brandon may be Uncle Robert's choice for me, but I have my own intentions clearly in mind."

"And what are they, may I ask?"

"To defy everyone and remain a spinster for life."

Her playful answer gave him a hearty laugh. "It's amazing, Jane! When I'm with you I learn to laugh again. I wish we had more time."

"So do I, Mr. Cordwyn. But I'm afraid I really must be getting home."

He took up the horse's reins and started the carriage again, this time stopping, at Jane's suggestion, a long block from the Prentice house.

I can't believe it's all over so quickly, Jane thought in dismay.

After a moment of silence, Simon spoke again. "Two things before you go, please. First, I'd like it if you'd just call me Simon. Mr. Cordwyn was your schoolmaster, and I haven't been that for years. Will you?"

"I'll try," she told him. "And the second thing?"

"Remember the last time we parted company? We agreed not to say good-bye. Just, 'till we meet again.' Let's keep it that way, all right?"

"Yes, indeed, that's much better. But when might that be, do you think?" Jane asked, hardly daring to hope that he could give a definite answer.

He shook his head. "Lord only knows. All *I* know is that I've never been able to get you out of my mind, and I can't help hoping that someday, somehow—" He broke off with a grimace. "I have no right to be talking like this. Not in these times, when our lives aren't even our own. Let's just promise each other— we do not, ever, say good-bye."

Jane could feel the color rising in her cheeks, but she kept her tone calm in replying. "Very well. I'll just say good luck and Godspeed, till we meet again." Then the solemn mood dissolved in another moment

140

of amusement as she added, "And in the meantime, I'll practice calling you Simon."

He was still chuckling at this as he got out and came around to help her out of the carriage. But his manner became serious again as he cautioned, "By the way, not a word to anyone that I've been here. It might seem a bit strange to you, but that's the way it has to be for now."

"I'm sure you have your reasons. Of course, I won't say a word. I promise."

Taking her hand, he held it for a moment and gently squeezed it as a smile crinkled his eyes. "Till we meet again," he murmured. Then, in an instant, he was back in the carriage, and after a cheery wave to Jane, he started off at a brisk pace, went around a corner, and was out of sight.

Jane walked the rest of the way home in a daze, wondering what, if anything, had just happened. So many times she had dreamed of such a reunion. Now her dream had come true—yet not really, not the way she had dreamed it. Plainly, he had wanted to say something important but for some unknown reason was unable to. He said he hoped that someday, somehow—what?

There was only one thing he said that we can both be perfectly certain of, she concluded. *That is that our lives are not our own.*

That night, Simon sat with Hugh and Lydia at their kitchen table in a dark and dismal mood.

"You should be pleased," Hugh remarked. "You saw her, she's lovely, and she's not married or even engaged to be."

"Yes," Simon replied. "She's even lovelier than I imagined. And my feelings for her, which I thought might be imagined, are very real. Still..." His mood showed no improvement.

"I know the trouble," Lydia said. "You feel you can't tell her the truth. She's still an English-born lady living in a Loyalist house. But that need not necessarily stop you, you know."

This only served to darken Simon's mood still further. "What are you suggesting—that I blurt out everything to her? That I say, 'I may not live long, Jane, but while I live I'm a man of distinction. I work for the rebel side, and the British would just love to put a rope around my neck.' That'll impress her! And how pleased she'd be that I'm helping those who are trying to destroy her comfortable English world here!" Simon slapped the tabletop angrily. "Damn, why did I get mixed up in this wretched business?"

Again Lydia answered. "Because there's a war, and we're all fighting, in our own way, for a good cause. Like it or not, love, so are you."

Silence descended upon them. There seemed nothing left to say.

Chapter 18

The Prentice family spent Christmas of 1779 at Rosewall, with exchanges of visits with Louis Lambert and his family, and other friends in the area. Mrs. Morley was brought from Goose Creek for the holiday and a brief reunion with Jane. But there was little festivity. The men talked grimly of the warfare they were sure was coming soon; the ladies tried to maintain a normal life. With shame and embarrassment, Louis Lambert finally admitted to Robert that Jacques had joined a Patriot militia company. As far as Louis was concerned, his brother had disgraced the family name. He vowed never to speak of Jacques again.

Robert shook his head in disgust. "Another good man wasting himself in madness!" To Jane, it meant just another good man risking everything for his ideals. There were so many of them to worry about.

On their first visit to Charlestown in the new year, the Prentices encountered an ominous rise in street disturbances. Taunts and insults were now shouted at Robert and his Loyalist friends whenever they went out on the street. One friend who dared to shout back at the rebels was dragged out of his carriage and knocked down. The British army continued its steady advance. The closer it came, the more belligerent grew the insults. Finally, Robert decided that he alone would make the occasional trips to town necessary to obtain the latest news. Jane and Clarissa would stay safely home at Rosewall.

In the next few months, the British encircled Charlestown from the landward side, skirmishing with the rebels around the city's edges. In April, a relentless cannon bombardment began, while the British fleet finally took over Charlestown Harbor, squeezing the city in an iron grip. Jane could get no news of the Ainsleys, nor of Hugh and his family.

"What do you suggest I do about it?" Robert demanded irritably when she told him she was worried. "I offered them refuge, and they all refused. What more can be done?" No one had an answer.

Each day, Robert roamed the house, impatient to find a way to help the British cause—but how? Gradually, a plan came to mind. And soon he found an unexpected opportunity to present it.

Jane was gathering flowers in one of Clarissa's corner rose beds one fragrant springtime day when a squad of British soldiers, in their splendid scarlet coats, galloped up the road. Jane stared through the heavy iron gate. In all her life in England, she had never actually seen a Redcoat soldier. The officer who dismounted and approached the gate was handsome, sandy-haired, and youthful. A curved saber hung by his side.

"Is this Rosewall, the plantation of Robert Prentice?" he inquired.

Jane nodded. "It is. How may I help you?"

"Summon your master, girl. I desire audience with him."

"Evidently you mistake me for a servant, sir," Jane said with a smile. "I am Jane Prentice, the owner's niece."

The officer blinked. "Ah—I do beg your pardon."

"I am dressed for gardening, so it's understandable. Here, my uncle and aunt are just coming."

Robert greeted the visitor with an enthusiastic handshake. "I'm Robert Prentice. Welcome, sir!"

"Thank you, Mr. Prentice. I am Captain Richard Fleming, aide to General Sir Henry Clinton, Commander in Chief of His Majesty's Forces in America. I bring you the general's greetings."

Robert's eyes widened. "I am greatly honored, Captain!" Robert hastened to introduce Clarissa to the British officer.

"Mrs. Prentice, charmed." The young Redcoat bowed.

"I take it you've met my niece, Lady Jane Prentice?" Robert asked.

"*Lady* Jane?" Fleming assessed Jane with fresh interest.

"Daughter of Edward, Third Earl of Almesbury, my late brother," Robert explained proudly. "Our family seat is in Hampshire. Perhaps you know it."

"Almesbury." Fleming studied Jane intently. "Yes, I've heard of it. It is an honor to make your acquaintance, Lady Jane." He bowed again, far more gallantly than he had to Clarissa.

Jane was mortified that her uncle had so brazenly tried to impress their visitor with the Prentices' aristocratic English background. Meanwhile, Clarissa immediately invited Captain Fleming up to the house. "Let us offer you some refreshment and a chance to rest." She smiled sweetly at him.

"Thank you, no, Mrs. Prentice. I cannot tarry long. We are contacting as many Loyalists as possible today, and we have much ground to cover."

"You may be sure of our loyalty," Robert declared stoutly. "I hope to meet General Clinton very soon, and to serve in any way possible."

"I am gratified to hear it, sir. I have just seen Mr. Lambert, who told me much the same. Most admirable, for a Frenchman, his own countrymen being allied with the American rebels. Would you say he's trustworthy?"

"Absolutely trustworthy, I assure you," Robert replied. "His forebears were Protestants, driven out of Catholic France by religious persecution. And now, Captain, if I may suggest a way I might be of service?"

"By all means."

"I gladly offer Rosewall to General Clinton as a

base of operations in this area. When Charlestown falls, rebel uprisings in the backcountry will surely follow. In that event, the protection of our massive wall should prove immensely useful, and we can provide ample victuals of the finest quality."

"Quite so, and many thanks to you. Should action develop out here, the general will remember your offer. In the meantime, we ask all Loyalists not to venture into Charlestown until the surroundings have been secured."

"You may rely on us, Captain," Robert vowed. "And, of course, we wish you all success."

"Thank you." The two men shook hands, then Fleming was eager to be off. "Mrs. Prentice? Lady Jane?" He gave them another low bow. "It's been a great pleasure. I hope that as soon as Charlestown is safely back in British hands, we may meet again."

"Perhaps we can receive you at our house there, Captain Fleming," Clarissa said with her sweetest smile.

"A delightful prospect," he replied, and he gave Jane a lingering look as he added, "especially if Lady Jane will be there."

For an instant, Jane considered advising the young man that she preferred not to be called Lady Jane. But that wouldn't do. "I'll be there, Captain."

"Excellent! Good day to you all, then." Captain Fleming and his soldiers departed in a flurry of pounding hooves.

"Attractive young man," Clarissa remarked. "Don't you think, Jane? He certainly found you attractive."

"Splendid fellow, the cream of English manhood!" Robert exclaimed as he secured the gate.

"However, Robert..." Clarissa looked troubled now. "I do hope the general won't accept your reckless offer. I don't relish the thought of my gardens being trampled by an encampment of soldiers."

Robert took her hand as they walked back to the house. "My dear, more important things are at stake here than gardens. History's being made..."

Jane heard no more. *When Charlestown falls,* her uncle had said. Not *if. When.* And Captain Fleming looked forward to meeting them at their house in town soon. They seemed so confident, so certain. Yet it was with a curious feeling of uneasiness that Jane turned back to the roses.

After weeks of merciless bombardment, Charlestown in May 1780 was so short of food that starvation loomed as the people's primary enemy. Exhaustion finally forced rebel defenders to bow to the overwhelmingly superior force. At eleven o'clock in the morning of May 12, the rebels marched out, sullen, still defiant in their hearts, but beaten. They stacked their weapons in surrender. It was one of the Americans' costliest defeats of the entire war.

News of the siege had reached Rosewall in the usual fragments—truth and rumor hopelessly mixed. Many nights, Robert paced the floor for hours, desperate for information. And many nights, Jane lay sleepless, worrying about those she cared about in the besieged city. She was tormented at being so safe while they were in such danger.

The day after the surrender, Louis Lambert banged on the Rosewall gate and rushed excitedly past Omar and into the house with the news. An elated Robert called for his finest champagne. He and the usually dour Louis celebrated at the dining room table late into the night, toasting King George, the victorious Redcoats, the return of lawful British rule, their wives, each other—anything they could think of—until the house rang with their drunken laughter.

Jane retired early, thankful that the waiting was finally over. At last, they could return to the city. She could find out how people had fared, and perhaps even find a way to help. The thought comforted her as she listened to the revelry downstairs.

She never even stopped to notice that she herself, a daughter of old England, felt in no mood to celebrate.

PART IV

Occupation
1780

Chapter 19

With the greatest pleasure I further report . . . that the inhabitants from every quarter repair to . . . this garrison [Charlestown] to declare their allegiance to the King . . . there are few men in South Carolina who are not either our prisoners or in arms with us.

— from General Henry Clinton's "Report on the Submission of South Carolina," June 1780

eneral Clinton's optimistic report was considerably exaggerated. In fact, barely two hundred people had come out to greet the victorious British as they marched into a city near collapse from weeks of bombardment. The streets, which normally would have rung with the cries of peddlers and the clatter of carriages, were almost deserted. All was quiet. But the calm surface concealed a smoldering reservoir of defiance.

Returning to the city, the Prentices found their Legare Street house again vandalized, greatly angering Robert.

The Ainsleys' home had been taken over by British soldiers, profoundly upsetting Jane. The Ainsleys had retired to Harriet's family home at Goose Creek. And Arthur, tainted by his association with known rebel leaders, was now officially a prisoner on parole.

"Be thankful they didn't clap him in irons in the Exchange Cellars as a traitor!" was all Robert had to say.

Jane walked over to Hugh's shop on Queen Street, but found it all boarded up. When she asked around the neighborhood, everyone eyed her suspiciously, claiming to know nothing about Hugh the cabinetmaker. She returned home in a cloud of gloom to find two guests in the parlor with Robert and Clarissa—Brandon, paying one of his brief periodic visits, and Captain Richard Fleming. They were savoring a pot of genuine English tea—a rare and precious commodity—that Fleming had brought as a gift. Both young men rose as Jane entered, each trying to outdo the other's show of gallantry. Brandon was fairly bursting with what he evidently considered to be the day's most important news.

"Jane! Captain Fleming's going to see about getting me a commission in the Loyalist militia. Soon I could be Lieutenant Ainsley!"

"How nice, Brandon." Jane sincerely tried to sound pleased. She was much more interested when Clarissa said, "Captain Fleming is working with the Board of Police, in charge of military security in the city. He's promised to look into Arthur's situation for us."

"That's very good of you, Captain Fleming," Jane

said, brightening. "Needless to say, we'd be terribly grateful."

"Not at all, Lady Jane. I'm glad to be of service if I can. And I'd be honored if you'd call me Richard."

She nodded. "Very well—Richard it is. And as long as we're on that subject, I prefer not to be called Lady Jane. Just Jane will be fine."

This brought a protest from Robert. "My dear! You're the daughter of an English earl, and as such—"

"Nevertheless, *Jane* you shall be to me!" Richard intervened, smiling. "I shall endeavor in all things to please you, Jane."

"About my brother, Richard," Clarissa coaxed.

Richard took a long sip of tea, then said, "Contrary to widespread opinion, we are not bent on vengeance here. We want only to bring all citizens of this colony back under the protection of their rightful king. Even the rebel militiamen have been released on parole—as long as they remain on good behavior, of course."

Jane breathed a sigh of relief, thinking of Peter Quincy.

"But prominent citizens like Mr. Ainsley, who may have influenced many to join the rebel movement, must be held accountable to some extent. I understand their so-called president, Rutledge, fled the colony in panic. Evidently your brother is made of sterner stuff, Mrs. Prentice."

"Or more obstinate stuff," Brandon muttered.

"However, his situation is not hopeless," Fleming went on. "Mr. Ainsley should immediately sign the

Oath of Allegiance, stating, 'I do acknowledge and declare myself to be a true and faithful subject of the King of Great Britain, and I will at all times hereafter be obedient to his government'—and so on. Perfectly reasonable, I'm sure you'll agree."

"Perfectly," Robert concurred. "My name is high among those who have gladly signed."

"So it is, sir. Unfortunately, Mr. Ainsley's has not yet appeared."

"Perhaps I could persuade him to—" Clarissa began.

"I wouldn't go to him, Mrs. Prentice." Richard shook his head. "You have your husband's position as a loyal king's man to consider. If you were seen contacting someone who's under suspicion—"

"But he's my brother!"

"I realize that, but do keep your distance. You could write to him, urging him to see the error of his ways. Meanwhile, be assured, dear lady, whatever can be done on your brother's behalf will be done."

"Thank you so much, Richard."

A few minutes later, Brandon announced that he had another appointment, and after taking leave of the others, asked Jane to walk outside with him.

Once they were outside, he turned to her with a troubled frown. "Be careful of Fleming, Jane. I fear he has designs on you."

"Brandon, you're not my guardian! I've got Uncle Robert for that, thank you, and I don't need instruction from you, too."

Brandon was taken aback but quickly recovered. "Very well, but I'm going to check on you often."

"Suit yourself," she said with a shrug. "Now, there's something I want to ask you. Have you seen your parents since the occupation began?"

"Ah, now it seems *you're* trying to be *my* guardian."

"I'm concerned about your parents, Brandon. Aren't you?"

"Of course I am. But Fleming told me the same thing he told Aunt Clarissa. If I want that commission, I'd better stay away from them."

"And you put that ahead of your parents! I'm disappointed in you."

Suddenly he was smiling indulgently as he took her hand. "Do not despair of me, my sweet. Imperfect as I may be, after we're married I shall be putty in your hands, and you shall make me over to your liking." After planting his customary peck on her cheek, he went on his way, Jane shaking her head ruefully as she watched him go.

Richard was just leaving, too. "Duty calls," he told Jane.

She stared coolly at him. "Tell me, Captain Fleming, do you have a family in England?"

"Yes, indeed, quite a large one."

"Then how can you be so indifferent to family ties, telling Brandon he must stay away from his parents, my aunt away from her brother?"

"It's for their own good, Jane, and that of everyone concerned, I assure you." He took a step closer. "And

157

if you persist in calling me Captain Fleming, I shall be obliged to call you Lady Jane."

No use in this, Jane thought. "Good-bye, then, Richard. It was nice seeing you again."

"Your aunt and uncle have urged me to come often. I said I would, but I really meant only if *you'd* like me to."

"Of course," she replied politely. "I'll be happy to see you again. Anytime."

"Then you most certainly will." He departed with a bright smile and a crisp military nod. Jane watched him disappear from view, fervently hoping that he meant it when he promised to interest himself in Arthur's situation. She decided she would bring it up with him every chance she got.

She was working at her writing desk when Clarissa appeared in the doorway. "May I have a moment, Jane?"

"Of course, Aunt Clarissa." Jane covered her paper. It was only an amateurish attempt at a poem, but she didn't need Clarissa reading it.

Her aunt sat down on the edge of the bed. "I'm sure you realize how fortunate we are to have Captain Fleming for a friend," she began. "Particularly with regard to Arthur. If Richard intervenes on his behalf, it could make all the difference."

"I'm sure it could," Jane agreed.

"There's Brandon's commission, and Richard's also promised to see if he can introduce Robert to General

Clinton. He can be enormously helpful to us in many ways—if he's so inclined."

"So it would seem."

"And the way I see it, that puts an important responsibility on *you*."

Jane blinked. "On me? I'm sorry, I don't quite follow."

"Oh, come now—surely you've noticed how attracted to you Richard is. I might even be a tiny bit envious."

"What on earth can you mean?"

"Isn't it obvious? Richard's interest in this family consists entirely of his interest in you. Therefore, it's of the utmost importance that you should—how shall I say it?—be *very* nice to him."

Jane stared, aghast. "Are you asking me to pretend that I care for Captain Fleming—to *deceive* him?"

"Oh, let's not put it quite that way. For all we know, you might develop genuine feelings for him. That would be lovely, and he'd make a fine catch. But no, I wouldn't ask you to spoil your arrangement with Brandon. Just keep Richard interested by letting him believe he might have a chance with you."

"Really, Aunt Clarissa, you do amaze me with your scheming!"

Clarissa smiled a superior smile. "We women have few tools at our disposal, Jane. Fortunately, we do have the ability to scheme, and we also have the ability to attract men. You have plenty of that. You just haven't learned how to use it. But very often it's the only way to entice our menfolk into helping us turn our schemes into reality."

Jane squirmed in indecision. "This all sounds so distasteful, I—"

"Jane—" Clarissa leaned forward, suddenly earnest. "Use your charms for Arthur's sake. Don't you remember his kindness to you when you came here a frightened orphan? Think about it. You might just save his life."

After long hesitation, Jane was ready to take a firm stand. "Aunt Clarissa, I will do all I reasonably can to persuade Richard to help us with Uncle Arthur's situation. But deliberately deceiving him is going too far. And since you mentioned it—whatever you and Uncle Robert may believe, I do *not* have an 'arrangement' with Brandon."

"Oh, I beg your pardon! Perhaps you have other plans that you haven't bothered to tell us about!"

"Only hopes and dreams, not plans exactly."

"What hopes and dreams?" Clarissa's eyes narrowed in suspicion. "Jane, are you meeting someone secretly? All those mysterious walks you're forever taking— where do you go?"

"Nowhere in particular. Just around." Jane could feel herself start to blush as her mind flashed back to the image of Simon turning to greet her last fall in Arthur's study.

"Meeting a secret lover, I shouldn't wonder!" Clarissa kept pressing. "I warn you, if Robert hears of such disreputable behavior, he'll—"

"Excuse me." Jane was on her feet. "I suddenly feel like going for another one of those 'mysterious' walks. Perhaps you'd like to follow me, Aunt Clarissa. Who knows, you might see something delightfully wicked!"

She paused long enough to enjoy the astonishment on Clarissa's face, then strode out the door and downstairs to the street.

This time Jane used her walk as a way of working off her seething resentment of Clarissa's accusation. How dare she, when *she's* the one who's had a secret lover! Naturally, it was flattering to be asked to assume an "important responsibility." But to deceive a decent, unsuspecting young man? Her innate honesty would make that quite impossible. And yet—

Use your charms for Arthur's sake . . . It's the only way . . . Remember his kindness . . . You might just save his life . . .

Jane felt trapped. She could not refuse to do anything for Uncle Arthur, whom she held in warmest affection. But how should she go about using her so-called charms on Richard and still be able to live with herself?

It would be the strangest challenge she had ever encountered.

Chapter 20

For hours a soft rain had drifted down from a black sky, but around midnight it ceased, and soon the scattering clouds only occasionally obscured a last-quarter moon. Even so, the dense forest at Merritt's Camp, on the North Carolina coast, would keep up a steady *drip-drip* all night long.

Stocky, shaggy-haired Billy Evans moved with extreme caution as he made his way up the soggy path that led from the river landing to the camp in the woods. His destination was the tent occupied by his boss—he who was known only as The Schoolmaster, but whose fame was widespread in these parts. At last, pausing in front of a small tent whose canvas walls glowed dimly from the light of a lantern inside, he spoke in a low tone.

"Sir? It's Billy here."

"Come in, Billy," was the muffled reply.

The young man entered to find Simon sitting on his straw pallet, working on his journals. "Nothing stirring out there, sir. Mr. Merritt's on watch."

"All right." Simon nodded toward a low stool, the only thing resembling furniture in the tiny chamber. "Care to sit a spell?"

Billy sat down. "Sir, why don't they come? The Spanish are usually right on time. But we've waited two weeks, and still no sign of 'em."

"It's a matter of luck," Simon explained. "One glimpse of a British warship in the area, and they'll turn and run. And if they think the British have discovered the landing site, they won't come back. We'll wait a few more days, then we'll give it up and leave."

"It's hard to sit around and wait. Mr. Merritt's gettin' pretty impatient. He says the Spaniards can't be trusted, anyway."

"Mr. Merritt doesn't trust anybody. Particularly me."

"Because you're a Northerner, sir?"

"That's part of it. But mainly because I refuse to carry a gun."

"Well now, beggin' your pardon, sir, but there he's got a point. War's a dangerous business, and I never heard of no soldier going without a gun."

"Well, since I don't carry one, I must not be a soldier. Soldiers kill their enemies, but I'm not interested in killing anybody. I smuggle weapons only because there's no choice, but I don't have to use them."

"I know you've told me that, sir, but it don't make no sense to me. Seems like when you work for one side against the other, that makes you a soldier, plain and simple."

"Not necessarily. I'd work for *both* sides if I could,

to keep all those wretched soldiers alive until their betters come to their senses."

"Come to their senses?" Billy was puzzled. "And do what, sir?"

"Sit down and work out their differences, which is what they should have done in the first place."

Billy shook his head. "You mean just stop the fightin', with no winner? That don't make no sense to me, neither. Fact is, lots o' things you say don't make sense. Like you plannin' to go back to Charlestown after we're done here. Why would you go back there now, knowin' the British have got it?"

"For personal reasons, I would."

"Hah! Lady reasons, I reckon. She must be mighty special."

This brought a chuckle from Simon. "Right you are, Billy. Now there's something we *can* agree on."

Just then their conversation was interrupted by another member of the camp calling urgently from outside. "Merritt's got a ship in sight, sir."

The two men in the tent were on their feet instantly, Simon taking up the lantern. "This could be it. Let's go."

A sluggish stream emerged from the woods at the river landing to meander across fifty yards of open beach and empty into the ocean. A miniature dock made of logs extended a few feet out into the slow-moving current. A skiff was tied there, and two lanterns hanging on a post created a circular oasis of yellow light. This was the domain of the tall, thin, hawkeyed George Merritt. When Simon and Billy arrived, Merritt and two of his men were staring intently out over the ocean. Beyond the frothy white line of a gentle surf, the dark form of a ship could be dimly seen, riding at anchor two hundred yards offshore.

"It's a two-master," Merritt reported to Simon. "Don't look like one o' Roca's, unless the Spaniards are tryin' to get tricky. I got a couple o' men down there keepin' an eye on it."

Simon lifted the cover of his lantern and blew out the flame, then addressed one of Merritt's men. "Put out your lanterns."

"Hey!" Merritt barked. "These men take orders from me, not you."

"All right, George," Simon replied patiently. "Tell them to put out those lanterns immediately."

A nod from Merritt was enough, and the lanterns were doused. Merritt then turned to Simon with a scornful smile. "What's the matter, Mr. Schoolmaster? You gettin' nervous?"

"What's the matter with *you*, George? You think it's smart to put up welcoming lights when you have no idea who's out there?"

"My guess is, it's a Dutchman. They put in here now and then."

"I see. And you're willing to risk your men's lives on a guess?"

Merritt's small eyes narrowed. "Listen, I been smugglin' here since long before you ever knew the meaning of the word. And I'm tellin' you, no ship ever put in here that didn't have friendly business with me."

"Maybe one has tonight," Simon snapped, and turned to Billy. "We need to get a closer look. You come with me, Billy. Everyone else, stay here."

"Wait a minute." Merritt grasped Simon roughly by the arm. "This is my land, damn it. *I'll* go get a closer look. *You* stay here."

Simon gave in with a weary shrug. "All right, have it your way. But get your men back up here under cover. They're too exposed out there."

Ignoring this, Merritt started for the beach, while the others stayed behind, Simon pacing restlessly as he waited. Soon a heavy cloud that had been obscuring the moon drifted off, and in the sudden rise of pale moonlight, Billy's sharp eyes caught something.

"Look there, sir. A longboat from the ship, heading for shore."

Simon stopped, squinting into the mist that hung over the ocean. "I don't like this," he muttered. "I don't like it at all." A few seconds later he exploded in fury. "Good God, the damn fools!"

One of Merritt's men on the beach had lit a lantern and was swinging it in an arc, its yellow glare reaching out just far enough to pick up the longboat, which was fast coming onshore.

Simon cupped his hands to his mouth and shouted. "George, tell them to put out that lant—"

His words were cut off by the percussive report of

a musket. The lantern on the beach spun crazily and disappeared into the water. Suddenly, the still night air was alive with gunfire, splashing, running feet, and harsh cries of alarm and rage. The heavy bark of muskets was answered by the sharper crack of rifles.

George Merritt came racing back. "Redcoats!" he yelled. "Run for it!" Halfway back to the forest cover, he stopped, drew his pistol, and turned to face the threat. At that instant he was struck with a force that shook his tall, gangly frame. He crumpled in the sand without a sound.

Simon ran for the fallen man. Merritt lay still, face-down, his right arm flung out, the hand still gripping his unused pistol. Kneeling beside him, Simon reached down to turn him over and felt warm, sticky blood.

From behind him came Billy's frantic shout, "Sir, look out!"

Simon glanced up just in time to see a British soldier running straight at him, bayonet raised to strike. One thought came to Simon's mind: *This man shot Merritt, and now he means to finish us both off with his bayonet*. No more time for thinking—his survival instinct took over. Wrenching the pistol from Merritt's hand, Simon fired just as the bayonet flashed in its downward thrust. The Redcoat grunted softly and pitched forward, falling across George Merritt's lifeless body. Simon dropped the pistol, and with his right hand clawed at what felt like a white-hot iron searing his left arm. Still on his knees, two bodies sprawled in the sand before him, he rocked back and forth in pain.

Then Billy's hand was on his shoulder, the young man's familiar voice close to his ear. "You hurt bad, sir? Can you stand up? If you can get to the landing, we'll take the skiff and..."

Billy's voice faded. The world began to spin crazily, and a great roar filled Simon's ears. Then silence, and everything went black.

Simon awoke to morning sunlight filtering through dense tree branches overhead. He was lying on his back, the weathered sides of a skiff limiting his vision on both sides. The small craft bumped gently against a bank. Dull pain throbbed in his left arm. Almost afraid to move, he groped carefully with his free hand and felt a thick bandage.

The skiff rocked slightly, and Billy's face appeared above him. "Glad to see you awake, sir. How you feelin'?"

"Terrible," Simon replied. "Where are we?"

"A mile or so up the river and into a side creek. I reckon we'll be safe here for now. And don't worry about your wound, it didn't go deep. I got the bleeding stopped and a bandage on it. You'll be all right."

Simon frowned, trying to remember, then winced as memory came rushing back in jagged, nightmarish images. A man lying wounded, perhaps mortally, in the sand before him. Another, his face contorted in desperate determination, looming over him with an upraised bayonet. The metallic glint of murderous steel. The blinding flash of a pistol shot. Then what?

"We was mighty lucky, sir, that's for sure," Billy continued. "The Redcoats all went chasing after Merritt's men down the beach, giving me a chance to get you over to the skiff. What happened after that, I don't know, but the camp's taken, that's sure, and Merritt's done for. So's the Redcoat who came at you with the bayonet."

"Oh, God...," Simon groaned.

Billy went on in his chatty way. "For a minute there, I thought you were done for, too, sir. That was a real close one. But, Lordy, what a shot you took! For somebody who don't carry a weapon, you were mighty handy with that one. You're a soldier right enough, and a dang good one." Getting no response, Billy glanced over and saw that Simon was staring into space. "Sir? You all right?"

Simon went on staring. "I shot a man," he said softly. "Shot a man I'd never even seen, possibly killed him. How can I live with that?"

"There you go, sir, makin' no sense again. Remember, he was comin' right for you, so it was either you or him. And like I said, it was one fine shot you took. My, my, just think how proud your lady friend in Charlestown will be when you tell her about it."

"She would *not* be proud," Simon replied darkly. "She'd be horrified. I'll tell her many things, but I will never tell her about that. Never."

"What d'ya mean, sir? That villain got just what he deserved."

"No, Billy, you're wrong. He was no villain. He

was some mother's son, just like you and me. Sent across the sea to fight in a war he probably liked no more than you or I do."

Billy sighed and gave up. "It's no use arguin' with you, sir. And I reckon you'll never be a soldier, after all. But I'll say this—you're one fine fellow. It's a privilege to work for you."

Simon managed a weak smile. "Thanks, Billy. And the same to you."

They fell silent then, Simon lying motionless in one end of the skiff, Billy lolling in the other end, arm over the side, fingers idly dangling in the placid brown water of the creek. It was a rare moment of peace and restfulness in the harsh life they led. But for Simon it was also a time for grieving—for his own lost ideals, and for two good soldiers, one American, one English, lying dead back there, together in the sand.

Chapter 21

General Clinton left Charlestown before Captain
Fleming could secure Robert's desired introduction. His replacement, General Cornwallis,
was not interested in Robert's offer of Rosewall Plantation as a backcountry military base. Robert swal-
lowed his disappointment and told Captain Fleming
that the offer still stood, in case the new commander
changed his mind. Fleming's inquiries in another area
were more successful, and soon Brandon was a lieutenant in the American Loyalist Cavalry. He was
grateful, but gratitude didn't stop him from being
upset over rumors that Jane was keeping company
with the English officer. He was waiting for her one
day when she returned from the city market, and one
glance at his face told her that something was wrong.

"Jane, I need to talk to you about a very serious
matter. I've heard you're being seen in public with
Captain Fleming. Is that true?"

"I've walked out with him a few times. Why do
you ask?"

"Why do I *ask*? I want you to desist at once, that's why I ask! It's humiliating for me that the young lady everyone expects to become my wife is going around with another man. Surely you can understand that!"

In the face of his anger, Jane drew a sad sigh and took his arm. "Walk with me a bit, please." As they walked slowly down toward the next corner, she spoke as gently and patiently as she could. "Brandon, I'm afraid you're deluding yourself about me, and it's partly my fault. I've let your mistaken impression go on far too long. But now I'm going to correct it, so listen carefully, please. Contrary to what 'everyone' expects, I do not intend to become your wife. What we are—and what I sincerely hope we can always remain, because I'm very fond of you—is good friends."

"Good friends!" He stopped, recoiling as if the words had struck him like a slap in the face. "After all we've meant to each other, all the happy hours we've spent together, all the dreams we've shared—"

"Now *you're* dreaming, Brandon. None of those things ever happened, except in your imagination. I'm truly sorry, but I think it's time you—"

"Enough, Jane. You've made yourself abundantly clear. So it's good friends, eh? Well! Perhaps I should start keeping company with Lucinda Dunning. You remember Lucinda. She's a lovely girl, she dotes on me, and quite frankly, she has a much more affectionate nature than you do!"

"Good. In that case, I hope you two are very happy together."

Bristling with anger, Brandon stalked away, while Jane, feeling at the same time relieved and a little ashamed, returned to the house.

Did I do the right thing? she asked herself. *Yes—but I should have done it long ago.*

Having decided to be "nice" to Richard Fleming, Jane had found to her pleasant surprise that it was easier than she had expected it to be. He was intelligent, thoughtful, gallantly well mannered, and altogether charming. They attended open-air concerts by the hired German band that traveled with the British army, plays at the Dock Street Theater, and social events in the Georgian mansion that served as the British Officers Club. They took long walks and talked of England, Richard speaking fondly of his family home in Essex, near London. It was quite enjoyable, except when Jane felt guilty thinking of her rebel friends.

But all hopes for Arthur Ainsley remained unfulfilled. Often Jane asked Richard about it, and each time he noted that Mr. Ainsley still had not signed the Oath of Allegiance. "He says he won't until his property is returned to him, and that's out of the question. No one can help him if he refuses to help himself."

Finally Richard himself brought up the subject, though in a roundabout way. During a walk one Saturday afternoon, he said, "I leave tonight for a week or two of patrol through the backcountry."

"Whatever for, Richard?"

"There's a great deal of rebel smuggling in these

colonies, you know. Naturally, my work with the Board of Police concerns such things. Speaking of which, I'm afraid Mr. Ainsley's situation is more complicated than I thought."

Jane felt a twinge of uneasiness. "What do you mean?"

"It's just that for years he managed to keep his store open most of the time in spite of an extremely tight blockade. How was that possible? He says only that he dealt with various suppliers at various times. Who they were and where they got their merchandise, he claims he never knew."

"That's understandable, isn't it?"

"I'm afraid not. One would have to be a fool not to suspect that those goods were illegally obtained. There's no proof, and I haven't said anything about this to Mr. and Mrs. Prentice, not wishing to worry them unduly. But the fact is, suspicions about Mr. Ainsley's activities are growing."

"That's absurd!" Jane declared. "I'm *sure* he's done nothing wrong!"

But that night she lay awake, wondering. *Kept his store open despite the blockade . . . How* had *Uncle Arthur done that? Received goods without knowing where they came from . . . Was that believable? And if his meeting with Simon last fall was really about how to run a store, why was it such a big secret?* She tossed and turned, trying to evade the questions. But they would not leave her alone.

———

Sunday mornings were normally quiet, with the cries of peddlers and the clattering of traffic largely absent from the street. Robert and Clarissa had gone to church and Jane had just finished dressing to attend a later service, when she was startled by an urgent pounding on the front door. With the maid, Nellie, off on an errand, Jane answered the door herself.

Standing on the stoop was a slender Negro lad she recognized as Luther, the stable boy at the Dudley place in Goose Creek, where the Ainsleys were living with Harriet's mother. Drenched in sweat from hard riding, the boy nervously twisted his cap in his hands. Jane steeled herself for bad news.

"Luther! What's happened. Why are you here?"

"Lordy, Miss, I never seen nothin' like it." Luther was trembling. "Them Redcoat soldiers come a-gallopin' into the yard at the crack o' dawn—I come runnin' to see what they want wid us—they kept shoutin' where's Mahster Ainsley. When I don't answer fast enough they knock me down—I's scairt half to death they gon' to kill me—"

"Stop it, Luther. You're babbling!" Jane came out on the stoop and grasped the boy's arms. "Just calm down and tell me what happened."

Luther gulped, trying without much success to calm himself. "'Fore God, ma'am, them Redcoats went bustin' into the house like they own the place. The missus, she come down an' say what you want. Then Mahster Ainsley come out, an' they grab him. They done arrested 'im and tooken 'im away."

"*Arrested* him! Taken him where?"

"I dunno, miss, but they left poor missus cryin' and wringin' her hands. She tol' me, Luther, ride fast to the Prentice house in Charlestown and tell 'em we need help, Mahster Ainsley be tooken away. I been ridin' ever since, seem like."

Jane tugged at his sleeve. "Come inside, Luther, and sit awhile."

"No thankee, ma'am. I got to go quick. Them soldiers guardin' the road say I got ten minutes to git in here an' out, or they's havin' my hide!"

Jane could keep him there only long enough to give him a drink of water, a coin for his trouble, and a hastily scribbled note for Harriet, saying they all stood ready to help in any way they possibly could. Then Luther sped off, leaving Jane, all thoughts of church forgotten, dreading the moment when she would have to tell her uncle and aunt the news.

But when they returned they had already heard, and knew even more than Jane did. They had learned that a number of men suspected of rebel activity had been arrested that morning, and the list of names nailed up on street corners included the name Arthur Ainsley. Clarissa was in tears and beside herself with worry, but Robert was stern in his judgment.

"Arthur brought this on himself," he muttered. "He thought he could thumb his nose at our lawful British government and get away with it. Now he'll learn otherwise, and it will serve him right."

Jane was shocked. "Uncle Robert! He's family! Can't you at least show a little sympathy?"

"Not for a man who insists on acting like a fool!" he snapped back.

"But couldn't you register a protest, or somehow try to help?"

"I cannot be expected to intervene now. I offered Arthur my help when I could, and he refused. Anything I tried now would only compromise my own position, and I couldn't change what has happened anyway."

"Your *position*!" Jane cried. "Is that all you can think about?" With Robert gaping after her, she turned and rushed upstairs to her room. Her mind was filled with a dark vision of Arthur as a prisoner, shackled in irons. And with this distressing thought came another: *Richard Fleming. He knew. He knew this would happen, all along . . .*

Chapter 22

Twenty-nine men, all prominent in the revolutionary movement, were arrested that Sunday morning in August. Accused of having engaged in acts of treason, they were taken aboard a prison ship anchored in the harbor. After three days, they were transferred to another vessel that would soon take them away. They would be banished to Saint Augustine, in the British-held province of East Florida, and would be forbidden, upon pain of death, to set foot in South Carolina again until the present hostilities had ended. And they should thank their lucky stars, their captors added, that their punishment was so light.

The prisoners would be permitted farewell visits from friends and family before the ship sailed. The night before, Clarissa and Jane sat up late.

"It's been a week since Arthur's arrest," Clarissa mused. "And Richard Fleming has not shown his face here once. You didn't do a very good job on him, did you, Jane? Well, perhaps I misjudged the man."

"Or me," Jane suggested quietly.

"Or you, indeed. I should have known you couldn't manage it. The whole thing was my mistake, so let's leave it at that. Now, about tomorrow. Robert thinks we shouldn't go out to the ship. I told him I won't let them take Arthur away without saying good-bye. What about you?"

"Unless he locks me in my room, I'm going!" Jane replied with spirit.

"I knew you would." Clarissa smiled thinly. "You see, I don't *always* misjudge you. I just hope we get to see Arthur, with all those people trying to get out to that ship."

"We'll get on," Jane vowed. "Even if we have to swim out there."

Just as Clarissa had expected, hundreds of relatives and friends of the prisoners were gathered on the docks the next afternoon. Many brought food or clothing. The occasion might have appeared festive, but a somber mood prevailed. Little was known of the exiled prisoners' destination except that it was an obscure outpost far to the south. If anyone knew that its harbor was dominated by a grim gray fortress containing a dank prison, they kept silent.

People were rowed out to the ship in small groups for short visits. Wives went first and were allowed to stay the longest. With hundreds of people awaiting turns, it was clear the process would last until evening.

Jane and Clarissa waited on the dock for Harriet to

return. She had been weeping but was otherwise composed.

"Arthur's in remarkably good spirits," she reported. "It's all a dreadful mistake, of course. Everything will be cleared up before long." Her eyes searched the crowd. "Has anyone seen Brandon? His headquarters said he has leave to come. It will break Arthur's heart if he doesn't."

"I'm sure he will," Jane declared firmly. *Or I'll never speak to him again,* she vowed silently.

Jane accompanied Harriet to her carriage. Rather embarrassed to say it, she told Harriet, "Uncle Robert sends his kindest thoughts and hopes you'll understand why he couldn't come today."

"Certainly, Jane, dear," Harriet replied. "We could hardly expect him to consort with criminals like us."

Jane was startled by the bitterness in her voice. She started to say she hoped to see Harriet again soon but was stopped by the same sharp tone. "No, Jane, stay away. Don't compromise Robert's purity! Someday we'll all be reunited. Arthur says so, and I must believe it, mustn't I?"

Harriet gazed for a long moment toward the prison ship far out in the harbor. Then she stepped into her carriage and, with eyes fixed straight ahead, signaled the driver to take her away.

Jane took her turn last. It was late afternoon by the time she climbed aboard the prison ship and found Arthur Ainsley on the crowded deck. *I will not cry,* she had vowed. *Weeping will hardly lift a prisoner's spirits.*

Arthur sat on a low stool near the stern. "Good of you to come, Jane," he said, rising to greet her. "You needn't have, you know."

"I wouldn't dream of doing otherwise, Uncle Arthur."

He offered her a stool near his own. "Sit down. Sorry there's nothing better here." He looked haggard, and his smile seemed forced.

Her own smile felt forced in return. Questions she longed to ask him swirled around in her head. *Is this really all a mistake, as Aunt Harriet says? Or are you guilty of illegal acts, as the British claim?* Instead, she asked only, "How have they been treating you?"

"Tolerably well," he replied. He tried to sound cheerful, but his mind was clearly elsewhere. "You haven't seen Brandon, I suppose?"

Jane had expected this question. "No, but he should be here soon," was all she could reply. "The road must be very crowded."

"That must be it." Arthur nodded toward the city basking in the late-afternoon sun. "You know, Jane . . . just before they took over, I walked all over Charlestown, and I was struck by how beautiful it is. How I never really appreciated it before. It's the same with the people I love. I'm not very good at saying this, but—"

"It's all right," Jane said gently. "I know what you mean."

Glancing around to make sure he was not overheard, he leaned forward and began to speak in a low voice. "Listen, Jane—we have a mutual friend from the

181

North. You saw him at my house last fall. He wrote to me recently that he expected to visit again this summer—in part to see you. But now certain papers of mine have fallen into the wrong hands and..." A guard was approaching, his sharp eyes examining the crowd. Arthur waited until he had passed by, then dropped his voice even lower. "If our friend contacts you, tell him for God's sake to get away from here and stay away until peace is restored. It's the same advice he gave me, and I was fool enough to ignore it. Will you do that?"

Jane was thunderstruck. Not only were her unasked questions answered, but another she hadn't dreamed of asking. "Y-yes, of course," she stammered.

"I know your loyalties must remain with the other side, but I'm sure I can trust you. Our friend's life depends upon it."

Jane was almost relieved when a guard whistled time's up a few minutes later. She and Arthur rose, and now his smile seemed genuine as he clasped her hands. "Take care of yourself, my dear. Remember, one day we'll be together in a happy reunion, all differences forgotten."

"We will, Uncle Arthur, we *will*!" Her vow not to cry crumbling, she gave him a hug, then quickly disappeared among the other departing visitors.

The crowd had dispersed, the launches that had conveyed visitors to and from the prison ship were gone, the dock was now virtually deserted. Still, Jane lingered. Part of her clung to the hope that Brandon would yet appear. It was too late now, but even so, she knew that someday it could make all the difference in the world for Arthur to know that his son had made the effort to come.

At the same time, she grappled with a stunning revelation. Arthur's warning for their "mutual friend from the North" had made it all too clear that Simon was wanted by the British on some serious charge— and what else could it be but smuggling? She had been prepared to believe it of Arthur. After all, he was a storekeeper in dire need of goods. But then, so was Simon now. He must have resorted to this as a desperate measure to protect his sister and her family from ruin. The gentle schoolmaster—an outlaw! Dazed by this startling knowledge, she paused by the low seawall and let her brooding thoughts roam.

What mysteries we are to one another. And for that matter, to ourselves. Uncle Arthur takes it for granted that my loyalties are all with the British. If only it were that simple! No doubt Simon assumes the same. How astounded he would be if he knew that after all this time I still don't know for sure exactly who or what I am . . .

She stood there for a while longer, watching gulls dip and soar over a quiet harbor burnished by a golden sunset. And observing this strangely peaceful scene, she thought how easily beauty and sadness can combine to bring a tear to the eye, a heaviness to the heart.

Brandon had not come. At last, with light failing and all hope fading with it, she turned away and started for home.

Chapter 23

Jane had just crossed the harbor road, heading for Legare Street, when she heard the distant clatter of a racing horse's hooves. She froze, listening. Could it be Brandon? Surely no one but he would dare ride like that along cobblestone city streets. The sound grew louder, and a moment later his great chestnut stallion, Warrior, rounded a nearby corner at break-neck speed. Jane waited, wanting to shout for joy, cry out in anguish, and wring Brandon's neck—all at the same time.

He was off his horse in seconds, rushing up to her. "Jane, where is everybody? Good Lord, don't tell me I've missed seeing Father!"

"I'm afraid so, Brandon. The launches to the prison ship stopped running an hour ago."

"Damn, what rotten luck! Now he'll be taken away thinking I'm a cad. And I'm sure you do, too."

"Well . . . you might have gotten here sooner."

"I meant to, believe me, I did. But everything went wrong."

Just as he was about to leave camp that morning, he told Jane, his company had been attacked by a band of roving rebels. A corral was set afire, and the attackers made off with a number of horses. Luckily, he was able to save Warrior. He and several others were then ordered to pursue the marauders—a fruitless effort that consumed the entire morning and delayed his departure for Charlestown until the afternoon.

"And now, after riding like a madman for hours—I'm too late. Eternal damnation to those dastardly rebels!"

Seeing that he was sincerely distressed over missing the chance to see his father, Jane offered a hopeful suggestion. "Why not go over to the Port Authority office and plead your case? You have a good excuse. Perhaps they'd make an exception."

He brightened immediately. "Excellent idea! But come with me, please. Whether this works or not, I do want a chance to talk to you."

It took only two minutes to walk to the Port Authority office a block away, where Jane waited outside with Warrior while Brandon went in. A few minutes later, he came out again, muttering furiously.

"Terribly sorry, they said, but for security reasons it can't be done. They wouldn't even let me send Father a note. What idiots!"

"Well, at least you tried, that's what matters," Jane said consolingly. "So come on home with me now."

"I can't stay. I have to get back to camp tonight."

"But you can rest awhile, have something to eat. Come on."

They walked along slowly, Brandon leading his horse by the reins.

"Was my mother here?" he asked after a moment.

"Of course she was. So was Aunt Clarissa. But Uncle Robert wouldn't come." Jane tried not to sound too disapproving in adding, "He feared it would compromise his reputation as a Loyalist."

"Oh, well, I understand that," Brandon said. "I have something of the same problem. It's not easy for me to convince my companions that I'm a good king's man when they all know my father's a flaming rebel."

"That must be very difficult," Jane allowed.

"How's my mother taking all this?" was his next question.

"She was very brave today. I was proud of her. And Uncle Arthur, too. He's keeping up amazingly good spirits."

"A man banished from his home and family, convinced that his only son has cruelly turned his back on him, was in good spirits? I think you've just told me a kindly lie, Jane."

"No, I mean it. In spite of all your differences, he never believed that of you. When you didn't come today, he didn't doubt that you'd been detained. And when he returns to us someday, he'll learn that he was right."

"*When* he returns? You mean *if*, don't you?"

"When, Brandon, *when*. He'll survive, and he'll come back. We must believe that. In the meantime, be concerned for your mother. She's fragile, and this has been a terrible blow for her. Please, go up to Goose Creek to see her as often as you can. I know it's difficult for you, but she needs you now more than ever before."

"I will. I promise you, I will." He was silent for a moment, falling into a reminiscent mood. "We've always been close, Mother and I. You should have seen her romp with me when I was a boy. Such fun we had. Father wasn't the romping sort, but he was always kind and generous. I had a happy childhood." Struck with a sudden welling up of emotion, he stopped abruptly and turned to Jane. "I never meant for things to be this way, you know. Father had his beliefs, I had mine. It was bound to happen that we'd become estranged. But I don't think my mother cares particularly which one of us is right. All she wants in this world is for her family to be together."

"I know, Brandon." Jane put a soft hand on his arm. "I know."

He had recovered his composure when he spoke next. "I believe I'll leave you here, if you don't mind, Jane. I don't feel like seeing Uncle Robert and Aunt Clarissa just now. Give them my regards, and tell them I'll come to visit as soon as I can, will you?"

"All right, if you prefer it that way."

"But before I go—" Stepping closer, he gazed earnestly into her eyes. "I want to thank you for speaking to me so honestly the last time we saw each other. I had no right to object to your seeing Captain Fleming. I don't consider him at all worthy of you—but that's not for me to say, and you had every right to slap my face and tell me to mind my own business. How like you, instead, to answer my anger with kindness and patience, and explain to me that we are good friends. And you're absolutely right. So, thanks to your honesty, we are both set free. I'm seeing Lucinda Dunning now. And I'm happy to say we're getting on just splendidly."

"Wonderful, Brandon!" Jane exclaimed. "That's good news, indeed!"

"Thank you. And now I must be off, so ... Fare thee well, good friend." This time his usual peck on the cheek was accompanied by a warm hug, then a final remark, which he couldn't resist. "But I still don't think Fleming's worthy of you."

In seconds, he was the dashing horseman again, waving his hat in a dramatic flourish as he and Warrior, man and mount as one, tore off at the same wild gallop that had brought them there.

Darkness was coming on by the time Jane reached home. Clarissa met her at the door, looking worried and a little suspicious.

"You were awfully long getting back, Jane. What were you doing?"

"Talking to Brandon," Jane replied, and went into the parlor.

Clarissa followed. "What? He came? What happened? Did he get to see Arthur after all?"

"Sad to say, he did not." Sinking into a chair, Jane

told of Brandon's late arrival, the reason for it, and of his failed attempt to get on board the prison ship. "At least he tried," she concluded. "We have to give him credit for that."

"Poor lad," Clarissa said sorrowfully. "What a shame, to make such a tremendous effort, and all for nothing."

Jane disagreed. "It wasn't for nothing. It'll mean a great deal to Aunt Harriet and, eventually, to Uncle Arthur, too. And it means a lot to me. I think more highly of Brandon now than I did before."

"Really?" Her curiosity aroused, Clarissa sat down. "You mean, highly enough to consider him as a possible husband?"

"Oh, please! Can't you get that idea out of your head, Aunt Clarissa? He's lost interest in me, anyway. He's seeing Lucinda Dunning now."

"Lucinda Dunning! Well, that's just bizarre. Compared to you, she's nothing but fluff. You know what I think, Jane? It's not so much that he lost interest in you. *You* lost interest in *him*."

"I never had any in the first place. Not that way."

"Who is it, then? Jane, I know there's someone in your secret thoughts. Who is it? Not Captain Fleming, I hope. Not after the way he betrayed us."

"Aunt Clarissa!" Jane's sharp tone stopped Clarissa cold. "Your brother is languishing out there on a prison ship, headed for God knows what fate. His wife is in deep mourning, and his son is wretchedly unhappy. And you want to discuss my marriage prospects!" She got to her feet. "Excuse me, please. I'm very tired. I want to lie down for a while."

With her aunt's grave eyes following her, Jane crossed the room and started upstairs, her leaden feet dragging with every step. Curled up on her bed a few minutes later, she began to regret speaking so sharply to Clarissa.

After all, she reminded herself, *it's only natural that she be curious about who's in my secret thoughts. And she's quite right, of course—someone is. He used to be a school-master, then he became a storekeeper, and finally a smuggler wanted by the British. But that's nobody's business but my own.*

Chapter 24

Loyalists like Robert Prentice were keenly aware that the British occupation of Charlestown was only increasing rebel resistance. When she went out on the street, Clarissa was openly taunted as "that damned Tory woman," although—curiously—this never happened to Jane. Perhaps Clarissa's always-grand appearance made the difference.

In the backcountry, rebel activity spread, as Robert said, "like weeds in an untended garden." A British victory over the Continentals near Camden triggered celebrations in Charlestown but did nothing to suppress backcountry troubles. Robert frequently had to rush out to Rosewall to deal with some crisis. He always returned more convinced than ever that the smartest thing he had ever done was to build the great wall around his plantation house. More than once, it saved his house from serious damage, if not destruction.

In September, soon after Robert's return from one of these emergency trips, Richard Fleming finally came to call. Jane had gone out to the city market, but Robert and Clarissa listened solemnly as Richard declared himself shocked at Arthur Ainsley's plight.

"I knew he was under suspicion, and refusing to sign the Oath of Allegiance wasn't helping him. But the arrest order came from Lord Cornwallis himself. I had recommended simply keeping Mr. Ainsley under observation, which might have led us to the smugglers' ringleader. We believe he's in South Carolina even now."

"So you're saying that *you* might have had my brother meet a worse fate than mere banishment," Clarissa remarked coldly. "Thank you very much, I'm sure. I shall take my leave of you gentlemen now."

"Never mind," Robert said mildly as she disappeared up the stairs. "You're an officer of the Crown, Richard. You can't be blamed for doing your duty, however unpleasant."

"I was only trying to explain that it's really the Continentals' smuggling ring we're after, not Mr. Ainsley himself," said Richard. "They run more supplies through the Carolinas than anywhere else in the colonies."

"Do they, indeed?"

"Their leader's devilishly clever, whoever he is. Always one step ahead of us. We almost caught him up near Cape Fear a few weeks ago, but he managed to slip through our fingers, curse the luck."

"Remarkable," Robert exclaimed.

"It is, when you consider that all we know about him is that he's called The Schoolmaster—not much to go on. But that's enough about my problems. How have you been faring lately, Mr. Prentice?"

"Not so well, I'm afraid. Last week marauders attacked Rosewall in broad daylight! They couldn't breach my wall, of course, but they made off with some livestock and burned down a barn. And in all this confusion, a third of my Negroes have disappeared."

Richard shook his head in sympathy. "The Negroes are becoming a problem for us as well. The poor wretches think the British will lead them to a paradise of freedom somewhere. God knows what'll become of them."

On this gloomy note, he rose to leave, adding, "I did hope I might see Jane. I'll admit I harbor tender feelings toward your niece."

"I realize that, sir. You'll find her at the city market. We have Nellie for that, but for some reason Jane likes to go."

As they reached the street, Robert had a last question for his visitor. "This so-called Schoolmaster—do you know if he ever lived in Charlestown?"

"As I said, we know nothing about him. Why do you ask?"

"Just curious." Robert flashed a smile. "Now, Richard, you must come to dinner soon. And don't worry, I'll square things with Clarissa."

They shook hands and parted, but as Richard walked away, Robert's smile vanished. "The Schoolmaster," he muttered. "How very interesting..."

———

The open-air market was a busy place where citizens of Charlestown could sometimes find fruit and vegetables. Jane had bought a few tomatoes and was just leaving when Richard fell into step beside her.

"So you're back, Captain Fleming," she said coldly. "Did you catch any of those awful smugglers?"

"We came close," he replied. "But no, not a one, I'm afraid."

"How regrettable," she remarked, breathing a secret sigh of relief.

"Look here, Jane, I know you blame me for what happened to Mr. Ainsley. But I swear, I had nothing to do with it." He repeated his protestation of innocence. "I had left orders that all those men be kept under observation," he explained. "It was only when I arrived back in the city last night that I learned that General Cornwallis had countermanded my order. What can I do? He's the commanding general. I'm only a captain."

"You boasted to us about your important position, Richard. You led us to believe that you had a great deal of influence."

"Obviously, I overestimated my influence. Please forgive me, Jane. It would distress me terribly to fall from your good graces."

Grudgingly she relented. "Well, we won't mention it again."

"Good. Now, on to more pleasant things. There'll be a ball at the Officers Club on Saturday night, and I thought, if you'll do me the honor—"

"No, Richard. I won't be going out with you anymore."

"What?" He pulled her to a stop. "Why ever not, may I ask?"

"You offered me an apology, and I accepted. Now I'll ask you to accept one from me. I've let you believe that I cared for you, because I thought it might be a way to protect Mr. Ainsley from harm. It was a mean and foolish thing to do, and I'm sorry. And I'm not going to do it anymore."

To her surprise, this made him chuckle. "Jane, my dear girl! You never deceived me. I never for one moment thought I had a chance to replace Brandon Ainsley in your affections. Not that I wouldn't like to, but—"

"Stop, Richard, and leave Brandon out of this. He has absolutely nothing to do with it."

"Oh? Perhaps Mrs. Prentice was right. She once told me she was glad I took up so much of your time. She had begun to suspect that on your long solitary walks you were secretly meeting someone. Is that true?"

Jane bristled. "Richard, I have grown fond of you, and I hope our friendship can endure. But if you speak to me that way, it will not."

"Once again, my apologies, Jane. That was an improper question, and I withdraw it. Now, about the ball on Saturday—"

"I have told you, I cannot." Her determined look set him back on his heels. "Listen to me, Richard. Mr.

Ainsley is not the only person I care about on the American side whose life has been devastated. There will be no plays or concerts for me, no more teas, dinners, balls, or entertainments of any kind. When all the people I care for can come back to normal lives, I'll come back, too. Not before."

Leaving him staring after her with a flabbergasted look on his face, she walked on, feeling lighter on her feet and in her heart.

As Robert had predicted, Richard Fleming was soon welcome again in the Prentice home. He and Jane were cordial to each other but no longer went out together. Jane returned to her old habit of taking long walks alone, seeming to withdraw into a shell of seclusion. Always watching, always suspicious, Clarissa spoke of her concerns to Robert.

"I'm sure she's up to something. It's high time she was married, but the way she behaves, it will never happen. First she chased Brandon away, and now she's doing the same with Captain Fleming. What can we do?"

Robert had no answer. Indeed, there seemed to be no solution in sight.

All Jane was up to on her walks was strolling down Queen Street, looking for signs of life at the cabinetmaker's shop. There never were any, until one bracing October morning when she ran straight into Hugh himself.

"Cousin Hugh!" she cried in delight.

"Hello, Jane! What a piece of luck, running into you like this. I've been hoping for a chance to see you."

"Where on earth have you been?"

"We've been staying with Peter's in-laws, up near Georgetown. I was trying to avoid signing the Oath of Allegiance but was afraid of what would happen to me if I didn't. Look at Arthur Ainsley, after all."

"That was a horrible shock. He's a very brave man."

"Braver than I. I finally signed the damned thing. Not that I've changed my mind about anything. It was just the only way I could safely get back to my shop. I do hope you'll pay us a visit soon, now that we're back."

"I'd love to. It's not easy, Uncle Robert feeling the way he does. But I'll watch for my chance and come when I can. In the meantime, give my regards to Lydia. And Peter, whenever you see him."

"Which isn't often," Hugh remarked glumly. "He's out there somewhere, but Lord only knows where. We just keep our fingers crossed for him."

"Of course. And speaking of people out there somewhere—you remember that gentleman we saw at the Ainsleys' house last year? Have you—"

"No, Jane, don't ask me that." Suddenly Hugh's face was a blank mask. "I can tell you nothing about him."

Jane stepped closer, her penetrating gaze holding him fast. "I know what he's doing. Uncle Arthur as much as told me before they took him away."

"Did he, now! Well, in that case—I heard from the gentleman about a month ago. He'd wanted to come to Charlestown this summer, but the occupation delayed things. But he plans to come back as soon as he can."

"Oh no!" Jane wrung her hands, suddenly agitated. "If he comes, you must tell him to go away and stay away! It's not safe for him here!"

Hugh shook his head. "I've tried that, but it's useless. In the first place, he wants desperately to see you again. And in the second place, who am I to lecture the Continental Army's chief of smuggling operations in the Southern colonies on the subject of safety?"

Jane stared. "He's . . . *what?*"

Hugh stared back. "I thought you said you knew."

"I know what kind of work he's doing. But I thought it was for his brother-in-law's store in Pennsylvania!"

"Good Lord!" Hugh clapped his forehead. "I've said far too much."

"You don't feel you can trust me, Cousin Hugh?"

He smiled an apology. "Of course I can. I'd trust you with my life."

A distant look came to Jane's eyes. "Just imagine! All the while I've been wondering what he would think of *me*. I'm supposed to be a loyal British subject, but more and more I find myself—"

"Drifting over to our side?" Hugh suggested hopefully.

"No. Suspended in the middle, not knowing where I belong."

"Be patient, my dear. Eventually it will all come clear to you."

On those words of hopeful advice, they parted company.

One afternoon not long after that, Clarissa sat in the parlor working at her needlepoint. Robert was at a Loyalist meeting, and Jane was off on another one of her frequent long walks. One day, Clarissa told herself, she would follow and find out once and for all what Jane was up to.

Glancing idly out the window, she saw a boy approaching the house. A moment later, she met him at the front door. "Yes, what is it?"

"Got a note for Miss Jane Prentice," he announced.

Clarissa instantly perceived a rare opportunity. "I'm Jane Prentice," she said, and reached for the note.

The boy waved it playfully in the air. "She's supposed to be a young unmarried lady. You don't look like that to me."

"Wait here." Clarissa disappeared, returning shortly with a gold coin, which she waved enticingly at the boy. "Does this convince you?"

"Ma'am, I'm convinced!" He grabbed the coin, handed over the note, and hurried away.

In seconds, Clarissa had scanned a few crudely scrawled lines.

Dear Miss Prentice,
  Your cousin Mr. Hugh Prentice sends you gifts of farm produce and news of his family. Will you come to

my lodging house at the address given below to receive
same? This afternoon, if you can?

   Mrs. Elinor James, Proprietor

Clarissa's maid, Nellie, was dozing in a kitchen chair when her mistress swept in. "I'm going out for a little while, Nellie. Back soon, I expect."

"Yes'm." The lady departed, and Nellie settled down to resume her nap. It was nice to have the house to herself occasionally. And for once, all was peace and quiet.

Chapter 25

The lodging house was in a shabby part of town, worlds away from Legare Street. Clarissa eyed it—and the shambling old woman who answered her knock—with distaste.

"Mrs. James? I'm Jane Prentice."

Mrs. James stared suspiciously at the fine lady standing before her, finally mumbling, "Well, come in." She led the way down a long musty-smelling hall and knocked on a door. When it opened, Clarissa Prentice and Simon Cordwyn stared at each other in mute astonishment.

"I had me doubts about this lady, sir," said Mrs. James. "But 'ere she came, so I let 'er in." When Simon made no reply, she shuffled away.

Finally Simon retreated into the room and sank heavily into a chair. "My God, what have I done?"

"Something not very clever, it seems," Clarissa observed, glancing over the threadbare furnishings. "That ridiculous note—was that Hugh's idea?"

"No. Hugh doesn't even know I'm here."

"Good. I'd hate to think a Prentice would stoop to such a cheap trick."

"Cheap trick?" He glared at her. "I sent Jane a note. You stole it—and then you have the gall to accuse *me* of a cheap trick!"

"Oh, Simon! How sad that we meet again this way. I've been suspecting Jane of seeing someone secretly. But I never dreamed it was you."

"And, indeed, it was not. I have not seen Jane."

"You'll pardon me if I don't believe that."

"Believe it or not, as you like."

"You know, it took me a long time to get over the way you just walked away from me. I was sure you'd come back one day. Finally, I realized it was just my pride that was injured, nothing more. And now you *have* come back—but this time, it's for little Jane!"

Simon grimaced. "You shouldn't be here, Clarissa. I must ask you to leave now, and—"

"Oh! I've found you out, so you order me away! You think it's that easy, do you?" Clarissa's voice rose in agitation. "I made a fool of myself once for love of you, and you cut me off like a useless, dead flower. Well, you can be sure I'm not going to stand by and watch Jane fall into the same—"

"Stop," Simon said quietly. A movement at the door had caught his eye.

"You can't bear to hear the truth, is that what you mean?"

"I mean we are not alone."

Clarissa spun around and saw Robert standing in the doorway. While she stood frozen in horror, he came strolling in. "I hope I'm not intruding." His words were courteous, but his tone was icy.

The color had drained from Clarissa's face. "Robert! I—uh—I was just—" Her hands fluttered like nervous butterflies.

"Visiting an old friend, I see. How very nice." He turned a glassy smile on Simon. "Good to see you again, Cordwyn. Will you be in town long?"

Simon shrugged. "That's hard to say."

"Long enough to come calling, I hope. Jane would be delighted to see her old schoolmaster again, don't you agree, darling?" Clarissa made no reply.

"You're so pale, my dear." Robert turned to Simon. "I'm afraid you'll have to excuse us, Cordwyn. My wife tires so easily. But do come to tea, my good fellow. Tomorrow at three? No argument now, we'll be expecting you. Shall we go, Clarissa?"

She stood silent for a moment longer, giving Simon a look as cold as a winter midnight. Then, as if sleepwalking, she left the room.

"Till tomorrow then, Cordwyn." Robert flashed another smile and followed Clarissa out.

When the landlady returned a few minutes later, she found her tenant slumped over the table, head in hands.

"Oh, dear! It wasn't the right lady after all, was it, sir?"

"No, Mrs. James," he muttered. "It most certainly was not!"

That evening Clarissa retired early, only to lie sleepless in bed. At last Robert appeared at her bedside like a shadow in the gloom around her.

"Headache any better?" he asked.

"A little, thank you," she answered weakly.

"Try to get some sleep. I'm sure you need it."

"How did you know I was there, Robert?"

"Sam Blaine was driving me home when I saw you heading into that low-class district. I got out of the carriage at the next corner and followed you. I haven't yet decided whether I'm glad or sorry that I did."

"That was quite a performance you gave, inviting Simon to tea. You don't really expect him to come, do you?"

"No, but I can play false games as well as anyone."

"How much did you hear?"

"Enough. Evidently, having invaded my domain once before, that scoundrel thinks he can return and invade it yet again."

"Ah, yes, your domain. I belong to you. Jane belongs to you. Rosewall belongs to you—everything belongs to you. Perhaps it's not so bad if a man learns his domain can be subject to invasion."

"Good night, Clarissa." Robert turned and started to leave the room.

"Robert, wait." She sat up in bed. "I'm sorry, I

shouldn't reproach you. But you've hardly said a word to me since we left that wretched place."

"I really have nothing to say, my dear."

"Nothing at all? Please, Robert! I admit there's a stain on my past, and I'm sorry you had to learn of it. But it all happened long ago. I'm married to *you,* and if you'll forgive and forget, I'll go on being as dutiful a wife as ever a man could—Robert! Hear me out!"

He looked back from the doorway. "I don't want a *dutiful* wife," he said. "I want a *loving* one." He closed the door softly behind him, leaving her staring into the darkness.

Jane also lay awake that night. She was thinking of her meeting with Hugh a few days before, and wondering about Simon. Would he dare return to Charlestown? Her heart hoped desperately that he would. Her head hoped even more desperately that he would not. Be patient, Hugh had said. But it was hard to be patient when she had no way of knowing what was going on.

She thought about Robert and Clarissa. They had barely spoken to each other or to her that evening, and Clarissa had retired upstairs immediately after supper. It was quite unlike them. They must have quarreled about something, Jane decided. Well, never mind. She settled down to sleep. Whatever was wrong between them would no doubt be cleared up by morning.

Captain Fleming, working late at the Board of Police, was surprised to receive a visitor close to ten o'clock.

"Good evening, sir. What brings you out at this hour? From the look on your face, it must be something serious."

Robert took a chair. "I do apologize for interrupting you here, Richard. But if you can spare a few minutes, I think you'll find what I have to say most worthwhile..."

Chapter 26

Jane was shocked and dismayed when Robert announced early the next morning that they would return to Rosewall that very day. "Today? Why so suddenly?"

"We usually go at this time of year, and the incessant raids out there require my immediate attention. Besides," he added, glancing darkly at Clarissa, "I've noticed that city life is unhealthy for well-bred ladies. The country is more beneficial, and we'll stay there from now on."

Jane shot a puzzled look at Clarissa but saw only a blank expression. "What do you mean, Uncle Robert?"

"No more questions," he snapped. "I'm going now to arrange for Nellie to join Sam Blaine's household. They have need of an extra maid. Meanwhile, you two pack up. We leave as soon as I get back."

He strode out, leaving Jane again searching Clarissa's face for explanation. "Something's happened, Aunt Clarissa. I know it has. Tell me!"

Clarissa smiled faintly. "Never mind, dear. We must obey quietly. Robert is king, and we are his subjects."

By late evening the family was again settled in at Rosewall. Robert ordered a bed made up for him in his study, far from the large bedroom he normally shared with Clarissa.

"I'm not sleeping well, you see," he told Cuba. "My tossing and turning disturb Mrs. Prentice."

Cuba was not one to question this departure from custom, and Clarissa clearly already knew its reasons. The mysterious tension filled the great house. Even more disturbing to Jane was the thought that a certain gentleman might come to Charlestown, and she would be thirty miles away at Rosewall.

Robert was off the following morning to report to Louis Lambert about rumors of General Cornwallis's planned sweep through North Carolina, Virginia, Maryland, and on to New York. Most Loyalists saw the British general as a conquering hero, but Robert Prentice scorned him. He regaled Jane and Clarissa about it later, as they worked on their embroidery in the parlor.

"That fool Cornwallis thinks he can crush all opposition before him. But the rebels have popped up like weasels, thumbing their noses after him at every crossroads between here and Camden. He just keeps racing north after the Continentals' General Greene, never noticing a thing!"

His mood hasn't improved, Jane thought, *but at least he's talking again.* Clarissa paid no attention to him.

Robert talked on. "Luckily, Brandon's cavalry unit is doing a fine job, I hear. Stalwart Loyalists like them will win this thing in the end, not vain military peacocks like Cornwallis. He covers himself in glory, leaving citizens like us to fend for ourselves! Very well. Louis Lambert and I have decided to form our own militia. Forty or fifty good men, gathered from miles around. Never fear, we'll defend ourselves!"

He paused for breath. "Now, did any messages arrive for me today?"

Clarissa finally glanced up from her work. "From whom, dear? King George, your fellow monarch across the sea?"

He glared at her stonily.

"No, Uncle, there have been no messages," Jane said.

"If one comes, summon me immediately." He stomped angrily upstairs.

But when the gate bell jangled half an hour later, Robert himself rushed out to answer it. Jane, watching from the parlor, saw him return shortly and hurry back upstairs. Burning with curiosity, she followed him and looked in at the open door of his study. He stood absorbed in a letter.

"Not bad news, I hope, Uncle Robert?"

Annoyed to see her standing there, he pocketed the letter. "Military matters," he growled. "They don't concern you."

Jane's tolerance for being dismissed in this way was

wearing thin. "Am I too simpleminded to understand military matters?" she asked sharply.

His scowl deepened. "I said, they don't concern you!"

"It seems, Uncle, that you think nothing does."

"I'm in no mood for your insolence, girl!"

This time his anger only made her bolder. "Indeed, you seem determined to keep me ignorant of all things," she continued. "Well, sir, you cannot. I have learned much, and continue to do so, despite your efforts to prevent it!"

Before he could reply, she rushed to her room and slammed the door behind her. *How long can this go on?* she seethed. *Sooner or later something's going to crack.*

That same night, something did.

Too upset to think of sleeping, Jane decided to write a letter to Harriet. She often did this, though it was not always possible to send the letter immediately. She had just begun when she heard Robert's ill-tempered growl and Clarissa's shrill, agitated voice floating up from downstairs. *Quarreling again,* Jane thought—but at least now she might find out why. She tiptoed to the top of the stairs and listened silently. The quarrel was becoming a shouting match. And what she heard took her breath away.

"How could you!" Clarissa cried. "Persecuting an innocent man—is that how you punish me?"

"Innocent, my eye! He's the worst kind of criminal, smuggling for the rebels!"

"You don't know that!"

"Don't I? Fleming lays out all the evidence in his letter. They're operating in the Carolinas, the ringleader's known to be from Pennsylvania, he's called The Schoolmaster, and they found a letter from his sister that showed his first name is Simon. Then who should suddenly appear in Charlestown? None other than Schoolmaster Simon Cordwyn! Not only meaning to wreck my family but to destroy my very—"

"What's happened to Mr. Cordwyn?" Jane cried out, suddenly appearing in the doorway. "When was he in Charlestown?"

"Tell her, Robert." Clarissa turned away. "She'll hear soon enough."

Turning to Jane, Robert spoke with grim deliberation. "Unfortunately, your former teacher has been running a vast smuggling network for the rebels. However, he's now in jail on a charge of treason."

"And all thanks to your heroic uncle," Clarissa added bitterly. "He told Captain Fleming where to find him."

"Thanks to *me*?" Robert snorted. "Do give yourself a little credit!"

"Yes, I'm to blame, too. Simon sent you a note, dear. I intercepted it and met him myself. Robert followed me and discovered him."

Jane's burning rage burst into words. "I don't know which of you I despise more! You scheming meddler, Aunt Clarissa! What right did you have to steal a letter? And you, Uncle Robert! You've always hated Mr.

Cordwyn! How you must have enjoyed betraying him! You're a *monster*!"

"How dare you speak to me like that!" he shouted.

"I should have dared long ago! I renounce you, sir! I renounce you both. You're no kin of mine!"

"Jane, I will not tolerate this kind of—"

"I will never speak to either of you again as long as I live!" Wild-eyed with fury, Jane flew back upstairs.

Stunned, Robert turned to Clarissa. "Has she taken leave of her senses? That scoundrel was after her, we know that. Could she have *wanted* him to be?"

Clarissa smiled calmly. "It's perfectly clear, Robert. She's in love with him. Probably has been since she first met him at Arthur's, years ago."

"And you mean to say she's nursed those feelings all this time? Why have I never seen it?"

"Because, like me, you have been a blind fool. Good night." With serene dignity, Clarissa left the room.

Robert stood staring around a cold, lifeless room meant to contain warmth and laughter. "Rosewall," he sighed. "Soon you'll be all I have left."

Nestled against the great stone wall near the front gate was the small cabin shared by Cuba and Omar. Omar's duties as gatekeeper were among his most important. Luckily for his master, he had a catlike ability to snap awake at the slightest noise—a talent that had foiled more than one rebel raid. That midnight, soft footsteps outside brought him instantly to attention.

In the dim moonlight, Jane was pulling at the gate's heavy bolt when Omar loomed up behind her.

"What you doing, miss?" His tone was gruff.

Startled, Jane gasped, but then answered firmly. "I'm going to the city."

"In the night? No, no, there be danger out there. Bad mens, wild animals. You get lost, fall down, die. You acting crazy, miss!"

"Maybe so, but I'm going anyway. I won't stay here any longer." She gave Omar a curious look. "Haven't you ever thought of running away? You and Cuba are both strong. You could do it. Go, Omar. Take Cuba and run! Why should you be the slave of someone who's no better a man than you?"

With a solemn shake of his head, Omar gave her a simple reply. "No, miss. Omar not run. Cuba won't run, and Omar not run without her."

Cuba had come out to investigate. "Miss Jane! What in the world—?"

"Young miss, she running away to Charlestown," Omar said.

"Lordy, child! Why?"

"I can't explain now," Jane said. "But if you are my friends, and I think you are, you won't try to stop me."

The two servants looked at each other and by some mysterious form of communication reached silent agreement.

"We not stop you, miss," Omar said. "But you not go by yourself. Omar get a horse, go with you, come back tomorrow."

Cuba nodded approval. "A good plan." To Jane she said, "I'll tell Master we found you gone in the morning, and Omar went to look for you."

It was settled. Omar pulled back the bolt and swung the gate open.

"Get back as soon as you can," Cuba told him. And when Jane tried to express her thanks to both, Cuba stopped her. "Never mind that, child. Go along now. No use standin' here talkin' 'bout it all night."

A moment later, Cuba silently bolted the gate behind them. She sniffed the air. There would be rain soon. A wild creature cried in the swamp to the north. Cuba hugged herself against the chill and hurried back inside.

In the elegant front hallway, the tall grandfather clock tick-tocked away the silent hours. And on the low settee beside it, a terse note lay folded, waiting for the first early riser to find it in the morning.

> *Dear Uncle and Aunt,*
>
> *I have gone to my cousin Hugh Prentice on Queen Street. I shall always be grateful for the kindness you have shown me, but I will never live under your roof again.*
>
> *Good-bye,*
>
> *Jane*

Chapter 27

Peering out a window at the sound of a knock at his front door the next morning, Hugh was alarmed by what he saw: a giant, stern-faced black man. Then recognition came, and he turned to Lydia, who was just coming downstairs.

"Good Lord, I believe it's Robert's man from Rosewall! What's his name? Omar. Let's hope it's not bad news."

Hurriedly opening the door, they saw that Omar was not alone. Standing beside him, but tottering as if barely able to stay on her feet, was Jane.

Lydia gasped at the sight. "Jane! What on earth . . . ?"

One on either side, they helped her inside and led her to a chair, where she collapsed while Lydia brushed her disarrayed hair out of her eyes and wiped her moist face with a cloth. "What's happened, love? Tell us!"

Jane opened her mouth to speak, but no sound came. The reply came, instead, from Omar, standing

215

in the doorway. "Young miss need food, water, and rest. Walk all night from Rosewall."

"*Walked?* All the way from Rosewall?" Hugh stared at the black man in disbelief. "Don't you have carriages there? Horses, at least?"

"Omar go for horse, then stop. Think. Horses in stable make noise, Master come out to see. Not good. Walk, only way."

"But why?" Lydia cried. "Jane, for heaven's sake— what's happened?"

At last Jane found an ounce of energy to speak. "I ran away," she said in a cracked and feeble voice.

Though there was still much to be explained, Lydia's motherly instincts told her that two tired and hungry travelers needed to be taken care of, and with this in mind she moved with brisk efficiency.

Omar was impatient to start back, saying, "Master be very angry with me." He tarried only long enough to drink two large cups of water and accept a hastily wrapped package of bread and cheese from Lydia. "Must go now," he announced, nodding his thanks, then looked expectantly at Jane.

Still unsteady on her feet, she rose and went to him. "Omar..." Words were suddenly hard to find. "What can I say? I shall be indebted to you forever."

He shook his head, disdaining her gratitude. "You safe now, miss. Be at peace."

A moment later he was gone, and Jane was standing in the doorway looking after him. Her eyes were glistening when she turned back to Hugh and Lydia.

"It may well be that I owe my life to him," she told them. "And in all those weary hours of trudging through the night, he concerned himself only with my safety. Never once asked why I was running away."

Lydia went to her and took her by the arm. "Come, love. We'll go upstairs now. And while I fix you a good meal, Hugh will get a bed ready for you so you can sleep for as many hours as you want."

Now Hugh was at her side as well, smiling his gentle smile. "And soon, my dear, perhaps you'll tell *us* why you ran away."

Helping her along step by step, they made their way upstairs.

Before that day was out, and while Hugh and Lydia were still trying to recover from the shock of the story Jane had told them, the news had spread through the city—the rebel smuggling agent known far and wide as The Schoolmaster had been arrested.

Hugh immediately began to make discreet inquiries, asking in every tavern, shop, and market where people gathered to gossip. But all he could learn was that the notorious prisoner was confined in the dungeon of the old Exchange Building, that the charge against him was treason, and that his trial was scheduled to begin in two weeks. Hugh tried to sound optimistic when reporting this to Jane and Lydia, but he knew that Simon's future looked bleak. No one expected a British military court to show leniency in a trial on charges of treason. For now,

Simon languished in a dark, filthy, airless cell, with no visitors allowed.

Meanwhile, Hugh and Lydia did their best to make Jane feel welcome. They cleaned out a storage area behind Hugh's workshop on the first floor and made a small but comfortable room for her. They tried not to ask too many questions, seeming to understand her absentmindedness and general lack of sociability as she settled in with them. Jane fretted that her presence would strain their scant supplies, but Hugh and Lydia were so gracious that she soon began to feel more at ease in this regard.

But they could do nothing to relieve her torment of worry over what Simon's fate might be—worries that, after all, they fully shared. Keeping herself busy, Jane soon realized, was the only way to avoid worrying herself sick. It was a kind of blessing that in the cabinetmaker's humble home servants were unknown. Seizing on this fact, Jane pitched in with the chores with such tireless energy that Hugh and Lydia were soon wondering how they had ever managed without her. All the while, Jane half expected Robert to appear, wanting to take her back to Rosewall. *He'd have to drag me kicking and screaming,* she told herself grimly.

In the end, it was Clarissa who came. Jane was sweeping out the shop one afternoon, about a week after her arrival, when a carriage pulled up and Clarissa looked out to greet Jane with a cheery smile. "Jane, dear. Hello!"

"Oh, hello," Jane replied coldly and went on sweeping.

"I brought you a few clothes," Clarissa said, trying again as her driver unloaded several bulky parcels.

"How thoughtful," Jane said. She could see Clarissa eyeing with distaste the ill-fitting dress and boots she was wearing, borrowed from Lydia. "I thank you. But I might as well tell you right now—I'm not coming back."

"I'm not here to ask you that, I promise. But won't you come for a little drive with me, so we can chat?"

Reluctantly, Jane agreed to a short visit. "We've both received letters from Brandon," Clarissa said as the carriage drove off. "I've brought yours."

"What does it say?" Jane asked curtly, accepting her letter but not glancing at it. "You're so good at reading my mail, you must know."

Clarissa winced. "I deserved that. I'm so sorry, Jane. I'd give anything to heal the hurt Robert and I have caused you."

Jane let that pass. "Well, what does Brandon say in *your* letter?"

"He's disgusted with General Cornwallis for giving up his push northward and making camp for the winter at Winnsboro. That appears to mean there'll be no more action till spring, and you know how hotheaded Brandon is—always itching to fight. As for me, I'm just thankful he's still safe."

"Amen to that," Jane agreed. Reports from soldiers in camp always renewed her worries about Brandon, and about Peter Quincy, fighting with the Patriots somewhere north of Charlestown.

Clarissa went on. "Robert's still working hard with Louis Lambert, trying to whip their scruffy militia into shape. He's determined to defend Rosewall as long as he can draw breath. I must say, I personally consider it rather foolish to love a piece of land practically as much as you love life itself. But he's my husband. And even though we've had certain difficulties, I'm trying very hard to be his devoted wife."

"How very touching," Jane said dryly, obviously not touched by this declaration of wifely devotion.

Clarissa sighed dejectedly. "Jane, dear, I have a confession to make. The quarrel between Robert and me wasn't just about his informing on Simon. There was something else, you see, something between Simon and me—"

"You mean the affair you and he had?" Jane asked casually. "I knew all about that years ago."

"What?" Clarissa was rendered almost speechless. "How did you know?"

"I heard you two whispering together one night in the Ainsleys' garden."

"And you never breathed a word? My God, how slow I've been to recognize your qualities! We all miss you terribly, you know. Especially Robert. He was furious with Omar for helping you run away."

"Omar is the main reason I'm still alive," Jane said firmly. "Please make sure Uncle Robert understands that."

"Oh, he does, I assure you. That's why Omar wasn't punished. It's just that your leaving like that was such a blow to him. You must realize, Jane, in his own clumsy way he loves you like the daughter he always—"

"Aunt Clarissa!" Jane's patience suddenly ran out. "I can't believe what I'm hearing. You sound as if you don't realize that it's thanks to *him* that Simon could soon be hanged as a traitor!"

"I was only trying to—"

"Well, you're wasting your breath. I haven't forgotten the awful things you both did. I told you I'm not coming back there, and I mean it!"

"I realize that, dear. And even though Robert is still your legal guardian, until you're twenty-one, he won't try to force you against your will. Just remember that he had no idea he was harming you in any way. He was devastated when he realized how important Simon is to you."

Jane could stand no more. "Excuse me, I think I'll walk back from here." Signaling the driver to stop, she stepped out of the carriage, then turned to say a final word. "Thank you for bringing my things, Aunt Clarissa. I am, as I said in my note, very grateful to both you and Uncle Robert. But I've crossed a bridge now, and there's no going back. Apart from that, there's really nothing more to be said."

Giving Clarissa no opportunity to reply, she walked rapidly away.

———

On her way home, Jane read Brandon's letter. In it he boasted about his magnificent Warrior and complained about "cowardly" rebels who wouldn't come out of the woods and fight. Jane wondered how these "cowards" could be the formidable adversaries they had proven themselves to be. He still regretted not seeing his father the day the prison ship sailed, and assured Jane that he was visiting his mother as often as possible.

"In closing," he wrote at the end, "I hope you will be pleased to hear that things are getting quite serious between Lucinda Dunning and me. But no matter what develops, dear Jane, I want you to know that the friendship I have with you is one I shall always treasure above all others."

All happiness to you, good friend, Jane thought, and, for the first time in many days, permitted herself a faint smile.

But the smile quickly disappeared when her thoughts returned to Simon, and the realization that his fate would soon be decided. She knew how grave was the charge of high treason but tried mightily not to think of it.

There was nothing left to do now but hope for a miracle.

Chapter 28

The trial of Simon Cordwyn before the British military court sparked more interest among the people of Charlestown than any trial in recent years. Hugh attended every session in the royal governor's building, faithfully reporting to Jane and Lydia all that transpired.

The first day belonged to the prosecution, headed by the British Army's Major Elliot. With principal witness Captain Richard Fleming, Elliot skillfully laid out his case, leaving little doubt that the former schoolmaster and the notorious rebel smuggler were one and the same.

On the second day, counsel for the defense—a British junior officer appointed by the court—argued that the evidence against the defendant did not add up to positive proof. He produced a string of character witnesses who had known Simon in Charlestown as a law-abiding, highly respected schoolmaster. One was cabinetmaker Hugh Prentice, who recalled how the accused had always condemned the rebellion as foolish and doomed to failure. Hugh swore that the same man could not now be guilty of treason.

Captain Fleming was gratified to see that there was no one important or influential among the defense witnesses. An obscure cabinetmaker was the best they could do. *Unbelievable,* thought Fleming, *that this man is first cousin to Robert Prentice, one of the colony's most distinguished Loyalist leaders.*

The young captain was supremely confident of the fine boost his own career would get from the successful prosecution of this case. Breaking the Continentals' most successful smuggling ring would be a real feather in his cap. With only one trial day remaining, all he had to do was sit back and wait for the congratulations to start pouring in.

On the third morning of the trial, Hugh was first in line for the spectator section. A summary of what had gone before was expected that day, followed by the verdict, either that same day or the next.

Soon after he took a seat, Hugh felt a nudge on the arm and rolled his eyes in disgust when he saw who had sat down next to him.

"I know what you think of me," Robert whispered before Hugh could say a word, "and you needn't tell me again now. Just tell me, how is Jane?"

Hugh's reply was chilly. "As well as can be expected, considering everything. Don't go near her, Robert. She won't stand for it."

"I won't trouble her, never fear." Robert leaned closer. "By the way, I hear you put on a fine performance yesterday. Almost had these gentlemen convinced that you never knew what Cordwyn was up to."

Hugh's manner turned from chilly to ice cold. "Robert, I know your part in this disgraceful affair. Years ago you cut yourself off from me. Now I'll return the favor. Get away from me. I'll not talk to you."

"I'm going, I'm going," Robert said, his own pleasant manner unruffled. "But do give Jane my regards, won't you? And Hugh, watch closely this after—"

"All rise!" the court clerk called out, and Robert's words were drowned out as the crowd rose for the judges' entrance. In solemn single file, they strode in, five in all, and took their seats at an elevated table at the front of the lofty chamber. Then: "Come to order!" Straggling spectators rushed for seats. To Hugh's relief, Robert had disappeared.

He studied the judges. All senior officers, they were ramrod straight and stone faced. And to them, Hugh thought in despair, we must look for justice and mercy! Major Elliot sat with Captain Fleming and several aides at a table to the right, the defendant and his counsel to the left.

After two days in court, Hugh was still shocked at Simon's appearance. His shirt tattered, his unshaven face grimy, he slumped in his chair staring hollowly at the table before him. He appeared to hold no hope—and, indeed, there appeared to be none. Hugh had not said this to Jane, although he strongly suspected that she knew.

Just as the tiresome case review came to an end, the trial of Simon Cordwyn took an unexpected turn. A commanding voice rang out from the back of the room.

"May it please the court, I beg to be heard!" A multitude of startled eyes, Hugh's among them, turned to stare as a man came forward, stopping only when guards blocked his way.

The five judges peered at the intruder, frowning. "What is the meaning of this?" the chief judge demanded. "State your name, sir."

The reply came promptly. "I am Robert Prentice of this city, and of Rosewall Plantation."

"Robert Prentice..." The chief judge pondered. "Your name is familiar to me, sir. Your reputation as a staunch Loyalist is well known. Do I take it that you wish to speak for the prosecution in this case?"

"With your permission, sir, I would speak for the defense."

A buzz of astonishment swept through the crowded courtroom. Major Elliot leaped to his feet, shouting, "My Lords, I object! This is most irregular!" The judges conferred with each other in whispers. As dumbfounded as anyone else, Simon sat up straight, staring blankly at Robert.

Finally the chief judge turned to Robert with a stern frown. "This is, indeed, highly irregular, Mr. Prentice. However, you may address the court if you make it brief. And be warned—we will not view it kindly if you have interrupted these proceedings for a frivolous reason."

Robert Prentice approached the judges' table with quiet dignity and a resolute look in his eye. The courtroom buzz quickly died as everyone in the crowded chamber waited breathlessly. And like a masterful orator, the unexpected witness held his listeners in thrall.

"Good sirs," he began, "I should like to speak to you today about the people of this colony. I have lived among them for more than twenty years, and I know them well. There is bitterness and resentment among them, and it threatens the safety of us all. Time and again, men are brought before you and accused of treason. Some are guilty, but many are victims of hasty, overeager pursuit, false evidence, human error. The people's bitterness grows, and rebellion flames anew. In the present case we have a man who a short time ago commanded the respect and admiration of all who knew him in this city. Now he comes before you charged with offenses no one can prove, and which are contradicted by everything known about his character—"

"My Lords!" Major Elliot sprang from his seat with another objection. "I beg to remind the gentleman that it was *he* who provided the information that led us to place the prisoner under arrest!"

"A mistake I will regret to my dying day!" Robert shot back. "I merely mentioned to Captain Fleming that Mr. Cordwyn was in Charlestown. I had no idea he would be arrested without proof of due cause, or brought to trial on such flimsy evidence!"

Sputtering, the prosecutor sat down, and Robert turned back to the judges. "Gentlemen, I do not presume to instruct you in the performance of your duties, or in your deliberations on the verdict you will deliver here. But I beseech you, listen to the people outside these walls. Most are loyal subjects of our king, but they decry as 'tyranny' any hint of injustice done in the name of the Crown. Do not give them cause to use that word again. I have known Simon Cordwyn for many years. And from everything I know about him, I would stake my life that an innocent man is on trial here. That is all I have to say. Thank you for your attention."

In the midst of confused silence, Robert turned on his heel and, with all eyes following him, strode rapidly out of the courtroom.

Chapter 29

O
rder!" bellowed the chief judge, and the pandemonium that had threatened to erupt in the courtroom subsided into an excited buzz. The judges then went into a huddle, whispering earnestly among themselves. The prisoner's mood had undergone a striking change. He conferred earnestly with his counsel, appearing to take an interest in the proceedings for the first time. Captain Richard Fleming's mood had also undergone a change. He now sat slumped at the prosecutor's table shaking his head, stunned at this incredible turn of events.

A recess then being declared for the day, Hugh raced home to Lydia and Jane, arriving out of breath from running, bursting with the news of the amazing scene he had witnessed. "Robert was magnificent! Who would have dreamed he would say such things! And that fool Fleming—he almost fainted!"

Jane was in a daze. "But what does it all mean?"

Hugh had a ready answer. "It means that Robert

knows what a low-down thing he did, and he's trying to repair the damage. And that takes courage."

"But you, too, spoke for Simon, as did others," Lydia pointed out. "What difference can one more voice make?"

"All the difference in the world!" Hugh exclaimed. "Robert is known as a leading Loyalist in this area. His word carries tremendous weight—far more than mine ever could." He turned to the shaking Jane. "The judges will deliver their verdict tomorrow morning. Only one more night to wait."

The longest night of my life, Jane thought.

Hugh was back in his seat in the courtroom gallery bright and early on the fourth day of the trial. In contrast to the dramatic scene that enlivened the day before, the closing session began on a dull, routine note. Once more came a detailed summary of arguments and evidence presented by both sides, with explanations of the laws each side thought should apply in the case. The chief judge then declared another recess—a few minutes of almost unbearable suspense that proved to be mercifully brief—after which he and his fellow judges returned to announce their decision.

The verdict: Guilty.

The sentence: Banishment to Nova Scotia, Canada, until hostilities with England had ceased.

The pandemonium that followed was beyond controlling. In seconds a stream of spectators poured out of the building, everyone loudly rejoicing or complaining. Outside, they gathered in knots, heatedly debating the matter.

It was not so much the verdict as the sentence that had spectators excited. Just as Saint Augustine, Florida, had been the topic of the crowd's curiosity several months before, the British province of Nova Scotia in the North Atlantic now became the subject of intense speculation. Some said it was a block of ice, frozen solid year-round. Others, who had heard that people actually lived there, claimed that it was a beautiful land of farmers and fishermen. But in that furious dispute, two points were agreed upon by all: No one had ever been publicly tried and convicted of treason and then received such a mild sentence—and this amazing outcome had to be due solely to the unexpected intervention of Mr. Robert Prentice.

Hugh was hurrying away from the courthouse to take the exciting news home, when Jane suddenly clutched at his arm. "Cousin Hugh, wait!"

"Jane! I thought you couldn't bear to come here."

This time it was she who was breathless. "I couldn't bear to stay away! I've heard what people are saying. Banishment—and to *Canada*! Is that true?"

"It's true." He grinned. "For such a serious charge, it's only a slap on the wrist."

"Thank God!" she cried. "Do you think they'd let me see him before they take him away?"

"Not likely, but let's try around back. They usually take prisoners out that way."

They made their way through the crowd but could

get no closer than thirty or forty feet from a small rear door. Jane strained to see through the throng of heads in front of her. Finally, two guards emerged with the shackled, half-starved prisoner between them. Jane gasped at the sight of him.

"Mr. Cordwyn!" she called. Her voice was lost among the shouts of the noisy crowd. "Simon!" she cried, waving her arms. "I'm here!"

Now he jerked his head in her direction, eyes frantically searching. "Jane! Wait for me, I'll—" There was no time for more. The guards hustled him toward an enclosed prison wagon and shoved him into the back, out of sight.

In tears, Jane turned to Hugh. "I saw him," she said. "I called to him, and he heard me. They wouldn't even let him speak, but I know he was trying to say, 'Wait for me. I'll come back for you.'"

"Then you heard all that really matters, didn't you?" Hugh smiled gently and took her arm. "Come now, let's go home and tell Lydia."

They threaded their way out of the crowd, never noticing Robert standing a short distance away. He watched them until they had disappeared from sight, then, head bowed, he walked off slowly in the opposite direction.

Early the next morning, Jane was shaken awake by Lydia. "Sorry to wake you, love. But you'll not believe who's come knocking at the door, insisting on seeing you. Of all people, that bloodthirsty monster Captain Fleming!"

Still half asleep, Jane winced. "Oh, no, please! Tell him to go away!"

"I did, but he won't. He says it's his last chance to see you before he sails for England tomorrow."

"Really!" Jane blinked herself awake. "All right," she sighed. "Tell him I'll be there shortly, would you?"

A few minutes later, Jane found herself strolling along the Charlestown seawall with the man who had proven himself to be Simon's worst enemy. "So you're sailing for England tomorrow," she remarked, unable to think of anything else to say. "Why so suddenly?"

"Who knows?" he replied glumly. "Perhaps it's my commander's way of punishing me for my failing to— But I'm a soldier, I can only follow orders."

They stopped and gazed out over the harbor.

"It's amazing, isn't it?" he mused. "How complicated life can be?"

She smiled faintly but did not look at him. "Very true, Richard."

He drew a deep breath, then began again. "Before I go, Jane, there are two very important things I want to say to you."

"If one is to justify your actions against Mr. Cordwyn, you needn't bother. You were doing your duty as an officer, I understand that."

"Good, thank you. Then I'll go on to the second one. From the first time I ever saw you—remember, that day at Rosewall? Good Lord, I actually mistook you for a servant! I've always held in my heart the hope that one day I might take you home to England as my bride."

Jane finally looked at him, but he could read nothing in her empty gaze. "I speak boldly because I must do so now, or never," he went on. "I always thought my chief rival was young Ainsley. But now I'm told it was none other than that schoolmaster! I must say, I resist believing that."

"Nevertheless, it's true, Richard. And it's not going to change."

"Jane, I appeal desperately to your good sense. How well do you know this Cordwyn? Do you really think you'll ever see the scoundrel again?"

"Captain Fleming," Jane said icily, "I do not require your instruction in this matter."

"Please, hear me out. Think of who you are—Lady Jane Prentice. That's *Lady* Jane Prentice. As my wife you'd also be a member of the distinguished Fleming family, with the most devoted husband you could ever desire. Give me your pledge, and I'll return within the year and take you home to England. And it *is* your home, Jane."

Jane's gaze drifted out to the distant horizon. "I often think of England," she said softly. "I loved the green hills and country lanes I knew as a child. They'll always be a part of me." As she turned to face him, Richard saw a light in her eyes he had never seen before. "I wish you well, Richard, truly," she said. "But now we must say good-bye. Because, you see, I'm doing exactly what you urged me to do—thinking of who I am. I wish I could explain it better. All I can tell you is . . . I'm an American now."

And before the flabbergasted Richard could recover his power of speech, she had turned and walked away.

Jane was surprised, too—both at what she had said, and at how right it had felt. She knew she would always love her native land and think with deep affection of the good people and beautiful places she had known there as a child. Something she had once read in a Shakespeare play suddenly came to mind: "Praising what is lost makes the remembrance dear." But it was all far away now, lost in faded memories that could never be relived.

"I'm an American now." She said it again, and liked the sound of it.

Her steps quickened by newfound self-knowledge, she hurried home to help Lydia get breakfast. It was a new day, and life goes on.

PART V

Storm's Fury
1781

Chapter 30

He arrived in the biting cold of winter, half starved and nearly frozen, at La Poissonnière—the Fish Kettle—the only public house in the tiny village of Mavillette. It was his good fortune that its owner, the stout, gray-haired Madame Duveau, was the first person he encountered. She listened to his story of banishment from the American colonies, gave him a steaming bowl of fish chowder, and then summoned prominent citizens of the community to come at once. Madame Duveau had an idea.

Mavillette was an isolated fishing village on the windswept west coast of Nova Scotia. Most of the villagers were descendants of early French settlers, forced to live as discontented subjects of the hated English king who now ruled their province. With this history, they might have looked with instant favor on one condemned by the British for smuggling for the American rebels. But they were clannish people, mistrustful of strangers. They gathered on long benches at rough, hand-hewn tables in La Poissonnière's main room and stared suspiciously at the bedraggled traveler. Once again, Simon Cordwyn was on trial.

If, as he claimed, a British ship had brought him as a prisoner to the port of Halifax, why had he trekked across the frozen peninsula, a journey no sane man would contemplate in winter? Simon replied that Halifax was on Nova Scotia's east coast, facing the Atlantic. He had to get to the west coast, facing the North American mainland. True, the great Bay of Fundy stretched endlessly to an unbroken horizon. But here, he said, he could at least feel that he had taken a first step toward home.

The villagers shook their heads and muttered among themselves. Hearing that Simon had once been a schoolmaster, they became slightly more respectful. Still, what if he were a British spy, sent to sniff out evidence of disloyalty even in this obscure corner of the empire?

Madame Duveau addressed her fellow villagers in a commanding tone. "Listen to me, *mes amis*. None among us can give our children learning. We have always needed *un professeur*. Suddenly one has appeared among us. Do you not recognize a miracle when you see it?"

She turned to Simon. "Monsieur Cordwyn, we will provide you with lodging and a classroom if you will start a school here. *Oui?*"

Simon had no interest in a permanent arrangement. But he had endured enough of winter travel in this land of ice and freezing mists. "Thank you kindly, Madame. I am honored to accept your offer. For now, that is."

"Splendid!" she cried. Ignoring Simon's hastily added *for now*, she began immediate plans for the future. "*Alors,* I will make this room into a classroom during morning hours, and next summer we will build a proper schoolhouse. Good! It's settled." She ordered a serving girl to bring cider and glasses, and soon, their suspicions put aside, the villagers were drinking a toast to *Monsieur le professeur.*

Simon sat amazed. He had discovered the dominant force in the affairs of this community—the strong mind and sturdy frame of Madame Duveau.

Simon was given a room at the inn, and his school was soon off to a shaky start. Books and writing materials were almost nonexistent. But Simon's gentle manner quickly put the children at ease, and his talent for improvising made up for the shortage of supplies. The class grew to fourteen, including Madame Duveau's two grandsons, their eyes bright with excitement over this strange new experience. Parents, observing the awakening of intellectual curiosity in their offspring, nodded in grudging approval and agreed that the coming of *le professeur* had indeed been something of a miracle.

Madame Duveau was pleased. Her idea was working beautifully.

_____

The dawning of 1781 brought short, dark days and icy storms that churned the sea into angry froth. With life outdoors at a standstill, La Poissonnière's public room was the center of local social life. On long winter nights, its timbers shook with the sounds of merriment, as villagers gathered almost every evening to drink and tell stories, with French heard more often than English. Simon, who had acquired a passable knowledge of French at Philadelphia College, watched the singing and dancing, participated in amiable conversation, and laughed politely at every joke.

But as popular as he was among these people, they all noticed that he was also a solitary man, given to private brooding. Several villagers spoke to Madame Duveau about it.

"It's only a little sickness for home," she declared. "Next summer, when we build a fine schoolhouse, he'll think no more about it."

How could she be so sure of that? they wondered.

"Because I will see to it," she snapped, dismissing the subject. Madame Duveau was accustomed to having her way.

By March, the fishermen were hard at work on their boats anchored in the harbor, for soon they would begin their summerlong sorties on the Bay of Fundy in search of tuna. But winter storms raged on into April. In the late afternoons, protected by woolen coat and fur cap, Simon trudged the hillsides. Madame Duveau often saw him out there, gazing westward across the water.

One raw day she put on her own heavy wraps and went out to join him. "You are unhappy, *mon ami*," she said. "Why is that?"

"Tell me, Madame. Does winter last forever here?"

She smiled. "No, no, spring does come. And with it will come flowering hills, bright blue skies—" She saw that Simon was not listening. "But, *Monsieur*, what is really troubling you?"

He turned to face her. "I met some travelers from Annapolis Royal this afternoon. Some sailors from a British frigate in the harbor there told them General Washington is about to join forces with the French for a major offensive. Meanwhile, Lord Cornwallis flounders in the South, not knowing which way to turn. Things are happening, Madame Duveau. Important things."

"And you want to return to that place, even though you were banished on peril of your life! Do you not realize what that would mean?"

"It would mean I would have to be much more careful in the future. I'm not a complete fool."

"Indeed, I hope not. You are fortunate to be well out of it, *mon ami*. Yet you still long for that endless, futile war!"

"On the contrary, Madame. I'd much prefer to live in peace as a schoolmaster. I was drawn into the rebellion against my will. And I'm still not convinced my countrymen can make independence work. But I am one of them, and for better or worse, I must share their fate. Besides..."

Madame Duveau waited. "Yes? There is something else?"

He nodded. "A lovely girl, in South Carolina."

"Mon dieu!" She was exasperated. "There are lovely girls right here. Choose one, marry her, and be happy! South Carolina—it is at the end of the world! Before you return, your mademoiselle will be wed to another!"

"That may be. But as soon as winter ends—if it ever ends—I must go."

"And how will you go, may I ask? By land? It is five hundred miles of trackless wilderness to the nearest settlements in the Massachusetts District of Maine. If you don't get lost and starve, you'll be killed by Indians or eaten by wolves. By sea? It's a hundred miles across here, rough and treacherous. I know of only one sailor who has the skill for such a voyage—my son Armand. And he will soon be chasing tuna all summer, too busy even to speak to you."

"Then what shall I do, Madame? I *must* find a way!"

"Mon ami, you must find a way to come to your senses! And you will, when you see carpenters building a fine schoolhouse. You speak of fate. Fate brought you here, and here is where you belong. You'll see— it shall be as I say." Permitting no dispute, she turned abruptly and walked away.

But she could not walk away from what she now knew in her heart. No miracle had occurred in the village that winter, and no schoolhouse would be built that summer. What was the use? It would only stand empty, a melancholy monument to her own failed dream.

―――

Spring came at last, the hillsides exploding in riotous color, and fierce storms giving way to bright days. The fishing boats put out to sea. Spring turned to summer, and Simon dismissed his students for a well-earned holiday. Now he began studying every map and chart he could find. He looked everywhere for someone who might know a practical land route to Massachusetts. Finding no one, he prowled the harbor, asking every fisherman who brought in his catch if he had ever sailed all the way across the bay. None had, and Simon was told that the only man who possessed the skills and daring even to think of such a thing was— sure enough—Armand Duveau.

Simon had never succeeded in becoming friends with Armand. Madame Duveau's taciturn son had sent his own boys to Simon's class only at the urging of his wife and the firm insistence of his mother. Armand admitted later that it was a good thing. But toward Simon personally he saw no need for friendliness. And when Simon now asked if Armand might consider taking him across the bay, he got a scowling reply.

"Monsieur, I am a fisherman, not a ferryboat operator. I haven't time for such foolishness!"

Obviously, Madame Duveau was right—no hope there. So Simon was taken by surprise when later that night, Armand knocked at his door.

Ignoring Simon's invitation to come in, Armand spoke curtly. "When can you be ready?"

Simon stared. "I beg your pardon?"

"If you can be ready at dawn, we'll sail for Falmouth, the nearest town of any size in Maine. I'll have two

245

crewmen, and if we catch a strong wind and good weather, we could make it in a few days. But you'd better be prepared for longer. Well? Can you be ready?"

Simon pondered this surprising development. "You said you had no time for this. What made you change your mind?"

Armand turned sheepish. "It was *Maman*. She said, 'Armand, once or twice in your life you will be called upon to do something more important than bringing in fish. This is one of those times. Do it.' *Maman* is a forceful woman, Monsieur."

Simon had to smile. "So I've noticed. Thank you, Armand! At first light, then—I'll be ready."

It was a cold, gray dawn, as if the world, having tasted summer, had decided to retreat to winter. Armand's sleek, twenty-five-foot sloop was moored at dock's end. Simon and Madame Duveau stood watching as his crewmen heaved the last few sacks of provisions aboard.

"The children will miss you," she said.

Simon smiled sadly. "They are young. They will forget. I'll remember them long after they've forgotten me."

Armand came to them. "We are ready," he said. He listened patiently while his mother lectured him about the weather, the wind, and not staying too long on the opposite shore. Then, with a quick nod to Simon, he scrambled aboard his boat.

Simon searched for appropriate parting words. "Madame Duveau, I . . . I hope you know how grateful I am for your many kindnesses. Indeed, I—"

She held up a hand to stop him. "Do not tire me with all that, Monsieur Cordwyn. You need only say good-bye and go."

He stepped closer, kissed her on each cheek, and said as simply as he could, "Good-bye, then, my dear friend. I shall never forget you, or the good people of Mavillette."

"*Mon ami,*" she murmured, her hand on his arm, "I am sure your lovely mademoiselle in South Carolina is waiting for you." Suddenly a warm smile illuminated her fine features. "You'll see. It shall be as I say!" She gave him a quick hug, held him with a fond look, then sent him on his way.

The powerful tide carried Armand's boat from shore like a leaf on a rushing stream. Madame Duveau retreated to a grassy hillside to watch the departure. It was the same spot where she had stood with Simon on a raw day weeks before, and had been forced, finally, to admit to herself that she was not, after all, in full charge of everything that happened in the village.

As she watched, the slanting rays of the rising sun found an opening in the clouds, transforming the dull gray bay into a sheet of burnished bronze. Madame Duveau liked what she saw—fine weather for sailing. *So be it,* she thought. *Dreams are born, dreams die.* She watched until the little ship had become a tiny speck on the immense canvas of sea and sky, then turned away.

Chapter 31

For Jane, the hardest season of the year had never been winter but the seemingly endless, steamy summers. But this year, she welcomed the return of summer as a soothing relief from anxious thoughts of Simon banished to a frigid northern land called Nova Scotia.

Slipping easily into the routine of life with Hugh and Lydia in Charlestown, she found it hard to believe that she had ever thought of the great manor house at Rosewall as home. She missed everyone there—even Robert, a little. But she truly felt that her present life was much more in harmony with her own modest nature. She had learned enough from Hugh, for example, to become an apprentice in his shop. The turning, shaping, and fitting of woodwork fascinated her. Hugh predicted she would become America's first woman cabinetmaker. She laughed, secretly thinking he might be right. But she made no secret of her gratitude toward the two kind and generous people who had welcomed her into their home with genuine joy. Except for the war—and Simon's absence, of course—life was almost good.

Hugh, Lydia, and Jane often talked of the war, and mainly of Lydia's son, Peter Quincy. He fought with an elite band of rebels led by Francis Marion, the Swamp Fox. From hideouts in the shadowy woods, Marion's men would dart out, inflict severe punishment on surprised Redcoats, then vanish again. Theirs was a harsh, often brutal existence—that much was known. Often, Marion's men went days with nothing to eat except for a few sweet potatoes. Constant worry about Peter's safety hung like an ominous cloud over Hugh's household.

Peter Quincy was only one of the people absent from Jane's life who were always present in her mind. Another was Harriet Ainsley. In August, it would be a year since Arthur's banishment, and Harriet had withdrawn into seclusion at Goose Creek. After coming to live at Hugh's, Jane began to make occasional trips to Goose Creek, both to visit Mrs. Morley and to keep a watchful eye on Harriet. At first, Hugh had insisted these visits were too dangerous, that the countryside was infested with roughnecks convinced that calling themselves Patriots justified any misdeed. A niece of the despised Tory Robert Prentice could hardly expect gentle treatment at their hands.

Jane was insistent. "I'd be pleased to have you come with me, Cousin Hugh. But if not, I shall go alone."

Lydia gave her husband some advice. "Remember,

love, this is the same young lady who walked all the way from Rosewall in the middle of the night. You might as well give in."

So Hugh hired a carriage and accompanied Jane on these trips. Luckily, the worst they encountered was frequent questioning by British patrols and rude stares from others on the road.

From her first day in Charlestown, Jane had been enchanted by the sunny disposition of the sweet-natured Harriet Ainsley, who had always been a source of comfort and kindness to all who knew her. Now Harriet welcomed her visitors to Goose Creek with her usual warmth, Hugh no less than Jane. And, of course, Jane was delighted to see Mrs. Morley again. Nevertheless, the Dudley house seemed unbearably gloomy. Except for Mrs. Dudley's upstairs apartment, and the rooms occupied by Harriet and Mrs. Morley, the old mansion gathered dust, silent and largely deserted. Harriet, with her husband banished to some far-off place and her soldier-son able to visit only occasionally, spent her time dreaming of the glorious day when her family would be together again. Meanwhile, her sunny nature remained hidden under a shadow. It was painful for Jane to see her this way.

On one occasion, Harriet confided to Jane that she and Brandon had quarreled on his most recent visit. "And the quarrel was about you, dear."

"Me?" Jane was taken aback. "Good Lord, what did I do?"

"It was your running away from Rosewall. Brandon was infuriated when he heard about it. And with me, because I said I admired what you'd done."

Jane sighed. "No doubt I shall receive my own good scolding in time."

Arriving one day in August, as the first anniversary of Arthur's banishment approached, the visitors found Harriet radiant with exciting news.

"Dr. Jeffers was in Charlestown last week and met a very high ranking British officer who talked of a general prisoner exchange. Arthur may be coming home soon! Needless to say, I'm floating on air!"

Jane privately wondered about the accuracy of this report but pronounced it wonderful news, and Hugh politely agreed.

"Just wait till Brandon hears!" Harriet glowed with renewed hope. "I've always known Robert lured him away from us. But I'm sure that once Arthur is home, Brandon will return to us, and we'll be a family once again!"

On their way home after this visit, Jane and Hugh remarked sadly on Harriet's unrealistic dream of a reunited family. And Jane wondered aloud about the prospects of a prisoner exchange.

"I've heard such talk before," Hugh told her. "It has never happened, and I see no reason to think it will now. And even if it did happen, my dear, it wouldn't include Simon. Arthur Ainsley was sent away on mere suspicion, but Simon was tried and convicted of treason. Don't hold false hopes—it will only bring you heartache, as it surely will poor Harriet. You'd best put the whole idea out of your mind."

Jane lapsed into silence, thinking of how easily hope could be raised, then cruelly dashed—not only for Aunt Harriet, but for herself as well. There was heartache enough for both.

One afternoon a week or two later, Jane returned from the city market to find Hugh and Lydia sitting glumly at the kitchen table.

"What's happened?" she asked, suddenly uneasy. "Is it Peter?"

It was Lydia who answered. "No, not Peter. Marianne, his wife. And the baby they were expecting in October."

Hugh added a few details. "Marianne has been living with her parents up near Georgetown, waiting for her baby to come. Last week, Loyalist thugs raided the farm, terrorizing the family. Everyone survived—or almost everyone. Marianne lost the baby."

Jane went tight-lipped. "Where's Peter?"

"Over at the Lion's Head, trying to drown his sorrows," Hugh told her.

Jane dropped her parcels on the table and headed for the door.

The Lion's Head Tavern was only a few blocks away, on the waterfront. Peter Quincy sat at a small corner table, staring morosely into a pint of ale. His once-strapping frame was lean and muscular, his weather-beaten face deeply lined. He did not look up when Jane approached.

"Hello, Peter," she said softly. "Remember me?"

He was slow to lift his eyes and, when he did, offered no hint of a smile. "Of course. Lady Jane Prentice. Sit down. Have a glass of flip."

"No drink, thank you. But I'll sit with you a spell, if I may."

"I heard how you left Rosewall and came to live here," he said after a moment. "Bully for you, Jane. It's good to have you on our side. And I suppose you've heard my happy news?"

"I'm so very sorry, Peter. Would you tell me what happened?"

"I'm sure I'll spend the rest of my life telling people." Staring into his glass again, he seemed to have difficulty beginning. "They weren't British, you know. They were black-hearted American Tories, in the pay of the damnable English king. Broke open a barrel of rum at the Wendells' and went on a drunken spree. Cuffed Marianne's father about, ransacked the house, threatened the family with swords. Marianne panicked and ran, but she stumbled and fell down a ravine. She wasn't hurt, but the baby—" Peter drained his glass and lurched to his feet. "I need another drink."

Jane stopped him gently. "Why don't we go walk by the harbor, instead? The air will do you good."

He grudgingly agreed, and they walked along the seawall, Peter staring at the ground. "It was a boy, you know. Seven months along—not far to go. But when he was born the next morning, he was—he was dead. We were going to name him Timothy, after my father. But they murdered him. Murdered him in the name of King George of England!"

"Don't, Peter!" Jane pleaded. "King George didn't kill your son, and neither did his troops. Those raiders were scoundrels, and there are plenty on both sides, as surely as there are victims on both sides."

"Victims?" Peter was outraged. "My son was a victim! Those damned yellow-livered American Tories are the scum of the earth, and I hate 'em all!"

Jane winced at his ferocious rage but remained calm. "Let me tell you about the Loyalist refugee camp Hugh and I see every time we go up to Goose Creek to visit Mrs. Ainsley. It's the most horrifying sight imaginable—hundreds of miserable people whose only sin was trying to remain loyal to their king. Whenever the British leave an area, good Patriots rise up thirsting for revenge. Those poor people had to run or be torn to pieces by their neighbors. Can you honestly say you hate them?"

"Yes, I hate 'em! They've gotten what they deserve. And one of these days, your high and mighty uncle Robert and his fancy wife will get what they deserve, too!"

After a strained silence, Jane began again, still calmly and patiently. "Please don't give in to blind hatred, Peter. It will destroy you. It's the madness of war you should hate. It doesn't care what side anyone's on.

Soldiers, citizens, people of all ages—even the un-born—and every one a tragedy. But this hatred be-tween Americans and other Americans is deadly. It could poison life in this country forever."

Peter snorted loudly and trudged on, but Jane could sense his anger cooling a bit. At last he spoke more calmly. "I'm too far gone to think clearly anymore, but I guess what you say makes some sense. Anyway, you're a tonic, Lady Jane. If Simon Cordwyn ever comes back here and makes you his wife, he'll be one lucky man."

"Well, thank you, Peter. And speaking of luck—I actually found a bit of meat in the market today, and I'll bet Lydia already has it on the fire."

He nodded. "Come to think of it, I could do with a bite."

"I'm sure you could." Jane tugged at his arm. "Tonight we'll make you a feast. Oh, and by the way—" Now she gave him a playful smile. "You're not supposed to call me Lady Jane. Just Jane, please, remember?"

At last he mustered a weak smile of his own. "Sorry, pretty lass, no offense intended. But to me you'll always be Lady Jane—as fine a lady as I ever hope to meet."

Jane hugged his arm as they walked on, pleased that she could help him enjoy at least a fleeting moment of cheer. But oh, the heartache! *Dear Lord,* she prayed silently, *let this be the last of it.*

Chapter 32

As summer dragged to a close, excitement filled the air in Charlestown. Hugh's friends often gathered in his workshop in the evenings to discuss reports from the North. Combined American and French forces were moving toward Virginia, where Cornwallis was holed up in the coastal village of Yorktown. No longer the mighty conqueror, the harried British general was now just trying to survive. Jane, hearing all this, could sense Patriot optimism growing. Hugh had warned her against false hope, but he was no longer following his own advice. The smell of American victory was in the air.

One day the stable boy from Goose Creek, Luther, appeared at Hugh's door, frantically looking for Jane. This time the sight of him made her go pale. "Oh no—what's happened, Luther? Is it more bad news?"

"Sorry, ma'am. It's Lieutenant Ainsley. He done got wounded."

"Oh, dear God!" Jane gasped. "Is it very bad?"

"Pretty bad, I reckon, ma'am. Doc Jeffers want to know can you come, young mahster keep askin' for you."

"Me?" Jane was taken aback. *Why wouldn't he ask for Lucinda Dunning at a time like this?* "Are you sure it's me he's asking for, Luther?"

"Oh, yes'm. Doc Jeffers say he keep callin' your name, over an' over. Doc got his hands full with young mahster's mama, too, kind o' goin' out o' her head, seem like."

Though momentarily stunned, Jane quickly focused on what she saw as her own duty. "I must go at once," she told Hugh, who had followed her to the door. A storm was brewing, but this time Hugh did not hesitate.

"I'll get us a carriage," he said quietly.

They arrived in late afternoon, in a driving rain that had turned the narrow dirt road into a river of mud. Harriet's elderly maid, Molly, met them at the front door, but her expressionless face told them nothing.

"Mahster Brandon restin' fairly easy this evenin'," she said. "You all come on in. I tell Doc Jeffers you here."

Dr. Jeffers soon joined the visitors in the parlor. A heavyset man in his early sixties, with gray hair and a quiet dignity, he lived nearby and had been the Dudley family doctor since Harriet was a girl.

"Thank God you've come, Jane," he declared in fervent greeting, then shook hands with Hugh, whom he knew from Hugh's previous visits with Jane.

"To be brief, Brandon took a musket ball in the midsection," Dr. Jeffers told them. "It went clear through, which is good in a way—it means there's nothing inside to be probed for. He's in the morning room, heavily sedated. In every waking moment he asks for you, Jane. Gets very agitated, and that's not a good thing. That's why I'm so glad you came."

"And I'm glad you sent for me, Doctor," Jane replied, and forced herself to ask a dreaded question. "What are his chances, do you think?"

He shrugged. "I've seen men recover from worse. I've seen them die from less. We do what we can, and hope for the best."

"Mrs. Ainsley and the other ladies—where are they?"

"I've taken Mrs. Dudley and Mrs. Morley to my home, where they can be looked after. But Harriet—" The doctor shook his head. "She won't go. She sits with Brandon for hours on end, waiting for him to wake up. This morning he did, but he didn't recognize her. She was so angry she smashed a porcelain vase out in the foyer, cursing Robert Prentice all the while. In her mind, this is all his fault."

Jane cringed at the thought of kind Aunt Harriet so sadly transformed. "I know how she feels about Uncle Robert," she said. "But he must be informed, and immediately! He and Brandon are very close."

"Like father and son, I've heard. That's just the problem. Harriet positively forbids me to send for him. Says she won't let him in the house."

"I'll talk to her. But first, may I see Brandon for a minute?"

"He's not a pretty sight," Jeffers warned her as he led the way.

Bare-chested, his midsection encased in a blood-stained bandage, Brandon lay on a narrow bed in what must once have been a pleasant room, opening onto a garden. His face was ashen, his eyes closed. The only sign of life was his labored breathing. Old Molly was in attendance.

"He ain't hardly moved for hours now," she said. "We jes' try to keep him comfortable."

Jane stared, for the first time grasping the full horror of what had happened. Leaning down, she spoke Brandon's name. There was no response.

"Thank you, Molly," she whispered, and went out.

Starting upstairs, she met Harriet, who was on her way down.

"Hello, Aunt Harriet." She tried to muster a smile. "I was just coming to tell you Cousin Hugh and I are here to offer what aid and comfort we can."

"Oh." Harriet blinked rapidly, as if confused. "You mean about Brandon. What do you think, Jane? He won't die, will he?"

"Goodness, no! He's young and strong, and Dr. Jeffers says he's seen people survive worse. I'm sure he'll recover."

"Well, thank you, dear. It was good of you and Hugh to come. I'm exceedingly grateful to you both."

"Not at all." Encouraged by Harriet's serene mood,

Jane moved on to the subject she wanted to discuss. "Aunt Harriet, I really think Uncle Robert ought to be—"

"Hush!" Harriet hissed with sudden fury. "That man's name is not to be spoken in this house!"

"But he ought to be told! We mustn't keep him ignorant of what's hap—"

Without warning, Harriet struck, the blow glancing off Jane's hastily upraised arm and grazing the side of her face. Jane gasped and stepped back, her cheek aflame not from injury but from disbelief.

"That loathsome man!" Harriet shrieked. "We have *him* to thank for this. He deliberately lured Brandon into—"

"That's not fair, Aunt Harriet! Brandon's an adult, he makes his own—"

"I will not listen to this!" Harriet's face was flushed with rage. "Adult, indeed! He was just a boy when Robert began poisoning his mind! If I see that man again, I'll—I'll kill him with my bare hands!" Wheeling about, she ran back upstairs.

Hearing Harriet's outburst, Dr. Jeffers and Hugh had emerged from the parlor. "You see what I mean," Jeffers said grimly, and started up the stairs. "Excuse me, I'd better look after her."

Hugh gave Jane an anxious look. "Are you all right?"

"Yes, perfectly," she said, trying to sound calm.

They returned to the parlor, where Jane sank unsteadily into a chair.

"Dr. Jeffers told me what happened," Hugh said. "It seems Brandon and another soldier were on patrol when they ran into a rebel ambush. They held their own and the rebels withdrew, but not before the other soldier was wounded and his horse killed. Brandon's horse, Warrior, was also badly shot up, but was still on his feet. Brandon could've ridden away, but, instead, strapped his companion on Warrior and sent them back to camp. Later a search party went to look for Brandon and found him lying in a pool of his own blood. Evidently the rebels had doubled back, shot him, and left him for dead. He was barely conscious when they found him, but roused himself to ask about Warrior and the other man. They told him the other man survived, but Warrior collapsed and died when they got to camp. That's about it. The fact is, Brandon saved the other soldier's life—but at what a cost to himself."

Jane sat unmoving, lost in a dark silence. "I thought I knew him," she said at last. "But I never dreamed he had it in him to do something heroic. And just think, Cousin Hugh. It could've been—" She stopped and gripped her temples, horrified by a thought she couldn't bear to put into words.

"I know," Hugh said quietly. "It could've been Peter who did it."

The doctor soon returned. "Mrs. Ainsley is quiet now," he reported.

"Dr. Jeffers—" Jane addressed him with a firm resolve. "I realize it's not my place to make decisions here. But I strongly believe that word should be sent to Rosewall at once. Today, if it's not too late."

Jeffers gave a ready nod. "I'm happy for you to make decisions, Jane. *Somebody* needs to. But unfortunately it'll be dark soon, and it must be a hard ride of several hours, even on a fast horse."

"Nevertheless, I have the feeling that time is of the essence here. Please be frank with me, Doctor. Don't you agree?"

After a moment of solemn hesitation, the doctor got to his feet. "I'll send a rider off immediately—with a lantern—and tell him not to stop till he gets there, daylight or no."

That night Jane sat at Brandon's bedside, gazing at his seemingly lifeless form and marveling that this was the same young man whose brash self-confidence had so annoyed her in the past. She had still not yet seen him conscious. No change, Dr. Jeffers repeated. No change, no change...

She had dozed off when Brandon's eyes finally opened. He peered fuzzily at her. "Jane? Is that you?" His tremulous voice was barely audible.

Instantly awake, she leaned forward and took his hand. "Yes, it's me, Brandon. Cousin Hugh and I came as soon as we heard. And Dr. Jeffers has sent word to Rosewall, so Uncle Robert should be here soon."

Brandon's feverish mind was drawn back to a dreadful scene he couldn't forget. "They killed Warrior, Jane. Finest horse that ever lived—they shot him as if he were a worthless old nag."

"I'm so sorry, Brandon. But you'll have other horses. Someday you'll have a whole stable of them, all as fine as Warrior."

He clung to her hand. "Stay with me, won't you? Please say you will."

"Of course. I'm all settled upstairs, and I'll stay here till—"

"No, I don't mean that. I mean *stay* with me—forever."

Jane's heart sank. Was it starting all over again? "I was wondering, Brandon," she ventured, "shouldn't we send for Lucinda Dunning? After all, with things so serious between you two, perhaps she ought to be—"

"Oh, no, please! That was all just a silly trick."

"Trick? What do you mean?"

"I just wanted to make you jealous. Lucinda never meant anything to me. It's always been you, only you, ever since the day we first met." He rambled on, not noticing that Jane had sagged in dismay. "What a fool I was to take you for granted, when I couldn't begin to be worthy of you. But I've changed now, I'm—" He sucked in his breath at a sudden stab of pain.

Jane dabbed at his perspiring brow with a damp cloth. "That's enough," she said firmly. "Get some rest now, we can talk about all this tomor—"

"No, no, this can't wait!" He strained to raise his head. "You must believe me, Jane, I've changed! I'm a man now, wiser and humbler. Finally worthy enough to ask you—will you be my wife? Promise me, and I swear I'll devote the rest of my life to your happiness."

"Brandon, I . . ." Jane's mind searched frantically for a way out. "This is hardly the right time for a proposal."

"On the contrary, it's the time more than ever . . ." His speech was labored. "Now more than ever, I need the promise of your love. Say yes, Jane, please. It will mean *everything* to me."

Jane hesitated for another long moment. Search as she might, there seemed to be only one escape. She took a deep breath. "Yes, Brandon. I give you my promise."

"Thank you, my dearest girl. It's a miracle—you've turned the worst time of my life into the best. I feel better already." A slow smile spread over his face as his eyes fell closed and his grip on Jane's hand relaxed.

Hugh had been listening from the doorway. "It's very late, Jane. Get some sleep, I'll take over here. Dr. Jeffers will be back before morning."

For a moment longer, Jane gazed at Brandon's haggard face. *How peaceful he looks now,* she thought. "Yes, all right," she said. "Thank you."

Hugh followed her into the foyer. "Jane, I didn't mean to eavesdrop, but—did you really say you'd *marry* him?"

Jane gave him a calm look. "Don't worry, Cousin Hugh. I never will."

"So you told a lie. It could come back to haunt you, you know."

"I hope and pray that it does. Then I'll have to say, 'I'm sorry, Brandon, but I've changed my mind. I cannot marry you after all.' And he'll be very angry and call me all sorts of rude names. But that would be when he's strong and healthy again. And maybe I'll have helped to save his life."

Hugh gave her an understanding nod along with a smile of fond admiration. "You're a wonder, Jane Prentice. Sleep well."

Sleeping well was something she could not do. The rain had stopped for a while, but around midnight it began again, pelting down relentlessly for hours longer. For Jane, the sound of rain had always had a soothing effect, but not this time. Even when she drifted off to sleep near dawn, her troubled mind still found no peace.

She dreamed of a broad and sunny field. On one side stood Harriet. On the opposite side, Robert. Suddenly a horse came galloping furiously toward her. It was Brandon's mighty Warrior. Harriet called to the dashing young rider to come to her, but her pleas were matched by Robert's shouts, urging him to come that way. Instead, the rider bore down on Jane, reining in his steed a few yards in front of her. She crouched, terrified, as the huge beast reared, pawing the air, nostrils flaring. And when the rider pulled off his hat and gave it a flourish, all she saw was a grinning skull.

She started to scream, but the scream that shattered her dream and brought her bolt upright in bed was not hers. It was Harriet's, and it came from downstairs. Jane raced out of the room and down the stairs, only to find Dr. Jeffers, his shirt splattered with blood, standing in the doorway of the morning room. Beside him stood Molly, softly whimpering. From inside the room where Brandon lay, Harriet's wails rose and fell like the cry of a wounded animal.

Exhausted, Jeffers stared at Jane as if unsure of how to tell her what she already knew. "Internal bleeding," he said hoarsely. "It came on suddenly and went out of control. There was nothing I could do."

Feeling faint, Jane sank down on the stairs, rocking slowly back and forth. *Is this another awful dream?* she wondered. Hugh appeared from somewhere, slipping a comforting arm around her shoulders.

"The doctor says he went peacefully, Jane. There was no pain."

She was deep in shock, barely able to speak. "That silly lie I told—I actually thought it might save him. How stupid of me!"

"Not stupid at all," Hugh assured her. "It was another act of kindness going unrewarded."

Jane was no longer showing any sign of hearing Hugh. She was staring across the broad foyer and out the open front door. The sun was rising and the rain clouds had disappeared, bestowing upon the earth a fresh, newly washed day.

"'What showers arise,'" she murmured. "How does it go? 'What showers arise, blown with the windy tempest of my heart...'"

Tenderly Hugh drew her closer. "My dear, I know how hard this is for you. But someday, when these bad times are over—"

"Someday, someday, *someday*!" She suddenly lashed out at him. Grieving would have to wait—right now, all she could feel was anger. "I'm sick of hearing about someday! I don't care who wins this hateful war! I just want the killing to stop!"

Then to her great relief, something hard and tight inside broke loose, and the merciful tears flowed.

Chapter 33

After hours of hard riding, Robert arrived shortly before noon, quickly tethered his horse, and hurried up to the house. Dr. Jeffers was waiting for him on the veranda.

"Mr. Robert Prentice, I presume? I'm Dr. Jeffers."

Robert made quick work of a handshake. "I came as soon as I could," he said. "How's Brandon?"

"I regret to say that he died early this morning."

Robert went pale and drew back as if struck. "Dear God—no!"

"I'm very sorry, sir. In the end, his injury was just too severe." He gave Robert a moment to compose himself, then continued, "He's laid out inside, and burial will take place tonight. Secretly."

"What do you mean, *secretly*?" Robert scowled.

"The Patriots control this area, Mr. Prentice. If a Loyalist is buried in the local cemetery, his grave will certainly be opened and desecrated. Brandon is known to have served the British. He must be buried here on the Dudley property, in a remote spot unknown to outsiders. It's the only way."

"Contemptible!" Robert spat the word. "Sneaking around in the dead of night to hide him away! He deserves a hero's funeral, right here in Saint James Church." But Robert knew in his heart that the doctor was right. "If that's not to be, then I'll pay my respects now and be on my way." He started for the front door.

Jeffers laid a gentle hand on Robert's arm. "Just a moment, sir. If I may have a word—Let's sit over here, in the shade."

Robert allowed himself to be escorted to a pair of cane-back chairs under a spreading oak. He was still scowling as the doctor spoke earnestly.

"The shock of these events has greatly unsettled Mrs. Ainsley. She blames you for Brandon's death, and there's no telling what might happen if she sees you. I must ask you, sir, not to enter the house."

"Harriet blames me?" Robert looked sad but resigned. "I shouldn't be surprised. She always insisted I forced Brandon over to the Loyalist side. But he was acting entirely on his own, believe me. I am not to blame."

"I'm sure not," the doctor said soothingly. "But it's most important that nothing upset Mrs. Ainsley further. You understand."

Robert glanced upward. Overhead, small birds twittered in the afternoon sunshine. "Birds sing," he murmured. "Deer play in the woods. Villains do their evil work and live on. But the youngest and fairest die." He seemed unaware of the other man's presence. "Am I really blameless? Or is that a lie I invented for my own comfort? If only he could tell me..."

Dr. Jeffers placed a hand on his shoulder. "Don't torture yourself, sir. Come home with me now. Miss Jane and Mr. Hugh are there, eager to see you. It's not far. I'll just go get my horse, and we'll be on our way."

Left alone, Robert stared intently at the house. "If only he could tell me," he whispered. Rising, he strode purposefully toward the front door.

Molly confronted him in the foyer, her eyes wide in alarm. "Lordy, Mr. Robert, suh, you not s'posed to be here!"

"Where's Brandon?" he demanded.

"You best leave quick, suh. Missus see you, she liable to pitch a fit!"

"Never mind, I'll find him myself." He brushed past her, went into the parlor, then came out again. "Damn it, Molly, where is he?" he barked at the cowering servant.

But it was Harriet who spoke next. "You dare invade my home, Robert Prentice?" She stood at the top of the stairs, looking like death itself in a long black robe. Sheer hatred blazed in her eyes.

Robert stepped forward. "I loved him, too, Harriet. May I not grieve?"

"Grief, sir, is for me, who had my child stolen away. Not for you, who stole him!"

Robert stepped closer, speaking softly. "My dear, what can I say? If you truly feel I'm guilty of that—"

"You are guilty, sir. There is no doubt! And just as you led my child to his death"—her hand emerged from the folds of her robe and leveled a pistol at him—"so I lead you to yours."

Molly rushed forward, screaming, "No, missus, don't!"

But her protest was drowned in a flash of lightning and an ear-shattering blast. Echoes returned from the far reaches of the house, and when they had died away, only Molly's terrified whimpering remained.

"Stop that, Molly," Harriet said severely. "Go find Dr. Jeffers and inform him that I have just shot Mr. Robert Prentice. Go!"

Molly fled, and Harriet turned her attention to her victim. Robert lay in shock, blood spreading across his chest. Groaning, he tried to rise, then fell back to the floor.

"Dear me," Harriet said without emotion. "I'm afraid I didn't quite accomplish my purpose. Still, in all modesty, I think I've done a valiant deed this day." Serenely calm, she made her leisurely way back up the stairs.

It was night—that much he could tell from the darkness that was held at bay by a single lamp burning off to one side. As awareness gradually returned, he realized that he was lying in bed and someone was sitting beside him. He squinted, forced his eyes to focus, and saw that it was Jane. Briefly he wondered where they were, and why she was there. As memory returned in a vivid, horrifying rush, he twisted and turned. Hot pain raged through his upper body.

"Jane— My God, Jane, we've lost—"

"Shhh." Her cool fingertips stroked his brow. "You've been badly hurt, Uncle Robert. Your arm and shoulder are all bandaged, and the doctor wants you to keep very still."

His eyes roamed. "Brandon . . . we've lost him. He died a hero, and they want to hide him away in the night like a common thief! Don't let them do it, Jane. Don't let them!"

"It's already done, and Brandon's at peace. So just let it be."

"God, what an abomination!" He closed his eyes for a moment as if trying to shut out unbearable thoughts. "That fine young man, cut down in his prime. And my cherished dream of you and Brandon, master and mistress of Rosewall. Those silent rooms at last filled with the laughter of children. But it was never to be, was it? Even if he had lived—"

"No, Uncle Robert, it was never to be. I'm so sorry, I know I've disappointed you in many ways—"

"Don't say that, Jane. I've never told you how very dear you are to me. And with Brandon gone . . ." He fell silent for a moment, almost too overcome with emotion to speak. "What about Harriet?" he asked then.

"Dr. Jeffers finally got her moved to his house and

gave her something to make her sleep. She has no memory of shooting you, and Molly claims she didn't see it. Can you tell us how it happened?"

He replied without hesitation. "It was an accident, and my fault entirely. I barged in without warning. Harriet came downstairs to investigate. The foyer was so dim, she didn't recognize me. Must've thought I was an intruder, got frightened, and fired. Simple as that."

"So dim? It was broad daylight, Uncle Robert!"

"You must take my word on this, Jane. *It was an accident.*"

"All right, if you say so. Do you think you could sleep now?"

His feverish eyes locked on her face. "Jane, please come home. Someday Rosewall will be yours altogether, and you're needed there."

"Please, Uncle Robert. You must rest now."

"I'm sorry about that unfortunate business with Cordwyn. When I found out what he meant to you, I tried my best to make amends."

"I know. Don't think about it anymore."

"Then for mercy's sake, come back to us. You left such emptiness behind. Clarissa, without whom I couldn't live, lies ill and—"

"Ill?" Jane was instantly alarmed. "With what?"

"Swamp fever, they call it. She's never been sick before, and she's—she craves your forgiveness, too. The whole world is falling down around us, with rebels prowling the woods like bloodthirsty wolves." Drained from the exertion of speech, he lay back, panting.

Again Jane's comforting touch was on his brow. "Please try to sleep, Uncle Robert. We'll talk about it tomorrow."

The suggestion that had failed with Brandon the night before was more successful this time. Robert's eyes slowly closed as sedatives drew him into a deep slumber.

A few minutes later, Jane joined Hugh and Dr. Jeffers in the parlor. "He's finally asleep," she reported to the doctor.

"Good," he said. "And likely will be, for ten or twelve hours."

"Did he say anything about the shooting?" Hugh asked.

"He says it was an accident," Jane replied.

"An accident! Are you satisfied with that?"

"Yes, I am. I see no reason to doubt Uncle Robert's word."

Hugh appealed to the doctor. "You find it believable, sir?"

"If Jane is satisfied with it," he replied gravely, "then so am I."

"Thank you, Doctor," Jane said. "So let's consider the matter closed. Now, how soon will my uncle be able to travel, do you think?"

"In a day or two, I'd say. He won't have much use of that right arm for months, but there's no reason he couldn't travel."

"Good. Because I want to take him home as soon as possible."

Hugh objected. "Jane, you said you'd never go to Rosewall again!"

"I said I'd never *live* there again, and I won't. But Uncle Robert needs to go home, and Clarissa lies ill with swamp fever. They need my help."

"Then I'll come with you," Hugh said, objections abandoned.

She smiled gratefully. "I hoped you'd say that."

"I'll provide an ample supply of medication for the patient," Dr. Jeffers put in, "and give you something for your aunt, as well. Swamp fever's quite common in the backcountry, but it shouldn't be difficult to treat."

"That's kind of you, indeed. So, we'll leave as soon as you say it's all right. In the meantime..." Jane sighed as she pulled herself to her feet. "I'm rather tired, so if you gentlemen will excuse me..."

They bade her good night, and as she went out, the doctor looked after her in open admiration. "She's a remarkable young woman, Mr. Prentice."

Hugh responded with a fond smile. "The most remarkable person, young or old, I have ever known."

Slowly climbing the stairs on her way to bed, every step an effort, Jane didn't feel at all remarkable. All she felt was mind-numbing exhaustion, and a desperate yearning for the sweet forgetfulness of sleep.

Chapter 34

On a golden day in late October, Hugh returned to Charlestown to find the city buzzing with excitement. News had come that General Cornwallis, his army half starved after a long siege by Washington's combined French and American forces at Yorktown, Virginia, had surrendered. The Lion of Britain, as his admirers liked to call him, was finally caged.

While Charlestown's British military government brooded over this calamity, the city's many Patriots danced in the streets and Loyalists kept out of sight. Where the war would go from here was still uncertain. But everyone knew that a major, perhaps critical, turning point had been reached.

Lydia greeted her returning husband with a barrage of questions. Why was he gone so long? What in the world had happened? And where was Jane?

Hugh told her the whole story—of Brandon's

death; of Robert being wounded; of Jane's decision to take him home; and of his own to go with them. Mrs. Morley had been taken to Rosewall as well. She had been unnerved by the horrors falling upon the Dudley house, and now that old Mrs. Dudley was living with the Jeffers family, she wanted to be with Jane again.

The journey to Rosewall—thirty-five miles and a full day's travel in a jostling carriage—had been an ordeal for everyone, especially for the wounded man lying helpless while mercilessly tortured by every bump in the road. And his state of mind was not improved by hearing from travelers on the road about the British surrender at Yorktown. Robert had scoffed, claiming not to believe it, but anyone could see that he was severely shaken.

"By the time we arrived at Rosewall that evening," Hugh said, going on with his story, "Robert had grown so weak he could scarcely move, and Clarissa was too ill with swamp fever to come downstairs. The only able-bodied people in the house were the two servants, Cuba and Omar. And would you believe it? That giant of a man, Omar, lifted Robert out of the carriage and carried him as tenderly as a baby into the house and upstairs to his room. A remarkable sight to see."

"I'm sure it was," Lydia agreed.

"Then, of course, it fell to Jane to break the news to Clarissa about Brandon's death, and Robert's being shot. She did it as gently as she could, but ill as Clarissa already was, she was hit pretty hard by it all."

Lydia nodded thoughtfully. "Well, it's a sad story you tell, love. That poor Ainsley boy—and his mother going mad like that and shooting Robert. They're not really calling that an accident, are they?"

"Robert insists that it was, Jane insists we take his word for it, and no one else has shown any inclination to question it."

"Then I guess that's the end of it. What worries me is, why didn't Jane come home with you?"

"With both Robert and Clarissa out of commission, she just feels she's needed there, at least for now. She'll come back as soon as she can."

"Robert won't try to force her to stay for good?"

"No, he knows better than to try that. My chief worry is that one day Jane might find herself trapped there, unable to leave at all. You know, that fortress of Robert's has come under attack before. Never by any major force, but things are different now. With Cornwallis finished and the Redcoats pulling back toward Charlestown, the Patriots are taking control in the countryside. Rosewall's fields are already ravaged— barns burned, crops destroyed, livestock and field hands all gone. But Robert will never give up. Every other Loyalist in America might be ready to admit defeat, but not Robert. Never."

"What on earth will he do?"

"Some time ago, he and a friend organized a militia group, thinking they can hole up behind that great wall of his and fight off any rebel attack. It's hard to believe they could find anyone who still wants to fight for the Loyalist cause. But he's got a whole troop of them, and they've set up camp right there on the grounds. Robert's certainly got the courage of his convictions. You can't help admiring that."

"Indeed, I *can* help it." Lydia got up to put the kettle on the fire. "Protecting poor addle-brained Harriet Ainsley by saying the shooting was an accident—that's all very gallant. But the rest is nothing but blind-fool stubbornness. I'll not waste a minute thinking about him—if only we could be certain Jane will be all right."

Hugh fell into a pensive mood. "It was strange, being there. I hadn't set foot in that house in years. I must say, I was treated with perfect courtesy. Still, I felt like an intruder. When Jane saw me off this morning, I was sorry to leave her behind but very glad to be going." He paused, shaking his head sadly. "When Robert and I came to America, we loved each other dearly, vowed to stick together always. What happened to us, Lydia?"

"War happened, love, and everything that goes with it. It's torn apart many people who belong together. Jane and Simon, for instance."

"It's funny, she hasn't mentioned him for such a long time. But as I was leaving this morning, she asked me if I thought he'd ever come back. I said he will, of course. But, in fact, we don't even know if he's still alive."

Neither felt inclined to pursue that gloomy thought. They knew there was no use in trying to peer into the shadows of the unknown.

Chapter 35

Often mockingly called a fortress, Rosewall had become one in grim reality. Strewn with tents and campfires and other paraphernalia of a military camp, the once-lush gardens now lay trampled under horses' hooves, wagon wheels, and the heedless boots of soldiers. True, the fifty-odd militiamen gathered from the surrounding countryside were soldiers only in the loosest sense. Ranging from gangly youths to old men, they had in common only their willingness to defy those who would overthrow British rule in America.

With Robert injured, co-commander Louis Lambert ran the camp. Three weeks after his "accident" at Goose Creek, Robert's right arm remained useless, his strength drained by the slow healing process Dr. Jeffers had predicted. Clarissa, meanwhile, hovered between sickness and health, one day well enough to be up for a while, the next too weak to raise her head.

Despite all this, good order still prevailed inside the

house. Thanks to the proven reliability of Omar and Cuba, Jane was able to concentrate on nursing her ailing aunt and uncle and trying to calm the frightened, endlessly hand-wringing Mrs. Morley. Robert required especially close attention. When Louis came to confer with Robert, Jane watched closely. When she saw that her uncle was tiring, she announced that he must rest and the meeting was over. Both men grumbled, but they obeyed. It was clear to all that inside the house at least, the youngest member of the family was in charge.

One unforgettable day, Jane had to take charge outside as well. She was alone in the parlor snatching a rare moment of rest late in the afternoon when Omar appeared in the doorway. "Trouble outside, miss," he said. "Mr. Ainsley come, but Mr. Lambert won't let him in the gate."

"Mr. Ains—" Jane gasped, rose, and flew out of the house. She found Arthur Ainsley standing just outside the gate, his horse's reins in his hand. A sentry stood with his rifle pointed directly at Arthur, while Louis Lambert shouted at the visitor that he was not welcome.

"How dare you, sir!" Pushing her way through the crowd, Jane confronted Louis, her eyes blazing.

"He's a damn traitor, Miss Jane!"

"He is Mrs. Prentice's brother, and you will treat him courteously! Omar, open the gate and look after Mr. Ainsley's horse," she commanded. In seconds she was in Arthur's embrace. "Praise heaven, you're back!"

"Repatriated, Jane," he said. "After fifteen months of enforced idleness that seemed like fifteen years."

His face was pale and haggard, his hair gone gray. Ignoring the sullen stares of Louis and his soldiers, she took his arm and escorted him to the house.

"I've been to Goose Creek," he said on the way. "I know what happened."

"I'm so sorry, Uncle Arthur. To be away so long, and then find all that when you return—it's awful for you. But you must know that Brandon did come to the harbor that day. He *did* try to see you before they took you away."

"Yes, I know that now—and it will always be a great comfort to me."

"Tell me about Aunt Harriet. How is she?"

He heaved a sad sigh. "She remembers nothing. The first thing she said to me was how glad Brandon will be to hear that I've returned."

Jane closed her eyes in pain. "Oh, dear God!"

"It hasn't been a happy homecoming, Jane. Not a very happy time here, either, as I can see. And Clarissa's ill, I'm told. How is she?"

"Better today," Jane assured him. "She and Uncle Robert will be very happy to see you."

"Maybe not, after they hear what I have to say," he replied ominously.

The reunion was strangely subdued. Clarissa tearfully embraced her brother while Robert gave him a left-handed handshake. Both congratulated him on his safe return and offered sympathy on Brandon's death and Harriet's sad condition. Arthur told how after being confined for fifteen months, he and his fellow prisoners were put on a ship and taken not home but to Philadelphia, where they were turned over to the American authorities.

The exchange of family news was very polite. But as they all took seats in the parlor and talk inevitably turned to the war, Arthur and Robert suddenly faced each other not as kinsmen but as sworn enemies.

"So, Arthur," Robert began, "why, after all, have you come here?"

"First, Robert," Arthur countered, "tell me who those surly men are, turning your beautiful gardens into a wasteland?"

"They are my company of Loyalist militia. They may not look like much, but they're first-class fighters. Now I repeat, why are you here?"

"I come as a representative of the American government, which—"

"American government? There's no such thing in South Carolina!"

"There will be soon. Governor Rutledge will be arriving back in Charlestown as soon as the British garrison there is withdrawn. I met with him in Philadelphia, and he appointed me his deputy in this district."

"Rutledge—that fraud! Once he called himself president of something-or-other, now he calls himself a governor. Spare me, Arthur. This is nonsense."

Arthur's tone hardened. "Listen to me, Robert. There's a huge Patriot force out there preparing an assault on Rosewall. They, too, are first-class fighting men, and in far greater numbers than yours. Soon they'll have you surrounded and cut off from the outside, and they won't leave until you wave the white flag of surrender."

"Oh, come now, Arthur. Do you imagine the possibility of a siege has not occurred to us? We've stockpiled food, water, weapons, and powder, and one of our militiamen is a skilled physician. We have everything we need."

"Everything, perhaps—except time. However valiantly you defend this place, you cannot hold out forever. Meanwhile, have you no concern at all for your family's safety?"

"Everyone here knows they can leave whenever they like, even the servants. I've made that perfectly clear. Omar and Cuba could join the household of friends of ours in Charlestown, but they choose not to go. As for Clarissa and Jane—ask them yourself. You'll find that no one is here against their will. Really, Arthur, this conversation is becoming tedious."

Arthur leaned forward, urgency entering his voice. "I beg you, Robert, heed my words. Loyalists all over the backcountry are surrendering and applying to us for safe passage to Charlestown. I'm authorized to offer you the same courtesy, and I strongly urge you to accept. If you refuse, the results will not be pleasant. Rosewall is one of the last Loyalist strongholds left in the state, and Major Thomas McNeal, the Patriot commander, will stop at nothing to have it. For the same reason, the British should be just as determined to help you hold it. Instead, they're nowhere to be found. Wake up, man! British rule in America is a lost cause!"

Robert's reply was calm. "You misunderstand, Arthur. I'm not only working to preserve British rule in America, I am protecting what is mine. I'll see them all in hell before I'll turn my home over to a gang of outlaws. And now, please excuse me. I tire so easily these days..." Pulling himself to his feet, he walked stiffly but with serene dignity out of the room.

Arthur turned to Clarissa. "My dear sister! Don't you realize you're married to a madman who's determined to destroy himself? Don't let him destroy you as well. For God's sake, come away with me, now!"

Clarissa considered her reply carefully. "It's very strange. For years, the more Robert doted on this place, the more I longed to be away from it, and him. But now that he's surrounded by enemies, his fortunes falling into ruin, I find myself drawn closer to him than ever before. God knows, I have not been the perfect wife. But I *am* his wife. Wherever he is, that's where I belong." She then rose with the same calm dignity Robert had shown. "Now I must excuse myself, too. My illness has left me exhausted. Thank you for coming, Arthur." She gave him a sisterly kiss. "Jane will see you out—unless, of course, she decides to go with you. If so, Jane, I do hope this time you'll say good-bye before leaving."

After she had gone out, the puzzled Arthur frowned across the table at Jane. "What did she mean, 'this time'?" he asked.

"A year ago, I ran away from here," Jane told him. "Went to Charlestown to live at Cousin Hugh's. I'm back now only temporarily."

"A year ago, you say." Arthur pondered this. "Let's see. Could Simon's banishment to Nova Scotia have had anything to do with that?"

"It had everything to do—" Jane stopped in amazement. "But that was long after you left, Uncle Arthur! How do you know about all that?"

Arthur came around the table to sit next to Jane and, after looking around to make sure they were alone, spoke in a near whisper. "You may be glad to know that Simon is now back in this country."

Jane almost fainted at the news. "*What?* I can't believe it!"

"He left Nova Scotia last summer, and he's now in Pennsylvania. I haven't seen him myself, but when I was in Philadelphia I met a friend of his who had. A Mr. Murphy, who once worked with him. He told me that Simon dragged himself into the city last fall, half dead after a long and perilous journey over sea and land from Canada. He went straight to his family's home in Lancaster. It seems his sister's husband, who'd been a British prisoner, had died, and the widow and her children were in desperate need. After helping out there, Simon was planning to stop in Philadelphia once more, then come down here as soon as he could. He told our friend there was a young lady here named Jane, and he wanted to find her." Arthur added with a smile, "I told him I know her."

Jane was too worried about Simon to react to this. "But how could he dare? What happened? Was he repatriated, or pardoned?"

"Neither. He had the good luck to make friends with some people in a fishing village, and with their assistance, he simply left."

"Then he mustn't come here! It's too dangerous!"

"I wouldn't worry too much about that. The rebel side controls the backcountry now. I left word with Murphy that Simon should come directly to Goose Creek. And wouldn't it be a delightful surprise for him if you were there when he arrived?"

Jane felt torn. "Oh, how I'd love to be! But I can't leave here yet."

"Why not? This place is doomed, Jane. Surely you can see that."

"I do see it. I am a little older and wiser than when you saw me last. But it's not just that. Uncle Robert and Aunt Clarissa took me in when I was a homeless orphan with nowhere else to go. Now they're the ones in need. I will leave here again one day, and for good, but I can't desert them now."

Arthur sighed and gave up. "That's so like you—I might have known. Well, I'm afraid I really must go."

They rose, and Jane accompanied him out to the veranda, where he stopped for a final word. "Take care of yourself, Jane. I can't tell you how much I hope to see you and Simon together one day. He's a fine man. Brandon—God forgive me—never came close to deserving you."

Jane barely held back the tears as she gave him a hug and watched him walk quickly away.

Omar found Jane later, again resting a moment in the parlor. "Mr. Ainsley want you to go with him, miss."

She roused herself with an effort. "He suggested that, yes."

"Bad times coming here. Why you not go?"

"Really now, look who's talking! I once asked you the same question, Omar. Remember what you said?"

"Cuba won't run, and Omar not run without her."

"Well, I feel that way about my aunt and uncle. They won't leave, and I won't leave without them."

He frowned in stern disapproval. "You be crazy, miss."

"I guess maybe we're all crazy here, Omar."

Omar shook his head as he left, and Jane smiled, watching him go. It always lifted her spirits to talk to Omar. He was so direct, so honest. Then her smile faded as her thoughts turned to Simon. The tug-of-war between her heart and head began again—the one yearning desperately for his return, the other hoping that he would stay safely away.

A few days after Arthur's visit, Jane was taken aback to encounter Louis Lambert's younger brother, Jacques, leaving the house.

"*Bonjour*, mademoiselle!" He grinned and winked, always ready to start a flirtation. "And who might this beautiful young lady be?" he asked, looking her up and down.

"I'm Jane Prentice, Mr. Lambert," she told him. "We met years ago, in this very house—the day we heard independence was declared, to be exact."

Amazed, Jacques stared at her even harder. "But Jane Prentice was a skinny little girl then, whose looks only hinted at great beauty. The young lady before me now is a ravishing woman, and deliciously curvy to boot. My word, time does do wonders!" His stare was turning to a brazen leer.

Jane blushed with embarrassment and even a touch of secret pride. But her curt reply was coldly formal. "I'm surprised to see you here, Mr. Lambert."

"No, no, mademoiselle!" He winced in mock pain. "It's my pompous brother, Louis, who is Mr. Lambert. I am Jacques, your devoted servant." He winked at her again, adding, "And a great admirer of feminine beauty."

"I see you were just leaving," Jane said, her manner still polite but her tone still icy. "Don't let me detain you." She started to move past him, but his hand on her arm stopped her.

"Oh, please, *do* detain me, my little enchantress! I remember when we met at that party. You were just a child then, no match for the delectable Clarissa. Now, I'm not so sure. I would so like to see her before I go. May I have that pleasure?"

"That's out of the question. She's unwell and mustn't be disturbed."

"Not even for someone who has adored her since he was a boy? What a pity. I should have liked to compare the two of you, to discover which is the lovelier. Now how am I to know?"

Jane's patience had reached its limit. "Surely, sir, you must be here for more important business than idle flirtation."

"Indeed, I came on behalf of the Patriot forces assembled not far from here to urge your uncle to surrender this camp or face an all-out assault. And what did I get for my trouble? My own brother insults me, and your uncle orders me to leave."

"Then by all means, do so."

"Gladly—if you'll come with me." Jacques stepped closer, a seductive smile creasing his lean weather-beaten face. "You can be my own personal prisoner. And I promise you, I shall treat you very, *very* tenderly."

Jane stepped back, glaring at him. "Three days ago, Mr. Arthur Ainsley, a respected Patriot leader, offered to take me away from here. He is a man of impeccable honor, but I refused his offer. That being so, can you imagine my contempt for yours?"

"I stand rebuked, mademoiselle," he said meekly, but his black eyes continued to glint with amusement.

"You do, indeed, sir. Good day." Jane disappeared into the house.

"A saucy wench, that one," Jacques said as a sentry escorted him to the gate. "She badly needs taming. If I could get my hands on her, I'd—"

But the sentry was not interested in this cocky rebel's leering speculations. Taking Jacques by the arm, he pushed him roughly out the gate and slammed it shut.

They arrived during the night, not with fifes and drums and a flourish of arms, but silently, under cover of darkness. Waking to a cold November dawn, Jane could see smoke from their campfires curling up out of the mist beyond the eastern section of the wall. The eerie silence felt menacing.

Suddenly the sharp crack of a musket shattered the stillness, followed an instant later by a shuddering thud as the ball struck the roof. With a gasp Jane drew back from the window. Silence fell again. It was only one shot, but it was enough. The attackers had announced themselves. The siege was under way.

Chapter 36

Within minutes, the Rosewall militia was mobilized. Lookouts on the stone wall scanned the outside terrain from wooden turrets. Robert kept watch from his third-floor observatory with his long handheld telescope. In the yard below, men nervously fingered their weapons. Hours had passed since the lone musket shot. It appeared that the Battle of Rosewall would be a battle of nerves more than guns.

In the late afternoon, the rebels finally opened fire on the guards at the gate. After a short but intense fight, several wounded attackers were carried away by their comrades, and three men lay groaning on the gravel path inside the wall. They were moved to the "hospital," a converted storage shed next to the main house, where they would be looked after by Mr. Warren. An old soldier with a little experience tending the sick and wounded, Warren was not exactly the "skilled physician" Robert had boasted of to Arthur.

The next morning, Louis reported that five men had deserted during the night. "The fainthearted soon quit," he growled. "And good riddance."

Robert was not comforted. "Yesterday our strength dropped from fifty-seven to fifty-four. And now we're down to forty-nine."

Around noon, the uneasy calm was broken by a burst of gunfire near one of the turrets, and Louis came to Robert with another grim report: The lookout in the turret had been killed. "Frank Lester, it was. Some villain with a torch got under the turret, apparently meaning to fire it. Lester must have stuck his head out to get a shot at the man and—"

"And made a perfect target of himself!" Robert growled.

"He did get the man down below first," Louis pointed out.

"One for one is not an acceptable exchange, Louis. They have far more men than we do! Now forty-nine has become forty-eight."

Jane seethed as Robert strode back to the house. "I heard all that, Uncle Robert. Good men have died, and you talk only of numbers!"

"This is war," he snapped. "Numbers mean the difference between victory and defeat. If that bothers you, perhaps you should have left with Arthur."

"Perhaps I should have," she replied sharply, and turned away.

A steady rain fell throughout that second day. There was no further sign of the enemy. Some militiamen declared that the big-talking rebels were discouraged and had slunk away defeated. Robert knew better. But he tried to sound optimistic when he visited the ailing Clarissa. It grieved him to see her laid low by her stubborn illness.

"Believe me, my dear, if I could choose between vanquishing our foes and having you back in the bloom of health, I would gladly choose the second."

"Thank you, Robert, but I fear you have no such choice," she said with a wispy smile. "Now tell me, how is it going out there?"

"The men think we've seen the last of the rebels. They could be right. We will prevail. That much is certain."

"No, it isn't," Clarissa replied. "What is certain is that whatever happens will happen to us together. And that's all that matters."

Coming in to bid her aunt good night, Jane paused in the doorway. Robert was kneeling beside the bed, Clarissa's arms around his neck. Jane turned away, unseen. *Something good comes from something bad,* she thought. *The worse things get, the stronger their love becomes.*

At that moment, in a forest clearing half a mile away, Captain Jacques Lambert stepped into the tent of Major Thomas McNeal, commander of the forces besieging Rosewall. "You sent for me, sir?"

McNeal, a burly man with brick red hair and a square jaw, handed him a letter. "A courier left this with my orderly this afternoon. It's from Arthur Ainsley."

Jacques began to read, mumbling aloud. "'As Governor Rutledge's representative for this district, I am authorized to instruct you regarding the campaign against Rosewall Plantation. Maintain your siege, but do not attack until my assistant arrives in a few days to instruct you further—'"

Scowling in anger, Jacques broke off. "Why, this is outrageous, sir! After sweating blood to capture this place, we should stand aside while one of Ainsley's cronies comes and takes all the credit?"

"Ainsley's a powerful man. We can't afford to ignore this."

A cunning glint came to Jacques's eyes as he handed the letter back. "But we could lose it. Since it wasn't put directly into your hands, it could've been soaked by the rain or blown away by the wind before you saw it."

"That's true, it could," the commander agreed thoughtfully.

"The next attack is ready, sir. Just say the word."

McNeal slowly tore the letter in half. "The word is dawn tomorrow."

At dawn the next day, the full horror of war burst upon the defenders of Rosewall. First came another assault at the gate. Suffering no casualties, the defenders quickly congratulated each other, convinced they had driven off the enemy. But the action at the gate was only a diversion. The real attack came in the rear. The turret on the south wall was set ablaze, and the guard was forced to abandon his post. Within seconds, rope ladders were flung over the wall. The unthinkable was happening: The great fortress was being invaded. Rebels, shrieking like demons from hell, swarmed over the wall to be met by other demons, the fierce-eyed defenders.

The two Rosewall commanders screamed themselves hoarse, urging their men on to valiant action. Their voices could barely be heard over the explosions of muskets, the clash and clang of swords and bayonets, the shouts and cries of soldiers in hand-to-hand combat. Men who had been neighbors just a few months before were now fighting a desperate battle to the death.

Inside, Omar calmly watched the battle through a crack in the boards he and Robert had nailed over the downstairs windows. The entire downstairs was now cloaked in a dusky gloom. Upstairs, Clarissa lay motionless in her bed, listening. In her room down the hall, Mrs. Morley cried hysterically, "Dear Lord, those bloodthirsty savages will slaughter us all!" Jane tried to calm her, but to no avail. *Thank God for Cuba,* she thought. Only Cuba, with her unquenchable cheerfulness, could keep Mrs. Morley from dissolving in panic.

After twenty minutes of ferocious combat, the Rosewall militia succeeded in repelling the invaders, who scrambled back up their ladders and away. But there was no celebrating among the victors. Dazed and exhausted, they surveyed a bloody battleground strewn with fallen soldiers, then turned to the grim task of separating the wounded from the dead, their own from the enemy.

Jane, who had come out to help, shuddered at the gruesome scene. Soon, kneeling beside a man lying facedown near the base of the wall, she turned him over—and drew back, gasping in horror. It was Jacques Lambert, barely alive, his shirt blood soaked, his tanned and weathered face unearthly pale.

"My God!" Cradling his head, she called frantically to a militiaman, "Get Mr. Warren, quickly! And tell Mr. Lambert his brother's here!"

"Do not trouble yourself, mademoiselle." Jacques smiled weakly. "To die in the arms of a charming young lady...What more could a soldier ask? Although..." His voice, and the light in his eyes, were fading rapidly. "I would have preferred...the lovely... Clarissa..."

Jane stepped back as Louis Lambert rushed to Jacques's side. He dropped to his knees beside his fallen brother. "Hold on, my boy! Warren will look after you. I beg of you, stay with us!"

But Jacques had floated away. Bending over the lifeless body, Louis bowed his head and sobbed in uncontrollable grief.

"I'm so sorry, Mr. Lambert," Jane said softly, laying a hand on his shoulder. But her words were as useless as the tears filling her eyes.

The rest of the day was spent burying the dead. It was hard for men saying farewell to fallen comrades to give the same respectful treatment to their enemy. But

Robert had ordered it, so they did their best. Robert presided alone over the burial ceremonies held in the southwest corner of the garden—Louis Lambert was nowhere to be seen. Jane gazed dully at Robert as he stood next to the shallow grave prepared for the dead soldiers—exactly where a glorious row of camellias had once bloomed. She knew the horror of this day would haunt her in nightmares forever. She also knew something else: It was time for Uncle Robert to face the truth.

Late that night when the house was quiet, she found Robert at his desk in the study, frowning over a list of figures. "Come in, Jane," he said. "I've just been calculating our losses. Six dead, ten wounded, three deserted. One of the deserters, I regret to say, is Louis."

"Really!" Jane exclaimed. "So *that's* why he wasn't at the burials."

"Yes. Losing Jacques just took his heart out of it, he said." Robert shrugged. "Well, every man must make these decisions for himself. So we're down to twenty-nine now, but the other side left nine dead and fourteen wounded today. In the end, we hurt them more than they hurt us."

"That must please you very much," Jane said acidly.

Robert sighed with long-suffering patience. "Jane, I know you think I'm made of stone, thinking only of numbers. But names and faces no longer mean anything to me—not since we lost Brandon. I used up all my grief on him."

"I grieve for Brandon, too, but that doesn't make me forget about everyone else. How many men must die for no good reason before you realize—"

"No good reason!" Robert's voice hardened. "You still don't know what we're fighting for? What have you been doing for the past five years?"

Fire came to Jane's eyes. "What have I been doing? Slowly, painfully realizing that I'm an American—*that's* what I've been doing! I now see many things very clearly, and for everyone's sake, it's time you saw them, too!"

Robert stared at Jane as if he had never seen her before. "Good God! You, too? Well, if it's all so clear to you—tell me, what should I see?"

Drawing a long breath, Jane answered in a sad, gentle tone. "That for you, Uncle, the war is over. It's over, and you've lost."

He glared at her. "Arthur was right," he muttered. "I should have sent you all out before. But it's not too late. Tomorrow out you go, all of you."

Jane shook her head. "That's impossible. Aunt Clarissa's too ill, and Mrs. Morley would die of fright. Besides, I'm not going to turn my back on you at such a time. Please, Uncle. Can't we discuss this reasonably?"

He rose slowly to his feet. "Tomorrow, with or without you, I continue the fight," he said between teeth clenched in fury. "That is all I have to say to you. Good night." And it was he who turned his back on her.

———

They say it's darkest just before the dawn, she thought, standing at her window hours later, staring up at cold stars that studded an intensely black sky. *Dear Lord, will the dawn ever come?* Soon, as she often did when standing at her north-facing window, she focused her gaze toward far-off Pennsylvania. *Simon . . . will I ever, ever see you . . . ?* The question was unanswerable—except, perhaps, with that ever-elusive *someday.*

Chapter 37

Major Thomas McNeal was angry. Angry at himself for allowing a foolish over-the-wall invasion that cost him twenty-three good men, including the excellent Captain Jacques Lambert. And angry at the stubborn master of Rosewall, whose defiance had cost so many lives. Now, however, McNeal finally had the ultimate weapon at hand. It had taken days to arrive, and backbreaking labor for a dozen men all night long to haul it into position. But at last, at the favored hour of attack—just before dawn—Robert Prentice would pay for his stubbornness.

"Ready, sir," the gun crew sergeant reported.

"Fire," snapped McNeal.

Within seconds, the cannon roared.

Jane, who had just fallen asleep after a restless night, sat bolt upright in bed. She had heard that earthshaking sound before, but never so terrifyingly close. A moment later, Robert shouted at her from the hall.

"Jane, I've got Clarissa. Call Mrs. Morley and get out! Quickly now!"

Major McNeal grimaced in annoyance. The first shot had sailed harmlessly over the plantation house. "Too high!" he barked at the gun crew. "Lower your sights fifteen degrees and prepare to fire again."

With Cuba's help, Robert established his sick wife in a makeshift bed beneath a tree far from the house. Suddenly he realized that Jane and Mrs. Morley had not followed.

"Where are those women?" he growled.

"I go get 'em," Cuba said, quickly returning to the house.

As Cuba reached the central staircase, the cannon boomed again. This time the great house took a direct hit, shaking all over.

Cuba peered into the gloom above. "Miss Jane? You up there?"

Jane's anxious voice came back to her from the top of the stairs. "Yes, but I can't find Mrs. Morley!"

Cuba hurried upstairs. "I find her, you go on out."

"Not till she's—"

"I find her, I said! Go on now, scat!" Cuba's sharp tone permitted no dispute. She took Jane by the shoulders and pointed her down the stairs.

Robert roamed the yard, warning his frightened men against their worst enemy—panic. He cursed the enemy outside. "Damn those villains! Cannon, for

God's sake! Who would have dreamed they'd resort to such a cowardly, dishonorable..." Fury choked him into silence.

Upstairs, Cuba groped along the dark, dust-filled hallway. "Mrs. Morley!" she called. "Where are you, ma'am?" She got no answer, but her keen ears picked up a pitiful wail coming from somewhere up above.

"Lordy, not up there!" she groaned. Cuba climbed the narrow staircase to the lofty room she had never before entered—the master's observatory. Mrs. Morley stood before the tall windows, arms uplifted as if appealing to heaven for salvation. A pearl pink dawn tinted the eastern sky. It was a pretty sight, in its way—and it was the last thing Cuba saw before the next cannonball struck.

Through his spyglass, Major McNeal studied the jagged ruins at the top of the house. "Excellent." He turned to his crew. "Now set your sights five degrees above dead level. We'll let the gun cool down a bit, then we'll go for the wall."

As Jane ran back to look for Cuba and Mrs. Morley, Omar emerged from the darkness and smoke in the house behind him.

"You not go in there, miss," he commanded.

"But Cuba, and Mrs.—"

"Omar found 'em." His voice was low, his noble features calm. "Ain't no use, miss. They both dead."

Jane froze in shock. *Please,* she thought desperately,

let this be just another nightmare to be endured. "No, Omar," she cried. "They can't be!"

"Your friend gone, miss. Cuba gone, too. Now, time for Omar to go."

"W-what do you mean? Go where?"

"Yonder." The black man gazed westward beyond the wall. "Over the far mountains, where the sun goes down."

Jane, who had once urged him to run away, now clung to his arm in a frantic effort to prevent it. "Omar, don't! You'll die out there!"

"You not worry, Omar find his way." Gently freeing himself from her grasp, he gave her a light pat on the cheek. "You good little lady, Miss Jane. Heart full of kindness. May blessings fall down upon you, all your days. Good-bye."

Blinded by brimming tears, Jane could only stare helplessly after him as he strode away, quickly disappearing from view. Then, just as she had when Brandon died, she sank down on the steps and rocked back and forth, lost in grief. *Blown with the windy tempest of my heart* . . . Those words of anguish kept coming back to her. Buffeted by the terrible tempest of the times, her heart was blown desolate and bare.

In the yard, Robert was trying desperately to rally his troops once more. "For God's sake, are you all cowards? Get up on the wall. Return fire!"

"How can we return cannon fire with no cannon of our own?" one of the men shouted at him.

"You have muskets!" Robert shouted back. "Use them! Use whatever you have—sticks, stones, your bare hands if you have to—but fight!"

Another man, clutching a flag made of a piece of tattered white cloth tied to a pole, spoke up. "Sir, we have done what mortal men can, but now it's time to—"

"To what?" Robert bellowed. "Submit, and cover ourselves in shame? Out of my sight!" He struck awkwardly at the despised white flag. As it spun out of the man's hands, the cannon's thunder rolled across the sky again.

The ground shook. The east wall quivered, and when the cloud of dust and debris settled, a huge crack zigzagged from top to bottom.

"The wall's going!" the men cried, running for cover. As he watched his men scatter, something snapped deep within Robert's fevered mind.

"Run, you yellow dogs!" he raged like a madman. "You may be beaten, but not I—never! Look how a true king's man defies the rebel horde!"

Brandishing a musket, he ran toward the east wall.

Scanning his target through a spyglass, Major McNeal could hardly believe his eyes. "Some lunatic's up on the wall waving a musket!" he told his gun crew. "Set your sights five degrees to the right, and fire away."

The great gun roared for the fifth time. When the dust cleared, the wall was cracked in another place, and the "lunatic" was no longer there.

"Now we'll let them think about it for a while," the major told his crew. "Perhaps they've had enough."

Jane was the first to reach her uncle, who was lying senseless at the base of the badly damaged wall. George Warren, the militia's physician, and another man were coming with a stretcher. Jane watched in an agony of suspense as Robert was carried off to the makeshift hospital. Unsure whether he was dead or alive, she breathed a sigh of relief when she saw his eyelids flutter. Barely conscious but still defiant, he mumbled, "Got to keep fighting. Never give up ... never ..."

An eerie silence had fallen over the grounds. In one corner, Clarissa lay very still on her pallet, either unaware of what was happening or no longer caring. In the yard, the remaining militiamen, leaderless and bewildered, milled about aimlessly. Jane's wandering gaze fell on the white flag lying a few feet from where she stood. And as she stared at it, a dreadful weight seemed to lift from her shoulders. Suddenly she knew exactly what to do.

When George Warren returned a few minutes later, he stopped short in astonishment to see the militiamen lined up behind a new leader, all heading straight for the gate. The guard drew back the bolt, and as the great gate swung open, the first rays of the rising sun glinted on its iron bars.

With the white flag fluttering high in the morning breeze, Jane Prentice led the vanquished defenders of Rosewall out to surrender.

Chapter 38

Although greatly pleased with his conquest of Rosewall, Major McNeal did not feel particularly generous toward its former defenders. He spent the morning restoring some order to the war-torn Rosewall grounds. In the afternoon, flanked by several junior officers, he set up his own "military court" in the dining room. Now he was grilling George Warren.

"I'm rapidly losing patience, Mr. Warren. Mr. Lambert, who's been in our custody since yesterday, has been most uncooperative. And my company doctor says that Mr. Prentice is unfit to appear before this court. That leaves you, as third in rank. What do you have to say for yourself?"

Standing stiffly correct, Warren replied with dignity. "I can say only that I cared for all the wounded as best I could. Yours, as well as ours."

"For which we are most grateful, sir. Nevertheless, the criminal refusal of this garrison to submit to our authority has cost many lives. You and everyone else involved will be held responsible. We will therefore—"

A soldier interrupted him to whisper a short message.

The color drained from McNeal's face. "Damn!" His mind raced. "All right, tell him to wait. I'll see him as soon as I . . ." His unfinished sentence hung in the air as he stared at the stranger who strode in.

"You will see me *now*," Simon Cordwyn said coldly.

There was dead silence as McNeal jumped to his feet. "I—I don't think we've met, sir."

"Then this will serve as my introduction."

Simon handed him a letter, then turned to the prisoner. "Mr. Warren? I'm Simon Cordwyn, assistant to the governor's deputy, Arthur Ainsley."

"Honored, sir," Warren replied with a nod.

"I'll want to speak with you later. Guard, escort this gentleman out."

Seeing the guard hesitate, McNeal hastily nodded to him. "Yes, we'll take a recess now." He handed Simon's letter back with a glassy smile. "It's a great pleasure to have you join us, sir. Indeed, we welcome your—"

"Major McNeal." Simon cut him off. "We must talk in private."

McNeal blinked. "Well, I've taken the parlor as my headquarters, so—"

"That will do." Simon strode out, and McNeal, his fellow officers staring in amazement after him, meekly followed.

Behind the closed doors of the once-grand parlor, Simon's simmering anger boiled over. "How dare you set yourself up as a minister of justice? You have no such authority, and you know it!"

"We suffered heavy losses here, Mr. Cordwyn! These criminals deserve to be punished!"

"They fought for what they believe in—just as you did. That doesn't make them criminals. Now, where is the Prentice family?"

"Mr. Prentice is in our field hospital. He fell from the wall during the fighting, and he's out of his head besides. The ladies are confined to their rooms upstairs. And lucky they are to have such comfortable quarters."

Simon's fierce look burned into the other man. "Major McNeal, you have inflicted wanton destruction on this house and caused needless loss of life, all in defiance of instructions sent to you in a letter from Mr. Ainsley."

"The devil you say!" McNeal pretended outrage. "I saw no such letter!"

"Didn't see it? Or chose to ignore it?"

"Look here, I resent your—"

"Either way, McNeal, I'm instructing you now. Your so-called court is disbanded. The Prentice ladies will be released from confinement and allowed free movement within the house. You and your men will immediately vacate."

This was too much for McNeal. "Dammit, Cordwyn, I'm in command here, and I'll not take orders from the likes of you!"

Simon drew a weary sigh as he thought back over his hectic career as a Continental agent. Why did the worst trouble so often come not from the British but from out-of-control fellow Americans?

"A word of advice, Major." His low voice carried an unmistakable threat. "When Mr. Ainsley and other officials arrive here tomorrow, they're not going to be pleased with what they find. You're already in trouble. Don't make it any worse for yourself. I'm going to interview Mr. Warren—and you're going back in there to tell your men to clear out. *Now!*"

McNeal scowled, but he knew when to quit. "As you say," he grumbled.

After his interview with George Warren, Simon started up the ruined stairs. On the second floor, everything was desolation—shattered glass, cracked walls, fallen plaster, overturned tables, massive roof beams jutting crazily through gaping holes in the ceiling. Stepping carefully through the rubble, he looked in at the first open doorway.

Pale and drawn, with a heavy woolen shawl over her shoulders, Clarissa looked nothing at all like the elegant lady she had once been. She sat in an armchair by the window and stared wide-eyed in disbelief when Simon stepped into the room. "Simon Cordwyn, as I live and breathe! I never expected to see you again."

"Hello, Clarissa. I'm sorry to hear you've been ill, and about the terrible things that have happened here."

"I'm getting better, thank you. But you can't imagine what we've been through! First we lost Brandon—"

"I know. I've just come from Goose Creek. It was shocking news."

"And now we've lost our Cuba, and sweet old Mrs. Morley. Poor dears, they died together."

"Yes, Mr. Warren told me. It's very sad. And where is Jane?"

"In Mrs. Morley's room. It's just down the hall, last door on the right. She's spent most of the day in there, seems to find comfort in it. There's no life left in her eyes, she's in such pain. Go on, don't let me detain you. Hurry and find her. And, Simon..." Her grave eyes held him a moment longer. "This time, never let her out of your sight again."

He found Jane curled up on Mrs. Morley's bed, fully dressed but apparently asleep. Kneeling beside the bed, he studied her face. She looked strangely peaceful. Then, as if sensing another presence, she opened her eyes and gazed at him. But her face was blank, her dull eyes, as Clarissa had said, showing no spark of life.

Simon greeted her with a smile, hoping to see a smile in return. "I hope I'm not disturbing you," he said softly.

She sat up with some effort, still blank-faced, staring at him. "Simon?" she murmured. "Is it really you?"

"Don't you know me?"

"You've been gone so long, I ..." Her voice trailed off.

"Yes, I have—far too long, and sick with worry

about you every minute of it. But I'm back at last, and thank God I've found you safe!"

Her empty gaze drifted across the room. "I shouldn't be, you know. So many have died here. Why shouldn't I have died, too?"

"Don't say that, Jane! We've both survived this war somehow, and the survivors have to carry on."

"I don't feel like a survivor," she said bleakly. "But if I am one, then you are doubly so. Being banished to the far north—was it awful?"

"Only because I was so far from you. But I was lucky. Some good people took me in and helped me to get back here. I'll tell you all about it later. Right now we need to talk about something far more important." He sat down beside her and took her hand. "I keep thinking of our first meeting, so long ago. That day you wandered into my classroom, you remember? You were so charming, I wanted to pat you on the head. Little did I realize, you'd eventually take possession of *my* head—and my heart, soul, and whole being. I don't know if you have any such feelings for me or not, but if you do..." He paused, waiting for some response. "Do you, Jane?"

She was slow to reply, gazing intently at him. "I'm thinking back to a long-ago day, too," she said finally. "To that day here at Rosewall, when you told me you were leaving, going back to Pennsylvania. Not a day has gone by since then that I haven't thought of you, wishing you were here with me. And yet... I've always felt that I hardly knew you."

"Well, there's a remedy for that now, and that's exactly what I want to talk to you about. We have the rest of our lives to get to know each other—in the best possible way—as husband and wife. That is, if you'll consent to marry me. And someday, when all this terror is over, we'll know what it feels like to be together permanently. Happily. In peace."

Still he waited. And looking into her eyes, he began to see a spark of will to go on living, faintly glimmering, gradually returning.

"Could it be, Simon? Could it really be?"

"It could if you say so, my dearest. And who knows?" He drew her into a sheltering embrace. "If our luck holds, maybe someday can even come soon."

"*Someday . . .*" She whispered the word—a word she had hated for so long but that now suddenly sounded like the promise of a golden dream. For now she finally knew what it meant. It meant her future life with Simon.

At last, they were almost there.

Epilogue—1782

Tragically, the Battle of Rosewall occurred weeks
after the British surrender at Yorktown had already made all further fighting pointless. The
British continued to occupy Charlestown for another
year, not leaving for good until December of 1782.
But long before that, it had become clear to everyone
that British rule in America was at an end.

Revenge against the Loyalists soon raised its ugly
head in South Carolina. Nowhere else had their resistance to the rebellion been so fierce, and nowhere else
were they punished so severely. Once-respected citizens became homeless, hated refugees, their homes
and property confiscated.

Robert and Clarissa Prentice were among the lucky
ones, taken in at Goose Creek by the Ainsleys, who
stayed on there while Charlestown remained occupied. In this quiet haven, Clarissa slowly recovered
and accepted their hard new reality with serenity. For
Robert, recovery was more difficult. His fall during

battle had left him with a limp, and his right arm remained useless from the gunshot wound. Harriet, still in her mental fog, believed that all Robert's injuries were received in the fighting at Rosewall.

Robert's deepest sense of defeat had come with the loss of his beloved plantation. Arthur used all his influence to try to obtain the return of Rosewall to its rightful owner. But although Robert continued to hold out hope that these efforts would eventually succeed, Arthur encountered only failure.

Meanwhile, Jane and Simon were happy just to be near each other. They began to make plans for the future, but first another separation would have to be endured. Simon traveled north to finish certain business in connection with his work for the Continental Army. Jane remained at Goose Creek, doing what she could to help, as always. They wrote to each other as often as they could and counted the days until Simon could return to South Carolina.

When he returned in the spring, wedding invitations were sent to Hugh and Lydia, and to Peter and Marianne Quincy. The Quincys sent back good wishes but could not come. Marianne was expecting again and was afraid to go far from home. Hugh and Lydia made the trip out from Charlestown, and when they arrived at Goose Creek, Robert greeted his cousin with a nervous half smile. After only a few awkward moments, they were friends again, reunited by the kind of happy event neither had seen in many years.

Jane and Hugh spent a few quiet moments together in fond reunion, during which Hugh presented her with a small package tied with a bit of yellow ribbon. "This came from the most unlikely of places, my dear," he told her. "But I still thought you might like to have it."

"Oh, Cousin Hugh, you know I wrote to you that people shouldn't bring us wedding presents," she admonished him gently.

He smiled. "I think you'll forgive my defying your wishes just this once."

Jane opened the package, and in it she discovered her little gold locket. Its slender chain was broken, but the tiny curl of her mother's chestnut hair lay inside, just as it had for so many years.

"My God," she breathed. "Where on earth..." The words caught in her throat as she looked up at Hugh, tears welling in her eyes.

"It was right there in our kitchen all along, lying in the dust under Lydia's wood box. When I tore that rotted old box out to make her a new one, there it was."

Overcome with joy and gratitude, Jane threw her arms around him. "Thank you so much, Cousin Hugh! For everything—and especially for the most wonderful present I could ever imagine."

The next morning, while her proud family beamed with pleasure, Jane and Simon were married in a simple but beautiful ceremony at Saint James Church in Goose Creek. With heads bowed beneath the British Royal Coat of Arms—emblem of an era that had passed into history—they solemnly vowed to love, honor, and cherish, forsaking all others . . .

Jane would always think of the few days following her wedding, spent at a small inn nearby, as a time of serene bliss. *Truly,* she thought, *love is one of the great forces of the universe.*

It was like returning to earth from paradise then, when they came back to the Dudley house, to stay there one more day before leaving to spend the summer in Simon's hometown of Lancaster, in distant Pennsylvania.

But first, a moment of quiet solemnity. In the afternoon, they walked to a remote corner of the Dudley lands and stood before a grave, the final resting place of Brandon Ainsley, Lieutenant, American Loyalist Cavalry, who had died a hero's death at the age of twenty-three. As they had so many times before, Jane's eyes brimmed with tears, while Simon held her hand. Neither spoke. The only sound was the chirping of birds in the forest. Words would have seemed a jarring intrusion on the deep peacefulness around them.

The next morning, they said their good-byes, climbed into the carriage given to them by the Ainsleys, and started their journey north.

The trip was long and grueling, over primitive roads, but Jane was dazzled by new vistas constantly opening up before her. Other parts of America were so different from lush South Carolina. She was charmed by the town of Lancaster, nestled in the rolling farmland of southern Pennsylvania. Hardly more than a rustic frontier village compared to the gracious Charlestown, it had a bustling vitality of its own. Best of all, Simon's sister, Becky, and her two children—Jack Junior, aged fourteen, and Frances, twelve—embraced Jane as if they had known her all their lives. As Simon had hoped, his young wife took a liking to his family, and they to her.

One day they all paid a visit to the nearby cemetery and stood somberly at another grave, that of Becky's husband, Jack Herndon. Released by the British after two and a half years as a prisoner, he had made his way home a broken man, his health shattered, and died a few months later.

"He was a good man," Becky said softly. "But, perhaps, a foolish one."

"He was a good man, and most assuredly a brave one," Simon declared.

And these, Jane silently recalled, *were just my thoughts that day at Brandon's grave.*

During that peaceful summer, Jane and Simon explored the town and walked all over the hills and fields that surrounded it, enjoying the beauty of the countryside. To Jane, it looked remarkably like England. She and Simon spent time at his sister's store, Herndon's Mercantile. She met many of his old friends and was impressed by their high regard for him.

But there was one serious matter that they still needed to decide. Simon had long dreamed of starting a school, and now was the time. But where? Jane could tell that he dreaded the question, fearing it might cause disagreement between them. *This won't do,* she thought. She decided to clear up the matter herself.

Her opportunity came late one afternoon toward the end of summer, when they stopped on a hillside during one of their walks and looked out over the town. "I've seen some good sites for a school here, Simon," Jane remarked. "What do you think?"

He stared intently at the green hills in the distance. "Yes, seems to me there are several that would be ideal. But I wouldn't make such a decision by myself. It must be made by both of us. And I know how difficult it would be for you to—"

"Simon, my dear, listen to me." She took his arm and turned him to look at her. "Years ago, when you left the South to come back here to live, you said it was because your sister needed you, and that was very admirable. But you had another reason, too, a far more important one. You said you couldn't live in a society that depended on slave labor. That must mean you wouldn't want our children brought up in that kind of society, either. Am I right?"

Simon considered his answer carefully. "Jane, I know that your kinfolk always treated their servants kindly. But it's still an evil system, and sooner or later it will have to end. It may not happen in our lifetime. Perhaps it will be our children, or their children, who have to face that terrible struggle—and a terrible one it will be. But when it comes, I'd like to think they'll be on the right side of it."

"So would I." Jane smiled into his eyes. "It's settled, then. Our new baby will be raised right here in Pennsylvania."

Speechless with delight, Simon gathered her into his arms, and they stood there together until the sun disappeared in a golden blaze below the dark green hills.

With no way to be certain that a letter would ever arrive safely in South Carolina, Jane worried over how to tell everyone there about her good news, and about their decision. She wanted to make one last trip south, but as the weeks slipped by the idea seemed less and less practical. The first chill of fall would soon sharpen the air. And besides, travel could prove excessively wearing, if not downright perilous, in her condition.

She and Simon were still pondering the problem when, one blazing August afternoon, Jane received a packet of letters Arthur had sent with a trusted friend who was traveling to Pennsylvania. There was a note from Arthur himself, another from Hugh and Lydia, and a third, somewhat longer, from Robert.

Arthur wrote that he and Harriet were still living at Goose Creek, anxiously awaiting the day—expected soon—when the British would evacuate Charlestown and they might return to their home. They had heard that it was wrecked after serving for years as a British military barracks. But of course, Arthur added, it can be restored. Harriet still sometimes fretted about why

Brandon never came to visit, but those lapses were growing less frequent. Arthur dared hope that eventually she would be her old self again.

Hugh and Lydia sent word that they were both well, and that Hugh's shop was prospering as never before. They were even thinking of moving to larger quarters. Peter and Marianne, they wrote, were expecting their baby in November, and might move on to Georgia in the spring. ("Foolish notion!" Hugh added in the margin. "Young people never know when they're well off.")

These brief communications were deeply appreciated by Jane. But it was the letter from Robert that held her the longest.

In Charlestown, 28 July 1782

My dearest niece,

I take up my pen in the hope this finds you and your husband well, and to inform you of events here. All hope of recovering Rosewall has been lost—the rebels recently sold it at auction. Its new owner, a wealthy planter from Beaufort, plans to knock down the wall, and since the name Rosewall will then be meaningless, to discard it. Clarissa and I do not wish to know what its new name will be. Indeed, we try not to think about it.

Recently we returned to Charlestown, and to our house on Legare Street—though, of course, as soon as the rebels retake the city, that property will be seized as well. The British are no longer an effective force here, and everyone expects them to pull out soon. When that happens, we Loyalists will be like lambs left to the mercy of wolves. Hundreds are leaving every day. Arthur is convinced we'll all eventually be allowed to return, perhaps even recover our property. But that is not for me. I am an Englishman, and if Englishmen are not welcome here, I will end my days in my native land. Clarissa and I sail for England in a few weeks. Clarissa is with me in this, and knowing that, I am content.

I am truly sorry for the grief I caused Arthur, and Hugh, and Simon. I acted as their enemy, and they repaid me only with kindness. From you, my dear, I especially beg forgiveness. I should not have tried to force you to remain a prim English girl. Believe me, it was only because I loved you too well.

Clarissa and I send you all our love, with fervent hopes for your happiness and good fortune in the new nation you and Simon will help to build. May the ocean we are about to cross never be so wide as to prevent English and American hands from being clasped in friendship, both now and through all generations.

Until we may meet again, I remain,
Your devoted servant and loving uncle,

Robert

Without a word, but with tears in her eyes, Jane handed the letter to Simon. He read it through quickly, then handed it back. His face was grim, and his voice dark with anger when he spoke.

"We'll live to regret this insane fury being directed at Loyalists. America needs all the brains, energy, and ability it can muster to turn this sprawling, disorderly land into a unified nation. And like fools, we're chasing away some of our best people."

"Thank you, Simon," Jane murmured. "I know it would mean everything to Uncle Robert to hear you say that. And when they send us word of where they are, I'll write and tell him that you did."

"So you don't want to try to get back there once more before they leave? There may still be time."

Jane shook her head. "There's no need." She held up Robert's letter. "Everything's already been said, right here."

So it was that the girl who had been born Lady Jane Prentice, daughter of an English earl, became the young wife and mother called Jane Prentice Cordwyn of Pennsylvania. But she would never forget the land of her heritage, and the tiny gold locket around her neck remained an unbreakable link to the old world she had left far behind.

And in that same spirit of sad, sweet remembrance, she never forgot the people and places she had known and loved in South Carolina. Visitors to the Cordwyn home years later never failed to admire the splendid bright red roses that covered the picket fence running the length of their garden. But to Jane, these roses were much more than a fragrant delight. They were a daily reminder to her of those who survived the war, those who did not, those who stayed behind when it was over, those who moved on, and those who sailed away across the sea—all of them living on in her memory. Omar and Cuba, too, who had been loyal friends when she needed them most, she always remembered.

No one ever knew what became of Omar. But his parting wish for Jane did come true. Blessings fell down upon her, all the rest of her days.

SUGGESTED
FURTHER READING

Davis, Burke. *Yorktown: The Winning of American Independence.* New York: Harper & Row, 1969.

De Pauw, Linda Grant. *Founding Mothers: Women in America in the Revolutionary Era.* Boston: Houghton Mifflin, 1975.

Fradin, Dennis B. *The South Carolina Colony.* Chicago: Children's Press, 1992.

Leckie, Robert. *The World Turned Upside Down: The Story of the American Revolution.* New York: Putnam, 1973.

McDowell, Bart. *The Revolutionary War: America's Fight for Freedom.* Washington, D.C.: National Geographic Society, 1967.

Miller, Lillian B. *"The Dye Is Now Cast": The Road to American Independence, 1774–1776.* Washington, D.C.: Smithsonian Institution Press, 1975.

Tunis, Edwin. *Colonial Living.* Cleveland, Ohio: The World Publishing Co., 1957.

READER CHAT PAGE

1. What did Loyalists like Robert and Clarissa Prentice and Brandon Ainsley have to gain by remaining true to the British Crown?

2. What were some grievances of Patriots such as Hugh Prentice, Arthur Ainsley, and Simon Cordwyn?

3. The Revolutionary War pitted family members against family members, neighbors against neighbors, friends against friends. How do you think you would react if you were in the middle of such a conflict?

4. Jane and her Aunt Clarissa have a somewhat strained, competitive relationship. How do these two women differ? In what ways are they similar?

5. Brandon Ainsley's Loyalist political views were much more extreme than those of his parents.

How must he have felt about his father being imprisoned for his support of the Patriots?

6. Why does Harriet Ainsley shoot Robert Prentice? Why does Robert later insist that the shooting was an accident?

7. What are Simon Cordwyn's feelings about slavery?

8. What did Robert Prentice hope to accomplish by gathering a small army of Loyalists at Rosewall?

9. Being born into English nobility, Jane is expected to stay loyal to the British Crown. However, after five years in South Carolina, Jane admits that she is "slowly, painfully realizing that I'm an American." What events precipitated Jane's reinvention of herself as an American?